UPSIDE DOWN WITH PAUL

The life of the Apostle Paul

Mark Morgan

Bible
Tales
www.BibleTales.online

Published in Australia by Bible Tales Online.
www.BibleTales.online
Last updated 19 August 2025

Upside Down with Paul

ISBN: (Paperback): 978-1-925587-37-1
ISBN (eBook): 978-1-925587-38-8
ISBN: (Hardcover): 978-1-925587-39-5

Parts of "Upside Down with Paul" are based on the text of the novelette "Paul in Snippets" by Mark Morgan (ISBN: 978-1-925587-08-1).

The text of Acts included in this book is quoted from:
The Holy Bible, Berean Literal Bible, BLB
Copyright ©2016 by Bible Hub
Used by Permission. All Rights Reserved Worldwide.

All other rights in this book reserved.
Copyright © 2025 by Mark Morgan.

No part of this publication may be reproduced or transmitted in any form or by any means, without permission in writing from the author.

Shelving categories:
English literature
Religion / Christianity
Religious / Christian fiction
Biblical / Bible-based fiction

Typesetting information:
Title: Trade Winds, 28pt.
Part headings: Droid Serif, 18pt.
Section headings: Arimo, 18pt.
Scripture: Tahoma; Headings, 10.5pt; Text, 8.5pt; Verse numbers, 5.5pt.
Sketches: Headings, STIX Two Text, 11.5pt; Text, PT Serif, 9pt.
Introductions and biographical information: EB Garamond, 10.5pt.
Snippets: EB Garamond, 10.5pt; Headings, Italic; Text, Regular.
Quotes from BLB documents in Introduction: Roboto, 8.5pt.
Headers: Trade Winds, 10pt.
Footnotes: EB Garamond, 8.5pt with parts Tahoma, 6.5pt.
Footers: EB Garamond, 10pt.

Cover picture: Saint Paul
by Bartolomeo Montagna (1482).

"I thank him who has given me strength,
Christ Jesus our Lord,
because he judged me faithful,
appointing me to his service,
though formerly I was a blasphemer,
persecutor, and insolent opponent.
But I received mercy
because I had acted ignorantly in unbelief."

Paul, from 1 Timothy 1:12-13

"And when they could not find [Paul and Silas],
they dragged Jason and some of the brothers
before the city authorities, shouting,
'These men [(Paul and Silas)] who have
turned the world upside down
have come here also' "

Leaders of a mob in Thessalonica, from Acts 17:6

To my ever-patient wife, Ruth

Contents

Introduction

Welcome to a study of the life of Paul in snippets, sketches, Scripture and summaries.

A predecessor of this book began its development in a 24-hour period back in 2016 when I was encouraged to take up an impossible writing challenge and write a novelette in 24 hours.

"Paul in Snippets" was the result – roughly 9,800 words of snippets from the life of Paul the Apostle, pasted onto a framework of the Acts of the Apostles.

For several years, I left it at that, but Paul is a complex and fascinating character. It's hard to leave him alone. About half of the book of Acts is dedicated to Paul's life as an apostle, but his letters include many other details that must be interleaved with Luke's record if we wish to understand the man better. This is a challenging task.

Eventually, the short novelette seemed utterly inadequate.

For a start, extra detail was needed, but then came the questions. How would others have seen him, interacted with him, resisted him, loved him, been frustrated or inspired by him? Did his enemies simply loathe him or did they harbour a sneaking admiration for this man who seemed unstoppable? Were people more likely to remember his miracles or his words? And what was it about him that enabled him to turn the world upside down?

These questions prompted the idea of sketches examining various scenes of Paul's life: snatches of a wider stage explored in more detail than scripture reveals, yet careful not to contradict scripture.

Forty-one sketches resulted, covering a wide range of Paul's experiences as a preacher.

Another component that seemed necessary was scripture itself. My goal in writing is to encourage people to read the Bible more, not to help people avoid reading it because someone else has read and summarised it for them!

Thus, I wanted a text of Acts that I could include in the final book without major copyright problems. The expansively licensed Berean Literal Bible (BLB) satisfied this requirement and all the scripture text in this book has been taken from this translation.

Please note that the BLB is written in US English, while the rest of the book uses Australian English.

All footnotes quoted from the Berean Literal Bible have the prefix "BLB:" followed by the verse number to which they relate. Footnotes relating to snippets, sketches or summaries have no prefix.

Some of the notes from the BLB refer to one or more of the Greek sources used in its translation, as is explained on the Berean Bibles website[a] and quoted below:

The Scriptures in their original form are God's inerrant word to us and to all generations. Scholars have sought to reconstruct these Scriptures by collating the manuscripts and sources deemed to be closest to the originals. For simplicity, we have footnoted significant variants between major collections of source texts. The following abbreviations are used in the footnotes to document differences among original language sources:

NA	Nestle Aland, Novum Testamentum Graece
SBL	Society of Biblical Literature, Greek New Testament
ECM	Editio Critica Maior, Novum Testamentum Graecum
NE	Eberhard Nestle Novum Testamentum Graece
WH	Westcott and Hort, New Testament in the Original Greek
BYZ	The New Testament in the Original Greek: Byzantine Textform
GOC	Greek Orthodox Church, New Testament
TR	Scrivener's Textus Receptus Stephanus Textus Receptus
DSS	Dead Sea Scrolls
MT	Hebrew Masoretic Text: Westminster Leningrad Codex Hebrew Masoretic Text: Biblia Hebraica Stuttgartensia
LXX	Greek OT Septuagint: Rahlfs-Hanhart Septuaginta Greek OT Septuagint: Swete's Septuagint
SP	Samaritan Pentateuch

The abbreviations above are included in the BLB footnotes quoted in this book. For ease of reading and consistency with the other content of the book, the italics used in the BLB to indicate extra words added by the translators are not shown in this book.

Various extra footnotes have been added to the text of the BLB to assist with understanding.

In electronic formats of the book, the words of Paul are in green while the quoted words of Jesus are in red.

Each component of the book is presented in a different way.

Each scripture passage has the passage reference as a heading and a bar on either side of the text. Verse numbers in eBooks are **bold brown**.

Each snippet is placed in a box with any references in a box above.

Sketches form the majority of the text and are numbered with titles.

---

a   See https://bereanbibles.com/about-berean-study-bible/greek-and-hebrew-sources/

PART ONE
Early Life

Tarsus

Paul of Tarsus is a famous man today, but it was not always so.

He did so much: travelling, working, teaching, writing, encouraging, and even suffering, that it is sometimes hard to believe all these things could fit into the life of just one man.

This is the story of a man driven to achieve. Driven first, if you like, by guilt, but expanding his vision so much along the way that you could never describe his stunning achievements as arising solely from guilt.

Here was a man of vision: a man who could never do enough to pay back his Lord and saviour Jesus Christ, and a man willing to do anything his Lord would have done to help his fellow believers.

Paul was an ordinary tentmaker,
but with an extraordinary faith.

❦

Acts 21:39; Acts 22:3; Romans 11:1; 2 Corinthians 11:22; Philippians 3:5; Acts 13:9; Acts 23:6

Tarsus was a city in the area of Cilicia, far to the north of Israel, yet Paul – a Jew – was born there. It was no unimportant city, and despite being a Jew, his father was a citizen of Rome. This inherited citizenship conferred immense privileges, privileges which Paul later took advantage of at times – but always with care.

Paul's heritage was in the tribe of Benjamin, the youngest of the children of Jacob. In accordance with the command of God through Abraham, he was circumcised when he was eight days old. His father was a Pharisee, the strictest sect of their religion. These were important details.

Jewish baby boys were named when they were circumcised, and at that time Paul was given the name "Saul", the name of the first king of Israel – the most famous son of all the tribe of Benjamin.

His parents must have had high hopes for him. He kept this name for many years, but shortly after his empire-wide work of preaching began, we suddenly read of him as "Paul" and the name "Saul" ceases to be used, except when Paul is retelling past events.

We know nothing of Paul's early childhood in Tarsus, but he grew up to be a well-informed and committed follower of the religion of his fathers. His knowledge of the scriptures no doubt reflects a home in which the ancient words of God in what we now call the Old Testament were treasured.

Although no-one knew it at the time, this Jewish boy – growing up in a foreign city far from the land of Israel – would contribute a significant percentage of the writings in the New Testament.

Jerusalem

Acts 5:33-42; Acts 22:3

Paul did not stay in Tarsus. His education took place in Jerusalem, sitting at the feet of a famous teacher called Gamaliel. There he learned to read, to write and to listen. His teacher was a wise man and laws defined his life.

The Law of Moses was the most important subject on the curriculum. Teachers must know the laws from start to finish, and Paul wanted to be a teacher. Obedience to it, and to the traditions which hedged it about, was vital. Law and tradition were his life. Soon, his zeal was noticed by the religious establishment. Paul's career began to blossom.

☙

Sketch 1 – Discussion about Saul

"Have you noticed my young student, Saul?" asked Gamaliel. "He has an incisive mind and an almost encyclopaedic knowledge of the words of the fathers."

"Yes," said a fellow greybeard. "I heard him the other day in discussion with that young reformer I'm unlucky enough to be teaching. He put him in his box beautifully. Quoted from many different rabbis as well as the law and the prophets. A very powerful presentation of our traditions and beliefs. I was impressed."

"Just the sort of student the chief priests have been looking for," said Gamaliel, comfortably. "A pleasure to teach."

"Wouldn't you like to swap students? You can have my reformer and I'll have Saul."

"No, I don't think so." The words suggested some reflection over the answer, but the tone of voice showed none. "It is unfortunate, dear friend, that you have a difficult student, but Saul is very much the right sort of student for me to teach. You know, he always asks the right sort of questions!"

"My student doesn't ask questions. He makes statements."

"Well, there's no doubt that Saul will be high on the chief priests' list of candidates when they're looking for new talent." Saul's teacher looked almost smug as he reflected on his star student's bright future.

"I heard that he's already been given a full scholarship and a guaranteed position amongst the next intake of lawyers."

"Your information is accurate. He is progressing quickly in Judaism – and deservedly so," said Gamaliel.

"He'll go far, there's no doubt about that." Gamaliel's friend looked at him shrewdly, smiled a little and added, "Perhaps he'll even outstrip his teacher."

Gamaliel's mouth stiffened for a moment, then relaxed again. "You may be right," he said slowly. "You may be right."

PART TWO
Before Christ

Stephen

Jesus Christ had lived and died and lived again. His followers had been transformed from timid, fearful admirers into true converts. Now, they were turning the Jewish religious world upside down.

The establishment tried to fight back. With reason and logic, they fought for the law of their fathers. It didn't work. These uneducated, ignorant country folk ran rings around the professors. Worse still, they performed miracles which couldn't be ignored.

If rational argument cannot win, violence often comes next.

Jesus' followers were beaten. It made no difference. They even had the audacity to rejoice in sharing the sufferings of their Lord Jesus. They continued to preach, continued to dispute, continued to win and continued to convince many. The number of their converts grew rapidly.

Stephen was one of the preachers – one of those who made life difficult for the leaders because his arguments could not be controverted. The Pharisees were uncomfortably reminded of Jesus and their attempts to best him in argument: it had never worked.

Paul was a Pharisee. A young man, but progressing quickly in his religion. Stephen disputed with many zealous Jews from far and wide, including Cilicia, home to the town of Tarsus. His opponents did their best, but it was no good, so then they did their worst. Lies and false witnesses were used to bring a case against Stephen and he was dragged into court.

Paul was never involved in the shadier parts of the fight against the followers of Jesus. Paul had a conscience, and he did his best to always keep it clear. The law forbade false witnesses – so others did the dirty work.

The trial was a farce. No attempt was made to seek truth. Death was all they sought: death for Stephen. When his answers could not be gainsaid, they shouted with one voice and attacked him, dragging him out of the court and out of the city. A barrage of stones, and it was all over. Stephen was dead.

The zealous ones had taken off their cloaks to free up their arms for the work. A studious young man stood and watched over a pile of nice clean clothes, while the zealous reduced Stephen to a lifeless heap of bloodied flesh and clothing.

Saul – that is, Paul – approved.

Acts 6:1-7:60

[Chapters 1 to 5 omitted: no connection with Paul]

Acts 6

The Choosing of the Seven
(1 Timothy 3:8-13)

[1] Now in these days when the disciples are multiplying, there arose a grumbling of the Hellenists against the Hebrews, because their widows were being overlooked in the daily distribution.

[2] So the Twelve, having called near the multitude of the disciples, said, "It is not desirable for us, having neglected the word of God, to attend tables. [3] Therefore brothers, select out from yourselves seven men being well attested, full of the Spirit and wisdom, whom we will appoint over this task. [4] And we will steadfastly continue in prayer and the ministry of the word."

[5] And the statement was pleasing before the whole multitude. And they chose Stephen, a man full of faith and of the Holy Spirit, and Philip, and Prochorus, and Nicanor, and Timon, and Parmenas, and Nicolas of Antioch, a convert, [6] whom they set before the apostles. And having prayed, they laid the hands on them.

[7] And the word of God continued to increase, and the number of the disciples in Jerusalem was multiplied exceedingly, and a great multitude of the priests were becoming obedient to the faith.

The Arrest of Stephen

[8] Now Stephen, full grace and power, was performing great wonders and signs among the people. [9] But certain of those from the synagogue called Freedmen, including Cyrenians and Alexandrians and of those from Cilicia[a] and Asia, arose, disputing with Stephen. [10] And they were not able to withstand the wisdom and the Spirit by whom he was speaking.

[11] Then they suborned men, saying, "We have heard him speaking blasphemous words against Moses and God." [12] And they stirred up the people,

---

a   Acts 6:9 – Tarsus, Paul's home town, was in Cilicia

and the elders, and the scribes; and having come upon him, they seized him and brought him to the Council.

[13] And they set false witnesses, saying, "This man does not stop speaking words against this holy place and the Law. [14] For we have heard him saying that this Jesus of Nazareth will destroy this place and will change the customs that Moses delivered to us."

[15] And having looked intently on him, all sitting in the Council saw his face as the face of an angel.

Acts 7

Stephen's Address to the Sanhedrin

[1] And the high priest said, "Are these things so?"

[2] And he began to speak: "Men, brothers, and fathers, listen! The God of glory appeared to our father Abraham, being in Mesopotamia, before his dwelling in Haran, [3] and said to him, 'Go out from your country and from your kindred, and come into the land that I will show you.'[a] [4] Then having gone out from the land of the Chaldeans, he dwelt in Haran. And from there, after his father died, He removed him into this land in which you now dwell.

[5] And He did not give to him an inheritance in it, not even the length of a foot; but He promised to give it to him for a possession, and his to descendants after him, there being to him no child. [6] But God spoke thus, that his seed will be a sojourner in a strange land, and they will enslave it, and will mistreat it four hundred years. [7] 'And the nation to which they will be in bondage, I will judge,' God said, 'and after these things they will come forth and will serve Me in this place.'[b]

[8] And He gave to him the covenant of circumcision; and thus he begat Isaac and circumcised him on the eighth day, and Isaac Jacob, and Jacob the twelve patriarchs.

[9] And the patriarchs, having envied Joseph, sold him into Egypt. But God was with him [10] and rescued him out of all his tribulations, and gave him favor and wisdom before Pharaoh king of Egypt, and he appointed him ruler over Egypt and over all his house.

[11] And there came a famine upon all of Egypt and Canaan, and great affliction, and our fathers were not finding sustenance. [12] Now Jacob, having heard there is grain in Egypt, sent forth our fathers first. [13] And on the second time, Joseph was made known to his brothers, and the family of Joseph became known to Pharaoh. [14] And Joseph, having sent, called for his father Jacob and all the kindred, seventy-five souls in all.

---

a   BLB: Acts 7:3 – Genesis 12:1
b   BLB: Acts 7:5-7 – Genesis 15:13,14

[15] And Jacob went down into Egypt and died, he and our fathers, [16] and they were carried over into Shechem and placed in the tomb that Abraham had bought for a sum of silver from the sons of Hamor in Shechem.

[17] Now as the time of the promise that God had sworn to Abraham was drawing near, the people increased and multiplied in Egypt, [18] until there arose another king over Egypt, who did not know Joseph. [19] Having dealt treacherously with our race, he mistreated our fathers, making them abandon their infants so that they would not live.

[20] In that time Moses was born, and he was beautiful to God,[c] who was brought up three months in his father's house. [21] And he having been set outside, the daughter of Pharaoh took him up, and she brought him up as her own son. [22] And Moses was instructed in all the wisdom of the Egyptians, and he was mighty in his words and deeds.

[23] Now when his period of forty years was fulfilled, it came into his mind to visit his brothers, the sons of Israel. [24] And having seen a certain one being wronged, he defended him and did vengeance for the one being oppressed, having struck down the Egyptian. [25] And he was supposing his brothers to understand that God is giving them salvation by his hand, but they did not understand.

[26] And on the following day, he appeared to those who were quarreling and urged them to peace, having said, 'Men, you are brothers. Why do you wrong one another?'

[27] But the one mistreating the neighbor pushed him away, having said, 'Who appointed you ruler and judge over us? [28] Do you desire to kill me, the same way you killed the Egyptian yesterday?'[d] [29] Now at this remark, Moses fled, and became exiled in the land of Midian, where he begat two sons.

[30] And forty years having been passed, an angel appeared to him in the wilderness of Mount Sinai, in a flame of fire of a bush. [31] And Moses having seen it, marveled at the vision. And of him coming near to behold it, there was the voice of the Lord: [32] 'I am the God of your Fathers, the God of Abraham, and of Isaac, and of Jacob.'[e] And Moses, having become terrified, did not dare to look.

[33] And the Lord said to him, 'Take off the sandal of your feet, for the place on which you stand is holy ground. [34] Having seen, I saw the oppression of My people in Egypt, and I have heard their groans, and I have come down to deliver them. And now come, I will send you to Egypt.'[f]

[35] This Moses whom they rejected, having said, 'Who appointed you ruler and judge?'—him whom God sent and as ruler and redeemer by the hand of the angel having appeared to him in the bush— [36] this one led them out,

---

c   BLB: Acts 7:20 – Or he was of great status in God's eyes
d   BLB: Acts 7:28 – Exodus 2:14
e   BLB: Acts 7:32 – Exodus 3:6
f   BLB: Acts 7:31-34 – Exodus 3:5-10

having done wonders and signs in the land of Egypt, and in the Red Sea, and in the wilderness forty years.

37 This is the Moses having said to the sons of Israel, 'God will raise up for you a prophet like me out from your brothers.'[a] **38** This is the one having been in the congregation in the wilderness with the angel speaking to him in Mount Sinai, and who was with our fathers. He received living oracles to give to us, **39** to whom our fathers were not willing to be obedient, but thrust away, and turned back in their hearts to Egypt, **40** having said to Aaron, 'Make us gods who will go before us. As for this Moses who brought us out from the land of Egypt, we do not know what has happened to him.'[b]

41 And in those days they made a calf and offered a sacrifice to the idol and were rejoicing in the works of their hands. **42** But God turned away and delivered them to worship the host of heaven, as it has been written in the book of the prophets:

> 'Did you offer slain beasts and sacrifices to Me
> forty years in the wilderness,
> O house of Israel?
> **43** And you took up the tabernacle of Moloch
> and the star of your god Rephan,
> the images that you made to worship them;
> and I will remove you
> beyond Babylon.'[c]

44 The tabernacle of the testimony was with our fathers in the wilderness, just as the One speaking to Moses had commanded to make it according to the pattern that he had seen, **45** also which, having received by succession, our fathers brought in with Joshua in taking possession of the nations whom God drove out from the face of our fathers, until the days of David, **46** who found favor before God and asked to find a dwelling place for the God of Jacob.[d] **47** But Solomon built Him the house.

48 Yet the Most High does not dwell in hand-made houses. As the prophet says:

> **49** 'Heaven is My throne,
> and the earth a footstool of My feet.
> What kind of house will you build Me, says the Lord,
> or what is the place of My rest?
> **50** Has not My hand made all these things?'[e]

51 You stiff-necked and uncircumcised in heart and ears always resist the Holy Spirit; as your fathers did, also do you. **52** Which of the prophets did your fathers not persecute? And they killed those having foretold about the

---

a   BLB: Acts 7:37 – Deuteronomy 18:15
b   BLB: Acts 7:40 – Exodus 32:1
c   BLB: Acts 7:42-43 – Amos 5:25-27
d   BLB: Acts 7:46 – NE, NA and Tischendorf the house of Jacob
e   BLB: Acts 7:49-50 – Isaiah 66:1,2

coming of the Righteous One, of whom you have now become betrayers and murderers, **53** you who received the Law by the ordination of angels, and have not kept it."

The Stoning of Stephen

54 Now hearing these things, they were cut to their hearts and began gnashing the teeth at him. **55** But he being full of the Holy Spirit, having looked intently into heaven, saw the glory of God and Jesus standing at the right hand of God, **56** and he said, "Behold, I see the heavens having been opened, and the Son of Man standing at the right hand of God."

57 And having cried out with a loud voice, they held their ears and rushed upon him with one accord, **58** and having cast him out of the city, began to stone him. And the witnesses laid aside their garments at the feet of a young man named Saul.

59 And as they were stoning Stephen, he was calling out and saying, "Lord Jesus, receive my spirit." **60** And having fallen on his knees, he cried in a loud voice, "Lord, do not place this sin to them."[f] And having said this, he fell asleep.

℞

Sketch 2 – Witness Statement

"I am Saul of Tarsus. I was asked to come and see you."

"Ah, thank you. I saw you at the execution of the heretic Stephen. To close the case, we need a statement from a witness who was not actively involved in administering the punishment. I'm sure you're aware of what we need: just a brief statement that describes the execution and a little about the crime that warranted such punishment. Would you be able to write such a witness statement for the High Priest?"

Saul agreed and the High Priest's agent produced a piece of parchment and offered him a quill and some ink. Saul wrote:

> Witness Statement:
>
> I, Saul of Tarsus, was a witness to the execution by stoning of Stephen, called a follower of The Way. He was a blasphemer who threatened to destroy Moses' Law and our nation, and deserved the punishment appointed by the High Priest and the council of Israel.

---

f   Acts 7:60 – Stephen followed the example of Jesus in Luke 23:34. This was an important prayer for Paul who was consenting to Stephen's stoning (see Acts 8:1).

The High Priest's agent sanded the parchment, then brushed it clean and rolled it up. "Thank you," he said. "That will make it all neat and tidy should the governor ask any questions."

"It's certainly best that we do the execution instead of having to convince the Romans that it is necessary."

"True. All too often, they refuse to cooperate or don't understand the religious background and allow condemned men to escape their deserved punishment."

"Well, this man didn't escape."

"No, and we're hoping that the rest of those followers of The Way will learn from his fate. We'd accept them back into Moses' fold if only they would recant."

"I suppose so" said Saul, thoughtfully, "but with the way they twist the Scriptures to make them contradict the rabbis, I sometimes wonder if we should refuse to consider any supposed repentance for such blasphemy. Is true repentance even possible for men like that?"

"Well, at least *he'll* cause no more trouble now. Was he really as good in debate and argument as I've heard?"

"Yes. He was absolutely brilliant," said Saul in frustration. "I disputed with him several times but could never defeat him – even though I had the power of an ancient truth and he was peddling some new lie about a dead carpenter."

"I've heard some funny stories about that carpenter. We don't seem to have been able to prove he was a fraud, then or since."

"Are you thinking of following The Way too?"

"No, but I'd like to know how he did his tricks and how his followers manage to be so convincing and determined."

"Evil has always pretended to be good. Anyway, now that this Stephen has been dealt with, it's time to see if I can get rid of more of them. I want to do all I can to clean up Jerusalem first, then I might even see what can be done elsewhere."

"I'm sure the High Priest will be pleased to hear that."

"We need to kill the leaders – the men like Stephen – and then lock up the followers until they recant."

Persecuting Believers

Acts 8:1-3

Acts 8

Saul Persecutes the Church

[1] And Saul was there consenting to [Stephen's] killing.

And on that day a great persecution arose against the church in Jerusalem, and all except the apostles were scattered throughout the regions of Judea and Samaria. [2] Now devout men buried Stephen and made great lamentation over him. [3] But Saul was destroying the church. Entering houses after houses and dragging off men and women, he was delivering them to prison.

[From verse 4 to the end of the chapter omitted: no connection with Paul]

Acts 8:1-3; Acts 22:4, 19; Acts 26:9-11;
Galatians 1:13; 1 Timothy 1:13

Stephen was dead, but the followers of Jesus did not give up.

Brave and godly men buried Stephen, then went about their business. They kept up the fight. It was never a physical fight; these followers of Jesus never fought their attackers, after that one lapse on Peter's part during the arrest of Jesus. Jesus' words rang in their ears: "He who takes the sword will perish by the sword."[a] Their focus was salvation, offered to those who were perishing but who chose a new way of life following Jesus. So they followed him: to dungeons and death, to beatings and torture.

Paul joined in the persecution. He became the public face of the relentless assault. He hounded the believers from house to house and from town to town. In prisons and synagogues, he did his best to make them suffer. He urged them to recant, and if they wouldn't, he cast his vote for the death sentence.

---

a   Matthew 26:52

> All over Judea and even to foreign cities, he mercilessly persecuted them in his madness against them.

☙

Sketch 3 – Arresting believers

Saul stopped outside the house then looked at the leading guard and gestured at the door: "See if they will open the door."

"Open up!" The temple guard spoke peremptorily, rapping on the door with his fist. There was no reply, and the door didn't move.

"I'm sure I heard people moving inside," said another guard.

"Open up!" Louder this time.

Still no reply. The second guard struck at the door with his club. "Open up or we'll break your door down!" he snarled.

"Let's wait a little longer. Give them a chance to respond," said Saul, mildly.

The door of the next house opened and a man looked out. Seeing Saul with the temple guards, he called, "What are you doing?"

"Our information says that heretics of 'The Way' meet in this house," answered Saul. "We have authority from the High Priest to enter such houses and arrest any we find celebrating this heresy."

"Well, they may have some ideas that the Chief Priests don't like, but they're good neighbours and they keep God's law much better than most. To be honest, many of the... ah... the people in the temple could learn something from them."

"They're heretics," said Saul, shortly. "If Moses and Aaron were alive, they would be with us, arresting the heretics."

"Whatever you say," said the man and closed his door.

The leader of the guards looked at Saul for guidance.

He gestured at the door again: "We've given them time. Open the door!"

"Come on, men," said the leader.

The guards began to use their feet and clubs on the door. It withstood their efforts, but gave an appearance of failing resistance.

A voice was heard from within, crying out, "I'll open the door!"

Saul smiled grimly as he signalled to the guards to step back. He was not concerned that those in the house would put up any sort of armed resistance – they never did. It was the only thing about them that made them easier to deal with. Their lives were exemplary, their arguments irresistible, their enthusiasm utterly contagious; but fortunately, their refusal to fight or resist arrest made it easy to drag them away and lock them in prison until the council had an opportunity to hear their case. And the council was never in a hurry. They had found that spiriting the believers away and making sure that no-one heard from them for some time had a far greater psychological impact on these ignorant sinners than holding confrontational trials where the temple authorities could be portrayed as unjust. The best part was that these poor simpletons never went to the Roman authorities to complain or to discover where their loved ones were hidden.

When the purge began, they had beaten such heretics in the synagogues and publicly executed men like Stephen, but it only seemed to win the villains more converts! Now the authorities had learned to use the prisons instead, and leave the unanswered questions to undermine their heretical faith.

Saul wasn't sure yet whether it was working or had just spread the cancer further into other districts and countries. One thing he was sure of: it *must* work. He would never give up until this disease was rooted out.

After a few moments, the door opened a little and a man slipped out, closing the door behind him. Saul had to admit that it was a brave gesture.

"What do you want, good sirs?" he asked, and his voice quavered a little.

"We have come to search this house for heretics. We have information that meetings of heretics are held here. Is this your house?"

"Yes, this is my house. We use it to give glory to God, not for any heresy."

"I have a warrant from the Chief Priests to search your house. Let us in and *I* will decide whether you are giving glory to God or practising heresy."

"Are you Saul of Tarsus?" asked the man, his face suddenly turning white.

"Yes, I am." Saul disliked the obvious fear in the man's eyes – it made him feel guilty, since the man appeared from all reports, including most recently from his neighbour, to be an honest, hard-working sort. Yet the carpenter had claimed to have authority to forgive sin[a] and to be the son of God,[b] and God himself had forbidden blasphemy against the name.[c]

It had been the same with that blasphemer Stephen, who called the carpenter, "the Righteous One"! Apart from that sacrilege, Stephen's words had been incisive and accurate – embarrassingly so, really. It was true that God's messengers and prophets had often been the target of persecution at the hands of the leaders of Israel. But the carpenter was no messenger of God, insisted Saul to himself. How could a righteous man claim to be the son of God?

"Are you going to let us into your house or must we force our way in?"

The man turned back to the door and opened it. "If you must," he said.

"We must," said Saul, pushing past him. "God's holiness demands it."

Beyond the door, Saul found a poorly-lit, low-roofed room in which a few men and women sat quietly. He knew that they must all have heard that he was Saul, but no-one shouted or screamed or leapt at him with a weapon. Though not a self-important man, he was sure that all of these people must be aware of his unrelenting attacks on their fellows, and would know that they had little chance of escape from a harsh punishment at his hands. In some ways it frustrated him that their behaviour was so admirable, so impeccable. Had they indulged in loose living or armed rebellion, unguarded speech or drunken revels, he could more easily have dismissed their convictions from his mind. As it was, their way of life made it harder to justify the beatings and incarceration he had inflicted on so many.

Best to get it over with quickly. Remember they're heretics. Rebels against Moses' law.

"Is that bread and wine on the table there?" he asked as his eyes adjusted to the dim light.

"Bread and wine are standard fare for the poor, your honour," said the man who had answered the door.

"They are also symbols of heresy when used by followers of The Way."

"We are just a poor family, sir."

"A big family, too," answered Saul, sarcastically.

"These are our friends, come to share a meal."

---

a   Matthew 9:2-3
b   John 10:29-36
c   Leviticus 24:16

"Are you followers of the Nazarene?"

"Yes, we are. Jesus is the son of God."

"That is heresy," said Paul, angrily. He looked around at his audience. "Does anyone else believe this heresy?"

"It is not heresy, sir, whatever you may call it."

"Are you all followers of this Jesus?"

"I am," said another man.

"I am," said another.

"I am," said the woman of the house.

"I am", "I am", continued the refrain until each of those present had declared their allegiance.

"If only you could be too," finished the man who had opened the door, softly. "If only."

Ignoring the man's temerity, Saul directed the guards to round them all up and take them to the temple courts where they would be separated and locked up until the chief priests were ready for their initial "interviews".

To Damascus

Acts 9

The Road to Damascus
(Acts 22:1-21; Acts 26:1-23)

[1] Meanwhile, Saul still breathing out threats and murder toward the disciples of the Lord, having gone to the high priest, [2] requested letters from him to the synagogues in Damascus, so that if he found any being of the way, both men and women, having bound them, he might bring them to Jerusalem.

[3] Now in proceeding, it came to pass as he draws near to Damascus, suddenly also a light from heaven flashed around him.

Acts 9:1-3; Acts 22:4-5, 19; Acts 26:9-11; Galatians 1:13-14

Synagogues in different countries had significant autonomy. Local elders settled local problems with little interference from the religious leadership in Jerusalem. But there *was* a central authority, and the high priest flexed his muscles from time to time.

Paul heard that the followers of Jesus had spread to many different cities and towns, and he was eager to apply his "methods" to believers in Damascus. The high priest was all cooperation, and letters of authority were duly signed and given to Paul.

It took the best part of a week to travel to Damascus, and Paul was champing at the bit. He couldn't wait to get his hands on the harmless, the innocent and the gentle. His attendants were baying for blood too.

Damascus was well in sight when the unthinkable happened. In a blinding flash, Paul met the man who simply *had to be dead*.

CR

Sketch 4 – Traveling

We'll be at the gates of Damascus soon, and then I can finally get on with what I came for. It's so much better keeping busy with important work. All this travelling time has me thinking round and round in circles.

Anyway, those rebels who think they can overturn our ancient religion must be stopped in Damascus too. I think we're in the process of getting them under control in Jerusalem and across Judea, but we can't ignore places like this. Heresy like this must not be allowed to infiltrate our Jewish culture. Hopefully, if we time it properly, we can break down their advances here and the whole movement will collapse.

But I keep asking myself: why are they so stubborn? Why won't they give up when it brings them so much suffering? And why are they so successful?

I'm willing to give them a chance to recant, but why are they so determined not to return to the faith? I have to admit that most of them are honourable people – amazingly so, really. If we could straighten them out, they'd be really good examples of what Judaism is all about. Yet they keep twisting Scripture to make it say that Jesus is the centre of God's plan.

How can this Jesus be more important than Moses? It sounds like he was an amazing man in some ways, but he caused so much trouble! Some of our leaders paint everything he did as black, yet the people I arrest paint him as white as light. If only I could've met him and heard his teachings – been able to make up my own mind!

But I missed out on that, and nothing can change it now.

So, Jesus is dead. I just can't understand how his followers can be so badly misled. How can they keep on believing in him and preaching about him when he's dead? Why do they talk about resurrection? They must know that he didn't rise from the dead – after all, it was their own leaders who went and stole the body. How can they claim he rose when they know he didn't? That's just dishonest! Besides, if he really *is* alive, how come nobody ever sees him? He spent plenty of time in the temple in Jerusalem before he died, so if he's alive again, why not now?

He's dead, dead, dead, and his followers should just admit it and get back to the true worship of God.

I can't help wishing that some of our own leaders were as upright, genuine and humble as many of those I've arrested. However, they believe such wrong things, so surely that must override the good they do? Enough. I'll keep on attacking them; do my best to help them to change, and stop them doing more damage.

Ah, it'll be good to get to Damascus after such a long journey. It'll be a relief to able to get on with *doing* something instead of having my thoughts tormenting me all the time!

PART THREE
A New Life

New Sight

Sketch 5 – The light

What is that light? Getting brighter and brighter! Light in the sky; it must be from heaven. What's going on?

Is this God's light? It must be the glory of God. Oh, I can't stand up any more! This is too much. I must kneel… no… get down on the ground. It's terrifying; I must hide!

"Saul, Saul, why are you persecuting me?"

Who's that speaking? Nobody I've been punishing can do anything like this! The light is so bright, it hurts. "Who are you, Lord?"

"I am Jesus of Nazareth, whom you are persecuting."

But Jesus is dead! And he was a man, not a blinding light. It doesn't make sense: but he's speaking in our language, and his followers claim that he's alive, and that he's in heaven. I can't deny that it's happening, so I'll just have to accept it for now.

"What shall I do, Lord?"

"Rise and enter the city, and you will be told what you are to do."

What's happening now? The light has gone. In fact, I can't see anything! Where am I? I'm still on the ground. Maybe if I stand up I'll be able to see.

I still can't see. Where is everyone? There's no sound of movement, no-one's speaking. "Who's there?" Oh, my voice is so quavery. Will anyone hear me?

"Sir, are you alright?"

"I can't see. Did you see the bright light?"

"Yes, sir. It was very bright."

"And did you hear his voice?"

"I heard a voice, sir, but I couldn't understand any words. Did you hear words, sir?"

"I heard words alright. Words from a dead man... but... then he can't be dead!"

"There's no-one extra here, sir, and no particular light either – not now. It must have been lightning, and what you thought was a voice must have been thunder."

"No, it was a voice. The voice of Jesus of Nazareth."

"But he's dead. Pilate killed him."

"Maybe – but that voice was him, speaking to me." How can that be? I'm blind after talking to a dead man who isn't here. It's ridiculous. I've got to go and... Calm down, Saul. Calm down. He told you what to do. Yes. I must go into the city, and once I get there, I'll find out what I'm meant to do.

"Are you all there, men?"

"Yes, we're all here, Saul. A bit confused, but well enough."

"Hurry, men. Lead me into the city. Take me to Judas' house."

"Yes, sir. Here's my hand."

☙

Acts 9:4-19

4 And having fallen on the ground, he heard a voice saying to him, "Saul, Saul, why do you persecute Me?"

5 And he said, "Who are You, Lord?"

And He said, "I am Jesus, whom you are persecuting.[a] **6** But rise up and enter into the city, and it will be told you that which it behooves you to do."

7 And the men traveling with him stood speechless, hearing the voice indeed, but seeing no one. **8** And Saul rose up from the ground, but of his eyes having been opened, he could see nothing. And leading him by the hand, they brought him to Damascus. **9** And he was three days without seeing, and neither did he eat nor drink.

---

a   BLB: Acts 9:5 – TR includes It is hard for you to kick against the goads.

Ananias Baptizes Saul

10 Now there was a certain disciple in Damascus named Ananias. And the Lord said to him in a vision, "Ananias!"

And he said, "Behold me, Lord."

11 And the Lord said to him, "Having risen up, go into the street called Straight, and seek in the house of Judas the one of Tarsus named Saul, for behold, he is praying, **12** and he saw in a vision a man named Ananias, having come and having put the hands on him, so that he might see again."

13 But Ananias answered, "Lord, I have heard from many concerning this man, how many evils he did to Your saints in Jerusalem. **14** And here he has authority from the chief priests to bind all those calling on Your name."

15 But the Lord said to him, "Go, for this man is My vessel of choice to carry My name before the Gentiles, and also kings, and the sons of Israel. **16** For I will show to him how much it behooves him to suffer for My name."

17 And Ananias went away and entered into the house; and having laid the hands upon him, he said, "Brother Saul, the Lord Jesus, the One having appeared to you on the road by which you were coming, has sent me that you may see again and be filled of the Holy Spirit."

18 And immediately something like scales fell from his eyes, and he regained his sight. And having risen up, he was baptized, **19** and having taken food, he was strengthened. And he was some days with the disciples in Damascus.

Acts 9:3-19

A light from the sky changed everything for Paul.

Jesus had to be dead. But he wasn't.

Paul just had to be right, didn't he? But he wasn't.

The light, the voice, the commands. How could Paul deny Jesus when he had spoken to him? Darkness came after the light. It had all been too much for Paul's eyes. He was blind.

Led into Damascus by his attendants, he struggled to come to terms with the new situation. Jesus was alive. He could no longer deny that!

But, oh! What had he done? The people he had persecuted: the beatings, imprisonment, torture and even death. What had he done? And now, what could he do?

Wrong, wrong, wrong. Everything he had been trying to do was wrong, and he wrestled with his understanding and his conscience. Guilt for wrongs which could never be righted. Sorrow for suffering inflicted on the innocent.

Paul could have given up then. But he didn't. He could have denied that he had ever met Jesus and continued with his plans in Damascus – except that he was blind.

Day by day in the house of Judas, Paul struggled, eating nothing and drinking nothing. Three days of black darkness, but with a growing insight.

After three days, he was ready, and Jesus sent a believer to prove it hadn't been a dream and to keep nudging him along a new path.

Ananias heard of his task with dismay. He knew about Saul. Had heard of the letters he was carrying and the authority vested in him. Ananias was no fool: he did not want to go. But Jesus was gently insistent, explaining to him that Saul was expecting him – by name.

Paul sat in his personal darkness, waiting for the knock to come. Would it come or was he going mad? But there it was, and the visitor was brought in and announced as "Ananias". Laying his hands on Paul, he called him "brother" and spoke of the Lord Jesus who had appeared to Paul. He knew it all, thought Paul. How?

Immediately something seemed to fall off Paul's eyes and he could see. What a difference a few days had made! If he had met this man a few days before, he would have been trying to kill him. Now, he was thanking him profusely and asking him to baptise him as the followers of Jesus were all baptised.

A new life was before him and new sight within him.

Sketch 6 – Three days

Three days of blackness. No message from Jesus, yet. It almost makes me begin to question my experience on the road. Yet I saw him; I heard him. He said I would be told what to do, but so far, I've heard nothing.

Did I imagine it?

I can't have. And after three days of thinking, I'm persuaded that Jesus really is the Messiah. All of those Psalms and prophecies in Scripture that fit with what happened to Jesus. How could I never have seen them before?

The gambling for his clothes. His pierced hands and feet. His silence in the face of false witnesses. The mockery of our leaders. Even his words just before his death, straight from the Psalm: "My God, my God, why have you forsaken me?" That's right, three days of thought and prayer have convinced me utterly: Jesus of Nazareth is the Messiah.

Yet until now I've dedicated my life to fighting him. "Kicking against the goads," he said. Oh, how right he was! I knew that the men and women I was attacking were genuine: just and righteous people. I knew it, but I fought it. What a fool I've been!

How long will I have to wait now? Many of those I put in prison are still there, waiting. Will I stay in this situation for years? I would deserve it. Perhaps that's what Jesus meant when he said I would be shown what to do. Perhaps he will teach me through years of blindness, forced to suffer as I have made others suffer.

I can never redeem what I have done. Nothing can justify or undo my actions. Innocent men and women have died because of me. Oh, God! Forgive me, although I can never deserve it.

A voice! "Sir, there's a man to see you. His name is Ananias."

Acts 9:20-22

Saul Preaches at Damascus

[20] And immediately he began proclaiming Jesus in the synagogues, that He is the Son of God.

[21] And all those hearing were amazed and were saying, "Is this not the one having ravaged those in Jerusalem calling on this name? And he had come here for this, that he might bring them, having been bound, to the chief priests."

[22] But Saul was empowered all the more and kept confounding the Jews dwelling in Damascus, proving that this is the Christ.[a]

---

a   Acts 9:22 – In Galatians 1:17-18 Paul explained that he went to Arabia after this, returning to Damascus almost 3 years later. Acts 9:23 describes this as "many days".

Acts 9:20-22

Paul did not waste time. Off to the synagogue he went, no embarrassment stopping him. People must be taught that Jesus was real, a living saviour.

Passages from the Hebrew scriptures now made perfect sense to him, and he could argue them clearly with any opponents. In just the same way as Stephen had bested his enemies, Paul could now excel. Conviction was in his voice and his words proclaimed a truth that made sense.

∝

Sketch 7 – Preaching

It was Saturday, the Sabbath, and the synagogue was full of people. Crowded.

Every Jew in Damascus knew that Saul had arrived in their city. Many knew that he would be attending this very synagogue – which is why it was more crowded than usual.

Saul was said to have brought letters from the High Priest to all of the synagogues in Damascus. For the traditionalists, his presence was a welcome relief. Surely this man would stop the rot: root out the poisonous weeds infesting their synagogues and drag the troublemakers off to prison in Jerusalem.

Since he had only recently risen to prominence, no-one in Damascus knew him by sight – hence the letters. Yet most had heard of his fame. A monumental intellect supported by an exhaustive knowledge of scripture and an irresistible determination, all wrapped up in a zealous commitment to the ancient traditions. His very existence had helped to sway many in the battle against those troublemaking followers of "The Way". In taking up the fight against Jesus and his followers, Saul had stopped those blasphemers from so easily sweeping aside the long-held understanding of Moses' law. With such a reputation, many pictured him as a repeat of the king whose name he bore: a handsome giant who would stand head and shoulders above his compatriots and lead them fearlessly against the enemy.

Yet as Saul stood surrounded by the leaders of the synagogue, it became clear something was amiss with this comforting picture. However much members of the audience craned their necks to see him, the prosperous bulk of the synagogue leaders hid him completely from sight. Could it be that this dynamic reactionary was, God forbid, *short*?

Bewildered onlookers exchanged looks of surprise.

"Hey, Cephas, he's not as tall as his namesake, is he?" whispered one of the audience to his neighbour, a noticeably diminutive man.

"Well, it's not height that makes a man, Joseph," responded Cephas, pointedly.

The first man smiled apologetically. "Sorry, Cephas," he said, "but you know that great orators are normally tall so that they stand out in a crowd."

"Perhaps this Saul will show you how wrong you are," answered Cephas.

"But can you hear his voice? asked Joseph. "It stands out alright, but those aren't the mellow, rich, inspiring tones of a powerful leader."

"You could be right, but why don't you listen to what he says? Surely that's more important than how he says it?"

"I suppose so, but true leaders are people that others can look up to." Seeing the flash in his pint-sized companion's eyes, Joseph waved his hand conciliatingly. "I mean metaphorically, Cephas. How he presents himself and how he says things are important."

Soon it was time for worship to begin, and the leader of the synagogue moved to the front, smiling and looking pleased with himself. "Brethren, we are gathered together once more on a Sabbath to celebrate our selection as a people by Yahweh, the creator of the universe and friend of our father Abraham. Of all nations under heaven, God chose *us* to be his people and gave us laws and commandments that keep us holy. You have all heard of Saul of Tarsus, defender of the faith and messenger of the High Priest. Brother Saul is among us today to deliver a message, though he says that it is not at all what he was expecting to tell us when he left Jerusalem.

"I don't know exactly what he means, so I'll be listening with everyone else as brother Saul speaks to us and delivers this 'surprising' message. Brother Saul."

Saul strode to the front, where he stood facing the congregation. Cephas and Joseph looked at each other. There was no doubt about it: Saul was small – and not exactly handsome, either.

As he introduced himself, describing his background as a member of the tribe of Benjamin, just like Saul the king, Cephas and Joseph exchanged glances again, for Saul's voice was far from sweet! Yet his movements were quick and decisive and his words full of energy. Saul was intense.

At times, an audience may analyse the speaker more than his words – but if Saul's audience was guilty of this for a few moments, it didn't last long. Within just a few sentences, he had their undivided attention.

True, his voice was neither honeyed nor euphonious, and, yes, he was small, but those eyes were irresistible – and how well he used them to engage the congregation's attention! It was as if he was able to see inside them, assess their responses and address their individual questions.

Smoothly, he moved from introducing himself to explaining why his planned work in Damascus had changed. He took his audience with him as he left Jerusalem, letters in hand and helpers at his side. He described his excitement and anticipation as he travelled towards Damascus. They forgot his height deficit and the timbre of his voice in the fascination of his story. Many felt discomfort, almost horror at the frank description of what he planned to do to any followers of The Way he found in Damascus. Yet overall, they were with him. After all, most of the followers of The Way, forewarned about the coming of their enemy, had stayed away – not that they were very welcome in the synagogue anyway.

"But then everything changed," said Saul, "and I want to tell you how." He looked around the synagogue, assessing his audience, deciding how best to present his experience. "I'm sure everyone knows that Jesus of Nazareth was killed by the Romans at the instigation of our chief priests." Saul looked around again, nodding a little to encourage their responses. It seemed that he was right: his listeners knew the background well. Saul continued, "Well, I was convinced that was where it had all ended for Jesus. A blasphemer had been killed, and that was that. That's what I thought, and I'm sure many of you feel the same." More nods.

"So you can imagine my utter shock when, as I was approaching Damascus, I suddenly saw a bright light, so intense that it was clearly no ordinary light. It was brighter than the sun, far brighter than my eyes could cope with. I fell down on the ground and heard a voice speaking to me. It was Jesus, and he had instructions for me.

"Now think about that for yourselves. I *knew* Jesus was a dead blasphemer – yet here he was alive in glory and telling me that I was choosing a hard path. And just to make sure that I couldn't question his presence or his power, when his light disappeared, I was blind. I had to be led into the city, and I stayed blind for three days.

"Brothers, what would you do in that situation? I had been a determined opponent of Jesus and his followers – but that was when I was sure he was dead." Saul's eyes challenged them all to consider what they would do if their own certainty was upended as suddenly as his had been. He appeared satisfied with what he saw, for he continued: "Now I know that he isn't dead. Oh, no! He's very much alive, and I can't deny it any more. So I had to understand what was going on. I endured three days of complete blindness, proof enough of the power of Jesus, and an inescapable reminder that I hadn't imagined that light!

"I've always believed the prophets and knew that the followers of The Way claimed Jesus had fulfilled many prophecies in our scriptures. Yet I dismissed this as nonsense even though I had to admit that their arguments were hard to disprove. In fact, Jesus told me that I was kicking against a sharp goad: fighting; struggling; wrestling; refusing to believe something that should have been completely obvious to me."

Saul scanned the congregation and then he held up three fingers. "I spent three days going over prophecies of scripture in my mind. How Moses said that God would raise up from among us a prophet like Moses, a prophet who would speak the very words of God. Isaiah said a virgin would conceive and bear a son. Micah said the Messiah would be born in Bethlehem. Zechariah spoke of the Messiah entering Jerusalem seated humbly on a donkey. Isaiah spoke of God's servant suffering and dying for others while many would think he deserved it.

"Jesus of Nazareth fulfilled all of these prophecies and many, many more. Every prophet in scripture provides prophecies or signs of Jesus. How could I have been so blind as to refuse to see them?

"So instead of *him* being a blasphemer, I found I was one myself. I had set myself up as a persecutor, spending my time fighting against God's word.

"And you, brethren, will you not listen to God? Don't do what I did and keep fighting against God and his son Jesus. The prophecies are clear. You know, there is even a prophecy in Psalms that God would not let his holy one see corruption. Do you remember that Jonah spent three days in the belly of a huge fish? But God didn't abandon him. Well, Jesus spent three days in a tomb, but God didn't abandon him either or leave him to decay. Jesus was raised from the dead, and now he lives, never to die again. I have seen him."

Saul paused again and Cephas and Joseph drew in deep breaths and looked at each other. Saul's message was challenging, alright. Certainly nothing like what they had expected to hear when they came to listen to Saul, the defender of Pharisaic tradition!

Should they rethink their own choices?

Arabia

> *Galatians 1:17*
>
> Shortly after this, Paul went into Arabia and his understanding and faith continued to grow. After some time, he returned to Damascus.

ℂℜ

Sketch 8 – Meditation

It's almost three years since I met Jesus, and so much has changed. Meeting him convinced me that he was real, of course, but I still didn't understand much about where he fitted into God's plan.

Since then, I've spent countless hours re-reading our scriptures with Jesus in mind. Little by little I've begun to see his position more clearly. Prophecy by prophecy, hint by hint, sign by sign, I've gradually realised how much Jesus was promised throughout scripture. All the prophets refer to him. So many promises include him in their fulfilment, from the Garden of Eden to the promise of Elijah preparing the way for him.

It's been slow in some ways, but it's been a continuous unfolding of truth for me. Now that I'm no longer fighting against it and denying it, it all makes sense. Scriptures that I never understood are now clear as crystal in Jesus, even the prophecies of his suffering.

I even see myself – my former self – and my accomplices in some of them. It's a painful experience.

How much punishment do I deserve for my past attitudes, when I was struggling against the truth? I can never repay Jesus or his followers for my behaviour.

Yet even though I now understand the enormity of my guilt, I'm so much happier.

But I think it's time to *do* something. I can't keep studying forever, even though I'm sure it's been necessary. When I saw Jesus, he told me that I would have to suffer for him, but I haven't done so yet, and I probably won't if I stay here in Arabia.

I feel that I'm finally prepared enough. I'm ready to get on with Jesus' work – the work Stephen was doing when we killed him. And I suppose that's when the suffering Jesus spoke of will start.

I can't wait any longer. I must go back to Damascus.

Back in Damascus

Acts 9:23-25; Galatians 1:17; 2 Corinthians 11:32-33

Back in Damascus, Paul's work prospered. Many opposed him, but none mastered him. He knew that Jesus was alive, and this truth about Jesus was spreading. After three years, his enemies took action and plotted to kill him.

Providentially, Paul heard of the plan and the other believers dreamed up a counter-plan. One night, after the gates of Damascus were shut, Paul was let down over the walls in a large basket. It's not hard to imagine how disappointed his enemies were when they couldn't find him the next day!

Safely away under cover of darkness, Paul escaped with his life as he would do many more times before his work was finished.

At this time, Paul had not met any of the leaders of the believers since his miraculous conversion. Jerusalem was the next place to visit.

Acts 9:23-25

The Escape from Damascus
(1 Samuel 19:11-24)

23 Now when many days had passed, the Jews plotted together to kill him, 24 but their plot became known to Saul. And now they were closely watching the gates day and also night, so that they might kill him. 25 But having taken him by night, his disciples let him down through the wall, having lowered him in a basket.[a]

---

a   Acts 9:25 – See 2 Corinthians 11:32-33

Sketch 9 – Paul's Escape

"Come in – and hurry!" hissed a voice, and the door opened a little wider. It was a dark night, but very little light spilled out to the top of the stone stairs on which five cloaked, shadowy figures stood. The last of the five looked around carefully, searching for any unwanted witnesses to their late-night excursion.

One by one, four of them slipped through the doorway into the house, leaving the last outside. As the door closed, he turned away from the door and stood guard. With his dark clothes and a cloak shadowing his face, he was invisible in the darkness.

Inside, a single oil lamp gave just enough light to allow the four new-comers to see and greet the opener of the door.

"May the Lord bless you, Jesse. Thank you for helping our beloved brother Saul to escape."

"Lydia and I are pleased to help, Matthias. She is with the two little ones in the other room, keeping out of the way, but she asked me to send you all her blessings."

"Greetings to you both," replied the other three.

"Ah, I hear Zechariah and Quintus – and Saul as well."

"That's right, and Mordecai is outside keeping watch."

"Brother Saul, I remember you saying that Jesus told you you'd suffer for his name. It seems to have started," said Jesse.

"Yes," said Zechariah, "but we're doing our best to make sure it doesn't end with his death here in Damascus."

"We'll get him out of the city alive if we possibly can," agreed Matthias.

"And I believe we can be confident we will," said Jesse.

"Of course," said Saul. "I can't do the work Jesus wants me to do if I'm dead! Then again, he never promised me I wouldn't suffer beatings like he did – quite the opposite. So although it's sure to be unpleasant if I get caught, I'm confident they won't kill me."

"I wouldn't want that hanging over me all the time!" commented Quintus.

"We may all suffer the same fate as Saul if they catch us trying to help him," warned Matthias.

"True," agreed Quintus, "but whatever happens, at least we know that God will look after us for our eternal good."

"Absolutely! And in a way that helps others to learn the way of salvation," added Saul.

"Well, as I was watching out of the window, waiting for you to arrive, I saw another reason for confidence: guards trooped by below," said Jesse. "Since they only come past once each watch, we've got a few hours."

"That's good news," smiled Quintus.

"Let's get on with our plan, then," said Jesse. "Can we say a prayer together before we open the shutters?"

"Good idea," answered Matthias. "Shall I?"

They all stood quietly while Matthias asked for heavenly help in their plans to save Saul. As he finished, the listeners echoed his "Amen."

"Let's get going," announced Jesse. "The large basket we talked about is next to the window with a rope attached. I've smeared plenty of tallow on the window ledge and the stone where the rope will rub against them, and there's a pot of it here too, just in case we need more. I haven't tried doing this before, but I think it should work."

"I haven't tried it either," said Saul, and the others could hear a smile in his voice. "Do you think I'll have to do it often from now on?"

"As long as it works, it's worth doing," said Matthias, "and maybe you *will* have to do it more than once."

"Put both feet in the basket, Saul," said Jesse. "I think it'll be best if you sit down, but don't let go of the rope just in case the basket starts to break."

"I'll try, but I haven't climbed into a basket like this since I was a kid," said Saul.

Jesse moved across to where the tiny oil lamp sat in a niche in the wall. "I'll just snuff this out," he said. "We don't want guards to notice the light, let alone see a silhouette of Saul climbing out of the window."

Total darkness fell inside the room for a few moments as quiet footsteps crossed the room. Jesse reached the window and fumbled with the shutters. Suddenly, a square of slightly lesser darkness showed where the shutters had been opened. Jesse struggled to pick up the awkward basket. "Can anyone help me with this basket?" he asked.

Saul and the other three men went to help, but bumped into each other in the dark. "Ow!" said Matthias, as he struck his toes hard against Zechariah's sandal, causing both to stumble.

For a few moments there was confusion and noise – enough to prompt Mordecai to open the door and ask what was going on. He was quickly reassured that there was no disaster and returned to his watch. Eventually, Zechariah and Matthias helped Jesse ease the basket out of the window while Quintus and Saul kept a tight grip on the rope, allowing the basket to hang only a little way below the sill of the window.

"Well, this is all very nice," groaned Quintus, "but we can't have Saul standing here holding the rope and being lowered down in the basket at the same time."

"Hmm. You're right," muttered Jesse.

"It's not funny that people are trying to kill brother Saul, or that they might kill all of us if they caught us helping him escape," said Quintus, "but I can't help laughing at our... ah... bumbling inexperience in this. I'm glad that we're relying on God to make it work, not our own expertise!"

There was a noticeable relaxation in the room after that. They still fumbled. They still made mistakes in the darkness, but never mistakes that mattered. Instead, they worked in the fellowship of shared danger and the confidence that Jesus their Lord had been through such dangers many times himself, as had the apostles and prophets. And while they had never been guaranteed personal safety, the numerous reports of miraculous deliverances were very reassuring.

Matthias, Zechariah, Quintus and Jesse now held the rope, with Jesse closest to the window so that he could guide it over the tallow-coated stones.

"Don't slip on the tallow," he warned as Saul got ready to climb into the basket.

✷ ✷ ✷ ✷

Saul climbed feet-first into the narrow window opening and crawled backward through the city wall, still more than a metre thick at that height. Jesse's house truly was part of the wall of Damascus, which provided Saul with the perfect opportunity to escape the governor's plan to capture him.

With his feet, Saul reached down from the opening into the darkness until he felt the basket with his toes. He placed both feet in its broad base and slowly transferred his weight into it, his fingers clawing desperately at the rope as the basket twisted and jerked uncomfortably. At last, everything seemed to settle down.

"Are you ready to lower me?" he whispered.

"Can you see any lights out there?" asked Jesse. "Any guards on their rounds?"

"No... I don't think so," said Saul slowly, looking around, "but it's very dark down there."

"Then we'll start lowering. Once you get to the ground, the rope will slacken and the basket may tip over – it's not completely flat down below. We'll try to stop lowering as soon as you touch, but you might end up falling out. If so, don't worry, there's nothing dangerous there."

"Thanks," whispered Saul.

The men lowered the basket as smoothly as they could, but it wasn't easy, even for four.

Saul endured a nightmarish descent as the basket scraped and bounced down the wall, one moment catching on a projection in the wall, the next hanging freely and spinning around or swinging like a pendulum.

Whether safety or capture awaited him, he had no idea, but he was willing to trust Jesus' assurance that he had work to do for The Way.

After a seemingly endless disorienting descent, Saul felt the bottom of the basket touch the ground. Jesse and the others must have felt it too, for the rope remained taut and Saul climbed out of the basket without too much trouble.

Relieved, he saw that there was no-one around. Nothing moved either.

Looking up, he saw the top of the wall silhouetted against a myriad of stars. He wondered if he could also make out a head looking down at him from the window. Yes, it was. That was a wave, barely visible in the darkness. The basket began to rise and soon reached the window. How could it be so quick when his descent had taken so long?

At the window, the basket stopped. After a few moments, it began to descend again, and soon his travel pack was within his grasp. With relief he lifted it out – it contained the things he needed most for his journey. The brothers would send his other possessions to Jerusalem after him once the excitement had died down.

After a prayer of thanksgiving, it was time for a cautious escape towards Jerusalem. The moon would rise soon, and then he would be able to see more easily – and be seen more easily, too.

He looked up and waved. He hoped the brothers would see.

High above, two arms seemed to wave, and the basket rose one last time.

The watchers above faintly saw an indistinct figure turn and walk away into the darkness. Saul was safely outside Damascus. The plot to arrest him had failed.

Their prayer had been answered.

Jerusalem – Briefly

Acts 9:26-29; Galatians 1:18-19

Paul was not universally welcomed in Jerusalem. The believers were afraid of him and his former friends had heard the unpalatable news of his conversion.

Barnabas made all the difference with the believers – he was not called the "Son of Encouragement" for nothing – and with his support, Paul was accepted into their fellowship. At this time, however, most of their leaders were not in Jerusalem, and Paul was only able to meet Peter (also called Cephas) and James, the half-brother of Jesus.

But nothing could convince Paul's old friends to accept him. They saw him simply as a traitor, not as a man who had found truth and was willing to admit he had been wrong.

Within a couple of weeks, they were plotting to kill Paul, so his visit to Jerusalem lasted only fifteen days. He was happy to have met the brethren he had, but he would have preferred to meet more.

Escape, again.

❧

Sketch 10 – Saul's friends

"Traitor!"

"You call me a traitor, Simon, but why would I turn traitor? Tell me how I am benefiting from being a traitor. Surely I must have a reason to betray my friends as you say I'm doing?"

"Not only your friends – your God as well!"

"Okay, I'll let that pass for the moment, but tell me, what benefit am I getting? What advantage have I had in making this change of beliefs?"

"You just want to be important."

"But the other believers in Jesus don't even know me, even though I became a follower of Jesus more than three years ago. So what advantage have I gained?"

"Probably someone paid you to change."

"Most of Jesus' followers are not rich men, though some of them were before they decided to follow him. They couldn't afford to pay me to join them. Have they ever offered to pay you to change?"

"I wouldn't listen if they did."

"You're dodging the issue. Listen, I left Judaism because I discovered that what I once thought was impossible was really a fact. Jesus isn't dead – he's alive. I've talked to him."

"Oh, yeah, sure. After all, people come back to life all the time, don't they? Particularly people who have been crucified for heresy."

"We were friends, Simon, why won't you listen to me?"

"Yes, we were friends, Saul – until you betrayed us all."

"How can you say I've betrayed you when I'm offering you all an opportunity for salvation? I was your friend and you trusted me, so why won't you now believe me when I tell you that I've met Jesus? I'm trying to help you! Why would you ever think I'm betraying you?"

"You've abandoned the faith and tried to lead us into worshipping other gods. Moses told us to kill anyone who did that."

"All I've done is to tell you that Jesus is alive. It's a fact I can't deny any more. Why won't you believe me? After all, as I've pointed out, his death and resurrection fulfilled predictions God made through many of our prophets."

"You're twisting their words."

"Many of them are so simple and clear that it's really hard to twist them! We all know that the soldiers tore up some of Jesus' clothes and cast lots for other items. Well, that's just what God predicted in the Psalms! And in enough detail that I couldn't twist it if I tried. Can't you just believe it?"

"Never! Your way of reading it is all wrong. This Jesus was executed for blasphemy! Why would God raise a blasphemer from the dead?"

"God raised him because he had promised that he would not let his holy one see corruption. Do you remember that in the Psalms? And

God also predicted that he would be killed unjustly, which is exactly what happened."

"The Romans killed him because he wanted to make himself king instead of Caesar."

"The Romans would never have killed him if our chief priests hadn't demanded that they do so. At the time, they didn't know what they were doing, but now they've heard from many witnesses that Jesus is alive, and they still won't believe it. I'm just one of those witnesses."

"He's not alive at all – it's just a big trick. You've heard the guards' reports: they went to sleep and his disciples came and stole the body."

"Did you also hear the report that the guards were paid to say that?"

"Who would pay them?"

"The very people who stood to lose their position of power and influence if Jesus of Nazareth rose from the dead. They also happen to be rich and able to fork out money like that."

"Didn't you say that some of Jesus' followers started off rich? How come they aren't any more? Have they been paying gullible innocents to join this sect you're promoting?"

"No, they've been helping poor people who don't have enough to eat because they're being persecuted. Look, Simon, I don't want to spend time in pointless arguing. You know I've already heard all the arguments you're putting forward. I used to believe them myself, until I met Jesus and found that he is the Christ. He spoke to me and asked me why I was persecuting him. Now I'll ask you the same. Don't you love truth? If you do, stop fighting it. In the end, I had to admit that I was wrong. Listen! Compare what Jesus Christ told us with what God said in the scriptures and you'll see that it matches. Start listening to Abraham and Moses, to David and Isaiah, to Jeremiah and all the other prophets. Stop fighting against the truth; stop denying the truth."

"Saul, you're the one who's twisting truth. We have history on our side – a consistent faith held by our fathers for more than 1,000 years."

"So why were our fathers sent into captivity, if our faith as a nation was so exemplary?"

"Because there were people like you around who kept breaking Moses' law and teaching others to do the same."

"Simon, Simon, you know the words Moses spoke about God raising up a prophet like him. Moses warned us that we had to listen to that prophet because he would speak the words of God – that we must listen or answer to God for not doing so. Jesus is this prophet. He spoke God's words and fulfilled many of God's prophecies."

"You sound like John the Baptist," snorted Simon with disdain. "But only the ignorant, common people accepted his fine-sounding nonsense."

"John warned the nation that God's prophet was coming. As you say, the simple people believed him. But those of us who thought they knew better wouldn't listen, and then we wouldn't listen to Jesus either. We were all sure that we knew better, so we rejected God's efforts to teach us."

"God wouldn't try to teach us to blaspheme!"

"No, but what if God's idea of blasphemy and yours don't match? What if we and our fathers have twisted God's words so that good looks like bad and bad looks like good? Please, just stop and think about whether that could happen."

"It couldn't. Moses' laws are clear and unchanging. You're trying to get rid of those laws just as Jesus did. He died for his crimes as he deserved, and I'm warning you – you'll soon be following him in that way too!"

"Simon, I beg you to listen! Please, just consider for a moment: what if I'm right? How would you check it?"

"I don't need to. We know that you're wrong! You were my friend, but Moses warned us that we had to be on our guard even with our friends. By the words of Moses, I will be doing my best to have you executed."

"How do you explain the miracles that Jesus and his followers have done? Are they not the work of God?"

"They are the work of Beelzebul!"

"And yet they are always used for good! Does that make sense to you? Countless miracles have been performed through the power of God's Holy Spirit as evidence that God himself is helping these people, yet you refuse to listen. How can God ever save you if you won't listen?"

"Moses' law will save us. And you'll find out soon enough whether God will save you, Saul!"

Acts 9:26-29

26 And having arrived in Jerusalem, he was attempting to join the disciples, and all were afraid of him, not believing that he is a disciple. **27** But Barnabas having taken him, brought him to the apostles[a] and related to them how he had seen the Lord on the road, and that He had spoken to him, and how in Damascus he had spoken boldly in the name of Jesus.

28 And he was coming in and going out with them in Jerusalem, speaking boldly in the name of Lord.[b] **29** And he was speaking and was debating with the Hellenists. But they were seeking to kill him.

a   Acts 9:26 – He met Simon Peter and James the Lord's brother (Galatians 1:19)
b   Acts 9:28 – For 15 days (Galatians 1:18)

Return to Tarsus

Acts 9:30

30 But the brothers having known it, brought him down to Caesarea and sent him away to Tarsus.[a]

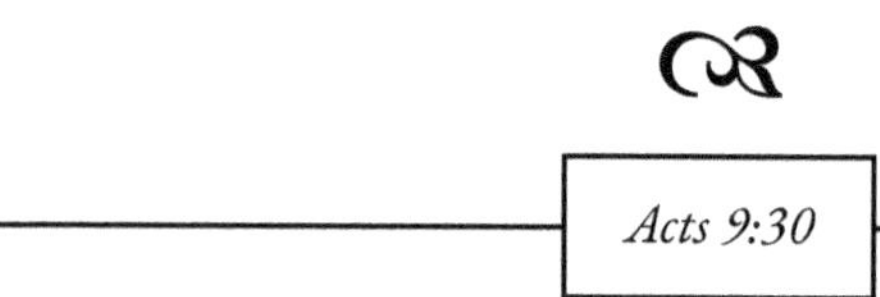

Acts 9:30

Paul was hurried away to Caesarea by the brethren, and from there they sent him on to Tarsus, his home town. It would be many years before he revisited Jerusalem.

With Paul gone, the believers in Jerusalem were left in peace.

Sketch 11 – Where's Paul?

"Hey, Barnabas, is it true that Saul of Tarsus became a Christian?" asked Rufus, a new believer. "I was wondering yesterday what had become of him, and Jonathan said he was now a follower of Jesus. It seemed so unbelievable to me that I had to check."

"Yes, Rufus, it's true. He changed after he met Jesus – it's hard to insist someone is dead when you've met them alive!"

"When was that?"

"A few years ago." Barnabas stopped and thought. "I suppose it must be about four years ago now."

---

a   Acts 9:30 – See Galatians 1:21

"Has he stayed a Christian, or is he one of those people who keeps changing?"

"Saul, keeping changing?" Barnabas laughed. "Oh, no! Saul isn't like that. Saul is..." He stopped and pondered for a few moments, as if trying to find the best words to describe the indescribable. At last, he continued slowly, "Saul is... very determined, very devout, very eager to serve God. Saul is resolute. Saul would never change without absolute proof that he was wrong."

"Then why did he go around trying to kill our brothers?"

"He believed he was doing what God would want, just as you do. The difference is that his conviction was wrong, whereas yours is right – as Saul found out for himself when he met the master, risen."

"So where is he now? He used to live in Jerusalem, didn't he?"

"He lived in Jerusalem for several years until he went to visit Damascus, but then he met Jesus and hasn't come back except for short visits. First, he went into Arabia: he wanted to make absolutely sure that his new beliefs were right and that he fully understood how the new information should change his understanding of the scriptures. He stayed there almost three years."

"You mean he spent *three years* checking his beliefs?"

"That's right. He's thorough, is Saul."

"Jonathan suggested that Saul was in Jerusalem again recently. Is that right?"

"Yes, that was last year. He was here for a while, but because he is what he is, he couldn't resist telling his old friends about his new convictions, and they – being the good friends they are! – tried to kill him. We had to smuggle him out of the city and send him home to Tarsus."

"Well, if he upsets people like that, maybe we're better off without him here!"

"You're not the first to suggest that sort of thing, Rufus. I thought about it a lot when I saw how much trouble came to believers after the death of Stephen. Some believers complained that Stephen had caused unnecessary trouble. They claimed he was too aggressive, too argumentative. Live and let live, they said, otherwise the rulers will use their position to persecute and kill believers. Don't look for trouble."

"That sounds sensible to me."

"Well, it's sensible up to a point, but trouble and persecution are inevitable if we're doing the work Jesus gave his disciples. Remember what he said: 'Go out into all the world and preach the gospel to everyone.' "

"Maybe, but Jesus our Lord managed to preach for three years before they killed him, whereas it sounds like Saul took only two or three weeks to upset people enough that they wanted to kill him. I don't want my family to end up in danger just because Saul is too confrontational! Preaching is all very well, of course, but...."

"All I can say is that many of God's prophets have been killed over the centuries, and that's included both confrontational people and timid people. I don't think you need to worry about it. After all, Jesus chose Paul to be one of his witnesses – and Jesus knows exactly what Paul is like!"

"True.... When you put it that way, I have to agree with you. Thanks for clarifying it."

"Jesus has work for Paul to do, and at the moment, that work is in Tarsus. And he has work for each of us to do, too, so let's get on with it, shall we?"

Antioch in Syria

Acts 11:19-13:2

Acts 11

[Verses 1-19 omitted: no connection with Paul]

The Church at Antioch

¹⁹ So indeed those having been scattered by the tribulation having taken place over Stephen passed through to Phoenicia and Cyprus and Antioch, speaking the word to no one except to Jews alone. ²⁰ But some of them were men of Cyprus and Cyrene, who having come into Antioch, were speaking also to the Hellenists, proclaiming the gospel—the Lord Jesus. ²¹ And the hand of the Lord was with them, and a great number, having believed, turned to the Lord.

²² Now the report concerning them was heard in the ears of the church being in Jerusalem, and they sent forth Barnabas to go as far as Antioch, ²³ who having come and having seen the grace of God, rejoiced and was exhorting all to abide in the Lord with resolute purpose of heart. ²⁴ For he was a good man, and full of the Holy Spirit and of faith. And a large crowd was added to the Lord.

²⁵ And he went forth to Tarsus to seek Saul, ²⁶ and having found him, he brought him to Antioch. Now it came to pass that they also gathered together an entire year in the church, and taught a large crowd. And in Antioch the disciples were first called Christians.

²⁷ Now in these days, prophets came down from Jerusalem to Antioch. ²⁸ And one of them named Agabus, having risen up, signified by the Spirit that a great famine is about to be over the whole world—which came to pass under Claudius.

[Verse 29 has been moved to between the end of Acts 14 and the start of Acts 15.[a]]

---

a The prophets' visit and Agabus' prophecy described in verses 27-28 above are probably in chronological order with the rest of the chapter, but the famine and its effects would be felt later, prompting the collection described in verse 29 to help the suffering brothers in Judea. Based on Galatians 2:1, Barnabas and Saul probably delivered this

Acts 12

[Verses 1-24 omitted: no connection with Paul]

[Verse 25 has been moved to between Acts 15:29 and 30.[a]]

Acts 13

Paul's First Missionary Journey (Acts 13:2-14:26)
(Second: Acts 15:36-41; Third: Acts 18:23-28)

[1] Now there were prophets and teachers in Antioch in the church being there, both Barnabas and Simeon who was called Niger, and Lucius the Cyrenian, and Manaen brought up with Herod the tetrarch, and Saul. [2] Now as they were ministering to the Lord and fasting, the Holy Spirit said, "Set apart then to Me Barnabas and Saul for the work to which I have called them."

Acts 11:19-13:2

It was several years after Paul had left Jerusalem in such a hurry that he met Barnabas again. During that time, believers had spread the word about Jesus north and south, with some preaching not just to Jews, but Greeks as well. When news of this development reached Jerusalem, Barnabas was sent to Antioch in Syria to check on the situation and make sure nothing got out of hand.

Barnabas, true to his name, encouraged the believers in Antioch, then went on to Tarsus to see if he could bring Paul into the unfolding work of The Way. Barnabas saw trouble brewing and believed Paul could help.

He got what he wanted. Paul returned with him to Antioch and they spent a year there teaching any who would listen. What a year of growth it was!

During that time, some prophets came to Antioch from Jerusalem and one of them, named Agabus, gave a prophecy through the Holy Spirit that a great famine was about to spread over the whole world. Over the next few years, this famine hurt believers and unbelievers alike.

---

aid during the visit described at the start of Acts 15 when they and others were sent to Jerusalem to discuss the question of circumcision.

a   This verse comes at the end of a section (verses 20-24) where Luke jumps ahead in time to report Agrippa's well-deserved death and the subsequent spread of the gospel (including during Paul's first missionary journey). Chronologically, it probably refers to the time when Barnabas and Saul returned to Antioch after the Jerusalem conference.

It was also there in Antioch that outsiders invented a name for believers that would spread across the world and endure through the centuries: "Christians".

It was a time of outstanding growth and spiritual development for all the believers. Some became prophets and teachers.

Once, as they were devoting themselves to service and fasting, a special message came from the Holy Spirit: Barnabas and Saul were to be sent away on a new project. No-one knew exactly what the task was or where it would lead them, but Saul was filled with anticipation. He had ideas: preaching and growth.

Sketch 12 – Ready to go!

"You got what you wanted, Saul!"

"Yes, Barnabas," answered Paul, rubbing his hands together and smiling an intense smile. "Where shall we go first?"

"We'd been considering going to Cyprus before the Holy Spirit told us to go out preaching, so I reckon it makes sense to follow those plans."

"Good. I'm looking forward to seeing if the Roman roads will make our preaching easier."

"It's an interesting theory of yours. There's no doubt they're excellent roads; amazing technology and well maintained. *And* they're the only ones that don't become quagmires during winter."

"Not to mention that they're also very direct, and often have soldiers stationed on them to protect travellers."

"Those soldiers might not always be a help!"

"Perhaps not, but I think they'll scare away robbers."

"True. Well, we'll see soon enough whether the roads are a help or not."

"Then let's sail off to Cyprus. You'll be able to start preaching in your homeland."

"My homeland? Sort of, I suppose. Is Cilicia your homeland, Saul?"

"No, not really. I suppose we've both chosen to spend a lot of time in Israel even though we were born outside it."

"Of course: it *is* the Promised Land!"

"Though neither of us have any inheritance there since our families settled elsewhere. At least now we might see some benefit from that – we're more used to living and travelling among Gentiles than most of the brethren. When should we leave, Barnabas?"

"I can leave tomorrow morning. What about you?"

"Me too. It won't be any surprise to my host – he was in the congregation when the call came."

"Mine was too. Do you have any loose ends you need to tie up? Any work to finish?"

"Just a couple of small jobs that I can finish today. Mending a tent and completing that decorated saddle bag I've been working on for a while. Then I'm ready to go." Saul clapped his hands together and grinned. "I'm looking forward to it."

"So am I," agreed Barnabas, smiling too. "I'll be glad to see Cyprus again. Particularly the beautiful scenery."

"I know what you mean – I miss some of the scenery around Tarsus. There are lots of bandits on the roads up towards the Cilician Pass, but it's a lovely area. Still, we're not going to sightsee: all that matters is finding people to preach to."

"Agreed. Now, I was thinking it might be a good idea to take some others with us. I expect we'll find a lot of people interested in hearing the truth about Jesus Christ, so having other believers with us to talk to them would be a great help."

"Hmm," mused Saul. "I hadn't thought of that. Is there anyone who'd be willing to go at such short notice? I don't want anything to delay our departure."

"I know what you mean, and I don't want to delay either. But I was thinking: my cousin John Mark is interested in preaching, so he might be able to come with us."

"Having a supporter sounds wise. Do you think he's the right man for the job?"

"Mark's a faithful young man – quite a lot like his mother. My only concern is that he's had a comfortable life in Jerusalem and I'm not sure we'll be very comfortable at times on this journey."

"No, I'm not expecting it to be easy."

"I think he should be able to learn to cope, though. Shall I ask him if he wants to come? He might not be able to."

"Yes, why not ask him?" said Saul. "The more I think about it, the more I like the idea of having a helper with us."

"I'll go and ask him now, and then I'll have to decide what luggage I need to take."

Saul threw up his hands in mock apprehension and said earnestly, "Just don't forget what Jesus said when he sent people out to preach: 'Take no gold, silver or copper in your belt, take no bag for the journey, nor spare sets of clothes or sandals.' We're not taking a cart and horses!"

Barnabas laughed, then inquired more thoughtfully, "Do you think we should still be following those instructions? After all, they were for people travelling in a small area, going from village to village. We might be spending several days at a time on boats or on the road. Won't we need to carry a bit more with us than they did?"

"I expect we'll be away for more than a year, so I reckon we'll need a full set of clothes to allow for different temperatures in different seasons. And we'll need some money too, if only to pay for our boat passage."

"Yes, I was thinking about the boat fare, too. I don't think I've got enough money to pay for my fare to Cyprus. What about you?"

"It'll be touch and go. Like you, I've been spending as much time preaching as I can, only working when I have to."

"We might have to work for a day or two in Seleucia to pay for our passage."

"Maybe, but even so, I don't think we should ask for money from the brethren here," answered Saul. "We can work while we travel, just as much as we need to cover our expenses."

"Jesus did say that the labourer is worthy of his hire, so if people are willing to feed us or give us lodging, I think we should accept it."

"I suppose so. But we'll be travelling among Gentiles in places we don't know, so I think we'll have to wait and see whether anyone offers any help or not."

"But since we're certain God wants us to go, we can trust him to look after us on the way."

As he spoke, an older man entered the room where the pair were talking. He waited until Barnabas finished speaking, then said, "Excuse me, brothers. Since God chose you two to go out preaching, I've been thinking what I can do to help. I want to give you some money toward your travel expenses." He offered some silver coins to Barnabas and continued, "Will you let me do that? I feel too old to go out preaching myself, but I'm excited that you're going and eager to help. Please!"

Barnabas smiled at Saul and Saul gazed at Barnabas, shaking his head slowly as if in wonder. Together they turned to the old man and Barnabas said, "You've just removed our first delay, Simeon. We thought we'd have to work a while in Seleucia to pay for our passage to Cyprus, but now we can go immediately!"

"If the Lord is willing, we'll leave tomorrow morning," said Saul. "Early."

"The elders are arranging a special meeting for tonight to lay their hands on you both and send you off with their blessing," answered Simeon.

"Thanks for telling us," said Barnabas, looking a little concerned. "I must go and find John Mark straight away or he won't have any time to make up his mind."

"Perhaps we should forget about asking him," said Saul. "Go by ourselves, just the two of us. After all, that's what Jesus told his disciples to do."

"I think our journey is a bigger undertaking, Saul. I think having someone like John Mark to help us will be invaluable when we're so far from home."

"Okay, if that's what you want, go and ask him. It can't hurt."

PART FOUR
The First Missionary Journey

Setting Off

All the brothers joined in a time of prayer and fasting, then laid their hands on Saul and Barnabas and sent them on their way.

John Mark went with them as well.

How could anyone know that by the time they returned, Saul would no longer be known as Saul, but Paul?

And how could anybody guess that the journey they were setting out on would become famous: still to be spoken of 2,000 years later?

It was the first of several preaching trips Saul-turned-Paul undertook in the company of many different evangelists, but Paul's would be the name associated with them all.

Paul's first missionary journey was underway.

Acts 13:3

[3] Then having fasted and having prayed and having laid the hands on them, they sent them off.

Cyprus

Acts 13:4

Leaving Antioch, Barnabas, Saul and John Mark went to Seleucia to catch a ship and sail for Cyprus.

ℭℛ

Acts 13:4-5

4 Therefore indeed having been sent forth by the Holy Spirit, they went down to Seleucia, and they sailed from there to Cyprus.[a] **5** And having come into Salamis, they began proclaiming the word of God in the synagogues of the Jews. And they also had John as a helper.[b]

ℭℛ

Sketch 13 – How to preach

A purposeful breeze filled the main sail, driving the ship onward. She cut through the waves, white water at her bows, her crew satisfied with their progress.

Barnabas, Saul and John Mark stood on the deck, shading their eyes against the brilliant sunshine, straining to see their target port as Cyprus opened out before them.

"We'll be landing in Salamis soon, and then we start telling the people of Cyprus all about Jesus, the Christ," said Barnabas, rubbing his hands together.

"How do we begin?" asked John Mark.

---

a   Acts 13:4 – Barnabas was a native of Cyprus (Acts 4:36)
b   Acts 13:5 – Also known as Mark (Acts 12:25; 15:37). Believed to be the author of the gospel of Mark. John Mark was Barnabas' cousin (Colossians 4:10).

"In Damascus, I went to the synagogue and was asked to speak," answered Saul. "It provided the perfect opportunity."

"And tomorrow is the Sabbath," observed Barnabas.

"We might not be welcome in a synagogue," said John Mark. "Have you thought about starting by healing some people?"

"That's not our main aim," said Saul. "Jesus Christ *taught* first. Miracles were never the main game."

"Saul's right," agreed Barnabas. "After Jesus fed the five thousand, multitudes came to him and he said they were just looking for food. He wasn't pleased – in fact, that was when he taught some of his hardest lessons."

"There's no doubt," said Saul, "the Lord Jesus came first to teach. Miracles followed – often because the people who came to listen had many problems and he felt sorry for them."

"We're not going to Cyprus to heal everyone's physical ailments. We're going to cure spiritual problems, particularly ignorance."

"So no miracles at all?" asked John Mark, disappointed.

"That's not what we're saying," smiled Barnabas. "Miracles are sure to come, but teaching about Jesus has to come first."

"What will we do the rest of the time? Going to the synagogue on Saturdays still leaves six days of the week."

"We can go to the market," said Saul. "I'll find tent-making and leatherwork to do and talk to the traders and customers while I'm at it."

"I don't have any trade I can pursue in a market," said John Mark. "Should I look for work as a labourer to pay for my food?"

"We're not short of money at the moment," answered Barnabas. "Our brothers and sisters in Antioch gave us money to cover our costs for some time. At the same time, Saul and I are both determined to support ourselves if we possibly can."

"We want to give people the gospel free of charge whenever possible," added Saul.

For a while, no one spoke. The ship was approaching the port of Salamis, and seabirds hovering above the ship filled the air with their mournful cries. All three had a feeling that they were on the cusp of something amazing. The Way had spread first throughout Israel and then through the neighbouring countries, but now... was it time for it to spread over the rest of the world?

"One thing I wonder," reflected John Mark. "On the Day of Pentecost, Jews from all over the world heard the truth about Jesus Christ and were baptised. Soon afterwards, most returned to their homes and took their new faith with them. Will we meet any of them on this journey?"

"That's a good question, cousin," said Barnabas. "I've often wondered what happened to all those people."

"We'll start to find answers soon," said Saul.

The ship was approaching the quay and the crew waited to spring into action and make the vessel fast. Christianity was about to enter a new phase.

Acts 13:5-12

Having landed at Salamis, it was time to begin preaching.

Straight away, Saul and Barnabas put into operation a method of preaching that they used for many years thereafter. If they arrived in a town and found a Jewish synagogue there, they visited it on the Sabbath. While there, they took any opportunity they could find to talk about the good news of Jesus from the scriptures, from witness reports and from Saul's own experience of Jesus.

In synagogues, visitors, particularly educated ones, were often invited to speak or read, and Saul made the most of that tradition. Sometimes, if he piqued their interest on a Sabbath, they also gave him opportunities to talk to them during the week.

Town by town, they made their way through the island of Cyprus until they came to Paphos at the far end of the island. News of their work had travelled before them and the proconsul wanted to hear the message from Barnabas and Saul directly. He was an intelligent man and Saul was enjoying explaining the gospel. However, a Jewish magician and false prophet was also present, and he did his best to stop the proconsul listening. Saul put up with this for a while, but then cursed the man and struck him with blindness in the name of the Lord. The proconsul was amazed and kept listening. The miracle achieved its purpose.

It was in Paphos that "Saul" changed to "Paul". From then on, he was always called Paul.

℘

Acts 13:6-13

[6] Now having passed through the whole island as far as Paphos, they found a certain magician, a Jewish false prophet whose name was Bar-Jesus, [7] who was with the proconsul Sergius Paulus, an intelligent man. He, having summoned Barnabas and Saul, desired to hear the word of God. [8] But Elymas the magician (for his name means thus) was opposing them, seeking to turn away the proconsul from the faith.

[9] And Saul, the one also called Paul,[a] having been filled with the Holy Spirit, having looked intently upon him, [10] said, "O full of all deceit and all craft, son of the devil, enemy of all righteousness, will you not cease perverting the straight ways of the Lord? [11] And now behold, the hand of the Lord is upon you, and you will be blind, not seeing the sun during a season." And immediately mist and darkness fell upon him, and going about, he was seeking someone to lead him by the hand.

[12] Then the proconsul, having seen that having happened, believed, being astonished at the teaching of the Lord.

---

a   Acts 13:9 – From this point on in the narrative, the name Saul is only used when Paul recounts earlier events, particularly telling of his conversion.

Perga in Pamphylia

Acts 13:13

13 And those around Paul, having sailed from Paphos, came to Perga of Pamphylia. But John, having departed from them, returned to Jerusalem.

Acts 13:13

Paul and his companions left Paphos and sailed to Perga where a sad and disappointing separation occurred: John Mark deserted them and sailed home.

Sketch 14 – John Mark leaves

"So we're agreed that tomorrow morning we travel north?" Barnabas looked at his companions for confirmation.

"That's what we've agreed, isn't it?" puzzled Paul.

"I'm just checking," said Barnabas, his eyes on John Mark, who was fidgeting.

"Ah, I'm not… That is, I'm wondering. I mean…" stuttered Mark.

"What *do* you mean?" asked Paul. "Haven't we talked this out already?"

Barnabas held up his hand soothingly. "Just let Mark say his piece."

"I'm going home," blurted out Mark.

"You're what?" queried Paul, frowning.

"I'm going back to Jerusalem. I'm sorry to let you down, Paul, but it's all too hard."

"What's too hard?" asked Paul, looking baffled.

"The stress, the uncertainty, the opposition, the worry. I don't think that I'm cut out for life as a travelling preacher." Mark looked ashamed and upset. He had been so eager to go on this preaching journey with his cousin and Paul, but it had turned out much harder than he expected.

"Look, Mark, it's up to you," said Barnabas, "but if you just hang on and stay with us, I'm sure you'll find it gets easier. God will give you strength and confidence if you can just keep trying."

"I just can't face it any more," replied Mark. "You've seen how angry some people get when we preach to them. One of these days we'll go into a town and someone will try to stone us. I just can't... I can't keep going. I'm too... too scared."

"Scared?" repeated Paul, blankly. He wasn't being deliberately obtuse – he simply couldn't understand how the events of their journey thus far could have inspired such fear. Later, after experiencing many far more traumatic incidents while preaching, he would begin to understand for himself how one could end up in such an extremity.

"If you feel like that," said Barnabas to his cousin, "perhaps it *is* better for you to go home. I'm sure God will have plenty of work for you to do in Jerusalem."

"That's true, I suppose," responded Paul, "but we'll miss your help. An extra pair of hands, an extra voice, an extra mind looking for opportunities and praying for guidance." He shook his head in disappointment. He couldn't help feeling that their current situation was safer than Jerusalem had been on his last visit! Yet Mark seemed to consider Jerusalem a safe haven – a place where he could feel at home.

Paul wasn't the only one who was upset at Mark's decision. Barnabas looked disappointed too – after all, it would certainly reduce their ability to preach – but he seemed to understand better. He knew that travelling through a foreign land where customs, language and behaviour were all different was not easy. After all, he had left his home in Cyprus to go to Israel!

Mark looked less distraught now that he had admitted his troubles and announced his plan to leave. It was as if a huge weight had been lifted from his shoulders.

"Will you need help to arrange a passage back to Judea?" asked Paul, willing to help, even if he couldn't understand.

"No, thank you," said Mark. "I'll see what I can arrange this afternoon. That is, unless you'd like me to help you get ready. I can find a ship after you've gone in the morning if you prefer."

"We don't have much to do before we leave," said Barnabas. "Just get some food, that's all."

John Mark booked a passage home that afternoon.

Antioch in Pisidia

Acts 13:14-52

Obviously, the stresses of such an uncertain task as preaching were more than John Mark could bear, but Paul and Barnabas could not give up so easily. They headed north to Antioch in Pisidia.

Once again, the Sabbath found them in a synagogue, sitting with the rest of the congregation. After the readings from the Law and the Prophets, they received a quick message from the synagogue officials: "If you have any words of encouragement for the people, please speak." Paul stood up and motioned with his hand for silence.

He spoke to them briefly of the history of Israel and how God had looked after them. Speaking of David, he referred to the offspring God had promised and introduced them to Jesus as the son of David. Crucifixion and resurrection completed his discourse, and the entire presentation was very well received. People begged them to come again the next Sabbath.

They did. So did almost the entire town, news of this new message having spread widely. A perfect opportunity for all to hear about Jesus.

However, the Jewish leaders were less happy with the good turn-out. Jealousy ate them up and they denied everything Paul and Barnabas said.

Paul and Barnabas responded with the devastating news that, although it was necessary for the Jews to be offered salvation through Jesus first, since they didn't want it, it would be offered to the Gentiles instead.

The Gentiles were pleased and many believed, but the Jews stirred up some important men and women to start persecuting Paul and Barnabas until they could drive them away.

As Jesus had suggested to his disciples, Paul and Barnabas wiped the dust off their feet as a sign of rejection and moved on.

Although they left trouble, threats and persecution behind, they also left behind some new believers, men and women filled with the joy of salvation.

ℭℛ

Acts 13:14-52

[14] Now having passed through from Perga, they came to Antioch of Pisidia, and having gone into the synagogue on the day of the Sabbaths, they sat down. [15] And after the reading of the Law and of the Prophets, the rulers of the synagogue sent to them, saying, "Men, brothers, if there is any word of exhortation among you toward the people, speak."

[16] And Paul, having risen up and having made a sign with the hand, said, "Men of Israel and those fearing God, listen: [17] The God of this people Israel chose our fathers and exalted the people in the sojourn in the land of Egypt, and with uplifted arm He brought them out of it, [18] and for a period of about forty years He endured their ways in the wilderness, [19] and having destroyed seven nations in the land of Canaan, He gave as an inheritance their land— [20] during four hundred and fifty years.

And after these things, He gave them judges until Samuel the prophet. [21] Then they asked for a king, and God gave them Saul son of Kish, a man of the tribe of Benjamin, for forty years. [22] And having removed him, He raised up David to them as king, to whom also He said, having carried witness: 'I have found David the son of Jesse a man according to My heart, who will do all My will.'

[23] Of the seed of this man, according to promise, God raised up to Israel the Savior, Jesus— [24] John having proclaimed before the face of His coming a baptism of repentance to all the people of Israel. [25] And while John was fulfilling the course, he was saying, 'Whom do you suppose me to be? I am not He, but behold, He comes after me, of whom I am not worthy to untie a sandal of the feet.'

[26] Men, brothers, sons of the family of Abraham, and those among you fearing God, to us the message of this salvation has been sent. [27] For those dwelling in Jerusalem and their rulers, not having known Him and the voices of the prophets that are being read on every Sabbath, having condemned Him, they fulfilled them. [28] And having found no cause of death, they begged Pilate to put Him to death.

[29] And when they had finished all the things having been written about Him, having taken Him down from the tree, they put Him in a tomb. [30] But God raised Him out from the dead, [31] who appeared for many days to those having come up with Him from Galilee to Jerusalem, who are now His witnesses to the people.

[32] And we preach the gospel to you, the promise having been made to the fathers, [33] that God has fulfilled this to us their children, having raised up Jesus, as also it has been written in the second psalm:

'You are My Son,
today I have begotten you.'[a]

34 And that He raised Him out from the dead, no more being about to return to decay, He spoke thus:

'I will give to you the holy and sure blessings of David.'[b]

35 Therefore He also says in another:

'You will not allow your Holy One to see decay.'[c]

36 For indeed David, having served the purpose of God in his own generation, fell asleep and was added to his fathers, and saw decay. **37** But the One God raised up did not see decay.

38 Therefore be it known to you, men, brothers, that through this One, forgiveness of sins is proclaimed to you. **39** And in Him everyone believing is justified from all things from which you were not able to be justified in the Law of Moses. **40** Take heed therefore, lest that having been said in the prophets might come about:

41 'Behold, scoffers,
and wonder and perish;
for I am working a work in your days,
a work that you would never believe,
even if one should declare it to you.'[d]"

The Gentiles Ask to Hear the Gospel

42 And they having departed, they were begging these words to be spoken to them on the next Sabbath. **43** And the synagogue having broken up, many of the Jews and worshipping converts followed Paul and Barnabas, who, speaking to them, kept persuading them to continue in the grace of God.

44 And on the coming Sabbath, almost the whole city was gathered together to hear the word of the Lord. **45** But the Jews, having seen the crowds, were filled with jealousy, and began contradicting the things spoken by Paul, blaspheming.

46 And Paul and Barnabas, having spoken boldly, said, "It was necessary for the word of God to be spoken first to you. But since you thrust it away and do not judge yourselves worthy of eternal life, behold, we are turning to the Gentiles. **47** For thus the Lord has commanded us:

'I have set you for a light of the Gentiles,
you to be for salvation to the uttermost part of the earth.'[e]"

a   BLB: Acts 13:33 – Psalm 2:7
b   BLB: Acts 13:34 – Isaiah 55:3
c   BLB: Acts 13:35 – Psalm 16:10
d   BLB: Acts 13:41 – Habakkuk 1:5
e   BLB: Acts 13:47 – Isaiah 49:6

48 And the Gentiles hearing it were rejoicing and glorifying the word of the Lord, and as many as were appointed to eternal life believed. **49** And the word of the Lord was carried through the whole region.

50 But the Jews incited the worshipping women of honorable position and the principals of the city, and they stirred up a persecution against Paul and Barnabas and expelled them from their district. **51** But having shaken off the dust of the feet against them, they went to Iconium; **52** and the disciples were filled with joy and the Holy Spirit.

Sketch 15 – Leaving

A large crowd moved noisily down the road out of Antioch, their loud, aggressive words directed at two men whom they pushed ahead of them.

"Get out of our district," shouted a voice.

"And stay out," snarled another.

"We don't want heretics here," came a slower but authoritative voice from the back of the group. From the group's response, it was clear he was their leader. His clothing showed him to be an important man in the city.

Anyone looking closely at the group would have noticed two distinct categories of people within it: the majority, well-dressed but unarmed; and the minority, the ones doing most of the shoving, well-armed.

As for the two men at the front – the ones being prodded and harried – they were dressed in the common working clothes of the working class. They weren't openly resisting, but they obviously didn't want to go, leading to frequent manhandling.

From time to time, more forceful shoves caused them to stumble and almost fall, but they still didn't complain.

Their clothes were certainly not new, but some of the large tears they sported probably were. Each man held tightly to a large bundle slung over his shoulder.

Suddenly, the smaller man received a particularly heavy push. He staggered and fell, dropping his bundle as he flung out his hands to break his fall. One of the armed men immediately kicked the bundle, catapulting it off the road into the drainage ditch, while another kicked at the fallen man, hitting him in the thigh.

Laughter rose among the group, but the man jumped quickly to his feet and scrambled to rescue his bundle from the damp earth of the ditch. He picked it up by the carry ropes and slung it over his shoulder again as the party came to a stop.

The laughter died down as the slow, authoritative voice announced, "This is as far as we need go, ladies and gentlemen. All except for you two," he added, speaking to the pair who had been the focus of so much undesirable attention. "You two must keep moving. Get out of our district and don't come back."

"If we see you back in Antioch again, someone might take matters into their own hands," said a woman's harsh voice.

"True, true," agreed the leader, "and our civil authorities may decide to take firmer action than the unofficial step we have taken today. Of course, some of us would be involved in the decision-making, and I'm sure it wouldn't be hard to convince our fellow councillors to take serious punitive action once they knew how much disturbance you two have already caused."

Paul faced the incongruous group that had driven them out of Antioch: Jewish religious leaders rubbed shoulders with pagan priests and important men and women from the city's upper classes. Catching his breath, he answered, "We have not caused any disturbance or rebellion. We have told you the solemn truth."

"Truth?" began a Jewish leader, his voice coldly contemptuous, screwing up his mouth until his beard jutted out.

The slow voice hushed him, then said, "We're not going into all that again. You two," he pointed to Paul and Barnabas, "are leaving our district *right now.*"

Paul was obviously about to speak, but the leader held up his hand. "Without further discussion," he ordered firmly, "or these guards will deal with you immediately." His eyes narrowed and his voice hardened as he concluded, "And if either of you ever comes back to Antioch, together or separately, you'll pay for it with your lives."

Once more, Paul looked as if he was about to speak, but Barnabas grabbed his arm. "Come on, Paul," he said, "let's go."

Paul pursed his lips, then sighed and nodded. "Very well," he said, bending over and taking off his sandals. He stood and banged them together, saying, "Since you reject God's offer of salvation, we shake the dust of your town off our feet as evidence against you."

Barnabas did the same.

They put their sandals back on without a word, then turned away from their persecutors. Packs over their shoulders, they walked away.

The watching group stood in silence for a while, then turned towards Antioch, strangely subdued. Perhaps they unwillingly acknowledged the significance of Paul and Barnabas' symbolic action.

Soon the crowd was out of sight and Paul and Barnabas were on their own again, following the road to Iconium.

"Why do our religious leaders choose to stir up hatred?" asked Paul.

"They just can't cope with new ideas," answered Barnabas. "Their entire life has been dedicated to maintaining tradition in the face of paganism and fighting off newfangled ideas. They can't see that these aren't new ideas at all, just the fulfilment of ancient prophecies."

"Our leaders fought Jesus, and now they're fighting us."

"And all because they don't understand that Jesus was presenting the only way of salvation, living a life that truly fulfilled the intentions and goals of Moses' law."

"I suppose you're right," sighed Paul. "They're wedded to their own traditions rather than God's truth. And when they hear anything they weren't brought up with, they reject it."

"Utterly."

"Almost without any attempt at thought."

"Thankfully, though, not everyone is like that, so now there are some new believers in Antioch."

"Which makes it all worthwhile," said Paul. "That's why we went there."

"And the enemy didn't kill us," smiled Barnabas.

"They didn't even hurt us," said Paul. As Barnabas questioned him with a look, he added, "At least, not much."

They walked in silence for a few minutes.

"Jesus warned me that I would suffer many things in his name," mused Paul. "It hasn't happened yet."

"Give thanks to God, then, and keep preaching – but don't go looking for trouble."

Paul laughed. "You're right. My suffering so far is trivial compared with crucifixion. In fact, I think we've both been looked after so that we haven't suffered as our enemies hoped."

"And we're free to go to Iconium and keep preaching."

"Will we ever go back to Antioch, Barnabas?"

"You heard their threats."

"True, but now there are believers to think about. Little children in the faith who will need support."

"Perhaps others could go there. Maybe some of the believers from Antioch in Syria could visit them. It wouldn't be so dangerous if people just visited to see the believers, rather than preaching publicly."

"Danger didn't keep Jesus away from Jerusalem."

"I'm convinced that we shouldn't run away from danger," said Barnabas, "but I don't think we should go looking for it either."

"I'm sure you're right. Danger will always be present if we preach Jesus Christ as the coming king. Most of the Jews reject him as Messiah and want to kill his supporters, the Romans consider him an enemy to the empire and want to kill his followers, and the Greeks say we're introducing a new religion and want to kill us for that."

"Fortunately, the Greeks also want to laugh at us because they think we're celebrating a loser, so that takes the edge off the danger we face from them!"

Iconium

Acts 14:1-5

Acts 14

Paul and Barnabas at Iconium

[1] Now it came to pass in Iconium, according to the same, they entered into the synagogue of the Jews and spoke so that a great number of both Jewish and Greeks believed. [2] But the unbelieving Jews stirred up and poisoned the minds of the Gentiles against the brothers. [3] Therefore indeed they stayed a long time, speaking boldly for the Lord, bearing witness to the word of His grace, granting signs and wonders to be done through their hands.

[4] Now the multitude of the city was divided, and indeed some were with the Jews, but some with the apostles. [5] And when there was a rush both of the Gentiles and Jews, with their rulers, to mistreat and to stone them...

Acts 14:1-5

Another new town, and again they followed Paul's standard procedure. When Saturday came, they went to the synagogue, talking about Jesus and grabbing the attention of any who would listen, whether they were Jews or God-fearing Gentiles. They followed up anyone who was interested, and soon they were speaking to large crowds of Jews and Gentiles. Many believed the good news, and Paul and Barnabas also performed amazing miracles – which helped convince even more.

However, the Jews who did not believe stirred up the crowds and drove them out of the synagogue.

The city was divided.

The unbelievers then got together with the rulers and plotted to mistreat and stone Paul and Barnabas – already an all-too-familiar situation – but they heard about it early enough to escape and flee to other towns.

❧

Sketch 16 – Is there any other way?

"By God's grace, we escaped again, Barnabas!" exulted Paul.

"Yes. If it weren't for God's grace, we'd be in our graves by now, wouldn't we?"

"It's amazing, but it's scary too."

"Don't think about it too much. We're heading for another town now... which one, Paul?"

"Lystra."

"Yes, Lystra, and... then we'll start all over again."

The joy and exultation were real, and the two missionaries were extremely grateful for God's care – but it didn't take much to remind them of their narrow escape from the brutal plans of their fellow Jews. They traversed the dry, flat, uncultivated land for quite some time in silence, passing occasional rocky outcrops. Infrequently they passed other travellers, but neither of them paid much attention. Their minds were held prisoner by the thought that echoed and re-echoed endlessly in their minds: when they arrived in Lystra, it wouldn't be long before another crowd was baying for their blood.

Even Paul, far more single-minded and optimistic than most and resigned to the task his saviour had appointed for him, couldn't rid his mind of the alarming probabilities.

"I wonder," mused Barnabas eventually, "is there anything we can do differently?"

Paul had no need to ask what he was talking about. "I'm pretty sure that unless we stop preaching completely, nothing will change the results."

"Can we *try* something different?"

"Such as?"

"Maybe we could start preaching somewhere other than in the synagogue?"

Paul didn't answer for a few moments. Then he sighed. "Perhaps we could, but the synagogue is the best place to find people who are interested in God and the good news."

"I know, but it's also the best way to attract the hatred of the Jews who won't listen."

"True... and they seem very good at inciting others to hate us, too."

"What a gift!"

The two friends laughed together, but humour alone wouldn't fix the problem. They continued on in silence once more.

"There's no point in going to a town to preach if we don't end up talking to the people who are interested!" Paul declared after a while.

"No, but there's also no future for our preaching if we get ourselves killed! So which is better: to preach to, say, 100 people in each of 20 towns over the next two years, or to speak to 1,000 people in Lystra tomorrow and then get killed?"

"You're right, of course, but I don't think it's quite as easy to keep things under control as you're implying. I never heard Jesus preaching, but I gather he had a lot of difficulty trying to balance the response of the crowd: at times he had to stop people trying to make him king, then at other times he had to avoid them stoning him!"

"Well, we haven't exactly had problems with people trying to make us kings!" laughed Barnabas.

"Which is good, because I've got no idea what we'd do if they did!"

"I don't think we need to worry about it, really. All we need to know is that Jesus made sure he stopped it, so we'd have to do the same."

"And crowds can be very fickle," said Paul. "Jesus entered Jerusalem with crowds of people cheering him on, then a week later they were demanding that he be killed."

"I don't think it was quite the same crowd, do you?"

"No, not entirely," agreed Paul, "but we've seen for ourselves just how quickly people can change."

They passed a milestone. Lystra was just two miles[a] away.

"Any other ideas of things we could do differently?" asked Paul.

This time it was Barnabas who sighed. "No, not really. We've got to preach the gospel, and that means some people will hate us. Nothing we can do will change that."

---

a   Roman miles were about 1.5 kilometres or 0.9 modern miles.

"And Jesus hasn't let us be killed yet, so he still has work for us."

"Yes. He still has people to save. I hope he has lots of people to save here."

"It's only the second day of the week, so we've got a few days before the Sabbath anyway. Let's start preaching."

They approached the gates of Lystra with mixed feelings.

Lystra

Acts 14:6-20

Entering Lystra, they continued preaching. By now they were quite familiar with the process that played out each time. But this time was a little different.

A man who had never been able to walk sat and listened intently to Paul. Paul saw that he had faith to be healed and said, "Stand up on your feet." Remember that this man had never walked in his life, so there would be all sorts of things stopping him, from weakness to fear. But he didn't let any of them put him off. He not only stood up, he leaped up and walked around.

Naturally enough, the crowd was amazed, and declared in their local language that the gods had come down to earth. They gave Paul and Barnabas the names of Greek gods, which upset the pair greatly. Things were spiralling out of control, with the priest of Zeus coming with garlands of flowers and oxen to offer sacrifices to them!

Paul and Barnabas did some hurried straight talking, but it was only with the utmost difficulty that they stopped the crowds from worshipping them. When they finally tore their cloaks in despair, this seemed to convince the crowd that they were serious.

You might think that if men could perform a miracle like this, they would also know how it was done. But the crowd wanted none of their explanation about a living God. Strange, really.

It was not long after this episode that troublemakers from Antioch and Iconium came on the scene. They won over the crowd (possibly still a little bit upset with what Paul had said about their gods), and stoned Paul. Thinking he was dead, they dragged him out of the city.

Perhaps he *was* dead, but whether he was or not, his work was not finished and when the disciples surrounded him, he stood up and went back into the city. A brave man indeed.

Now Paul had suffered just as Stephen had done on that terrible day years before – a day Paul could never forget. Like Stephen, Paul too had been beaten to the ground with stones of hatred, but unlike Stephen, he had survived to preach another day. Was it repayment for his involvement in the stoning of Stephen? If so, then he was paid back double. Not only did he suffer the horrors of stoning, but he also had to endure the lengthy recuperation as bruises and cuts slowly healed. Paul's suffering for Jesus had well and truly begun.

The next day, Paul and Barnabas left Lystra.

Acts 14:6-20a

[6] having become aware, they fled to the Lycaonian cities Lystra and Derbe, and the surrounding region, [7] and there they continued preaching the gospel.

The Visit to Lystra and Derbe

[8] And in Lystra a certain man was sitting, crippled in the feet, lame from the womb of his mother, who had never walked. [9] This man heard Paul speaking, who having looked intently at him and having seen that he has faith to be healed, [10] said in a loud voice, "Stand upright on your feet!" And he sprang up and began to walk.

[11] And the crowds having seen what Paul had done, lifted up their voice in Lycaonian saying, "The gods have come down to us, having become like men." [12] And Barnabas, they began calling Zeus; and Paul, Hermes, because he was the leading speaker. [13] And the priest of Zeus, being just outside the city, having brought oxen and wreaths to the gates, was desiring with the crowds to sacrifice.

[14] But the apostles Barnabas and Paul having heard, having torn their garments, rushed out into the crowd, crying out [15] and saying, "Men, why do you do these things? We also are men of like nature with you, proclaiming the gospel to you, to turn from these vanities to the living God, who made the heaven and the earth and the sea and all the things in them, [16] who in the generations past allowed all the nations to go their own ways. [17] And yet He has not left Himself without witness, doing good, giving to you rains from heaven and fruitful seasons, filling your hearts with food and gladness."

[18] And saying these things, they hardly stopped the crowds from sacrificing to them.

[19] But Jews came from Antioch and Iconium, and having persuaded the crowds, and having stoned Paul, they dragged him outside the city, supposing him to have died. [20] But the disciples having surrounded him, having risen up, he entered into the city. And on the next day he went away with Barnabas to Derbe.

❦

Sketch 17 – Leaving Lystra

"How are you feeling after an hour of walking, Paul?" asked Barnabas.

"Surprisingly, the walking seems to be making most of it feel a bit easier," croaked Paul, his words slurred. "I can count all of my ribs, though."

"It must be tough, but you're doing well," said Barnabas, sympathetically. "Your face is a mess, though. Can you see anything through those slits of eyes?"

"Don't make me laugh," groaned Paul. "The ribs, you know, and my lips…"

"Sorry."

"You wanted to try something different in Lystra. Happy with the results?" Paul's slurred speech was quite different from his normally precise diction, and this time it took Barnabas a few moments to work out what he was saying.

"Oh, I suppose it proved what you were saying before we arrived: it probably doesn't matter much how we preach. If we preach about Jesus, we're taking up a cross like he did, and we could suffer just the same result."

"True. How far to Derbe?"

"Another 80 miles or so.[a] About three days' journey, normally."

"Maybe four at the moment."

"Or five, or however long you need. After all, people might be more likely to listen to what you say if you don't look like a battered wreck. Perhaps by then they'll be able to understand more of what you say, too."

Paul groaned again. "I thought you were meant to be Barnabas the Encourager!" he said.

"Normally," laughed Barnabas. "But some people don't need encouraging, they need slowing down, bringing back to reality."

"The way my feet are feeling, I don't want to think about the reality of walking 120 kilometres. And how can my backside be so badly bruised?"

---

a   Approximately 120 kilometres or 75 modern miles.

"Don't forget, they dragged you out of the city and dumped you, Paul. Two men holding an arm each – you can guess which part of you was scraping on the ground. It's amazing that your tunic is still intact, not to mention what's underneath!"

Derbe

Acts 14:20b-21a

And on the next day he went away with Barnabas to Derbe.

The Return to Syrian Antioch

[21] And having proclaimed the gospel to that city and having discipled many...

Acts 14:20-21

Derbe was yet another town where Paul could tell others about Jesus. Many heard his message and quite a few became disciples of Jesus as Paul and Barnabas were.

And then it was time to move on again, going back over their path to board a ship and return to Seleucia.

Sketch 18 – Return

"I think I can see Lystra in the distance," said Barnabas. "Are you still determined to go and see the brothers there?"

"Of course," said Paul, sounding a little puzzled by the question, given the strength of his assurance the last time it was asked.

"I know we've been through it before," replied Barnabas, "but I have to make one last effort to convince you. They stoned you in Lystra! If they stoned you last time, do you think they'll hesitate to do it again? Can't you see how risky it is?"

"Don't worry, Barnabas." Paul stopped, and when Barnabas halted beside him, Paul put his hand on Barnabas' shoulder. Paul had a piercing eye when he wanted to make a point. "I know just how risky it is, but there are some positives as well, and those are what convince me to do it. Our brothers and sisters will be encouraged by seeing us. They'll be glad to know we've been to Derbe and left without being stoned or attacked in any way. They'll also be glad to hear that there are plenty of new believers in Derbe too, and that the word of Christ is spreading as it should."

"That's true, but what about the men who did their best to kill you?"

Paul began walking again. His decision was made. As far as he was concerned, further discussion was fine if it could help convince Barnabas, but it would not materially affect his own choice. "We know many of them were men who'd followed us from other towns, and they won't be in Lystra any more – after all, they thought they'd killed me. Don't worry, Barnabas, I'm sure we'll be safe. Anyway, I want to spend most of our time there with the believers, not preaching. Any preaching we end up doing will be to Gentiles – the Jews have had their chance."

"Don't forget, there were Gentiles in that crowd too, Paul. It wasn't only Jews who threw stones at you!"

"No, but they were the ones who led the attack. If they hadn't been there, I doubt anyone would've attacked me."

"You could be right, but I'm also a bit concerned that we'll make life more difficult for the new believers if we stir up trouble in the town again."

Paul patted Barnabas on the arm as they walked. "Don't worry, brother," he said with a smile. "If the Lord Jesus still wants us working for him, everything will be alright. We take care of what we can take care of, and he'll take care of the rest."

"I suppose that's true," admitted Barnabas. "He took plenty of risks himself with enemies who wanted to kill him. Yet despite their best efforts, they couldn't kill him until the time planned by the Father."

"So then, let's get on with it: head into Lystra and start encouraging our brothers straight away," insisted Paul.

Barnabas gave up.

It wasn't long before they reached the gate of Lystra. No-one attacked them, no-one stopped them – indeed, no-one even seemed to recognise them, although Barnabas recognised two of the soldiers who stood on guard beside the gate. They had been on guard when Paul was dragged out of the city, presumed dead, and had merely stepped aside and watched impassively.

Once inside, Paul and Barnabas eagerly made their way towards the house of one of the earliest believers. The town streets were busy, however, and on one occasion, they even had to stand aside and wait as a cheering, chanting procession wended its way past them towards the city gate.

"What was that about?" breathed Barnabas to Paul as the tail of the procession passed by.

"I don't really know, but I think they were heading towards the temple of Zeus outside the city. I recognised some of the men and women from when they wanted to sacrifice to us. Remember how they called you Zeus?" laughed Paul.

"Yes, and you Hermes. Ah well, it looks as if our attempts to steer them away from idolatry failed. They're still wedded to it."

"Perhaps it didn't work for them, but it did work for brother Quintus, so let's get to his house as quickly as we can."

Hurrying through the streets, they reached the door they sought and Barnabas knocked. Knowing the volume of Paul's ordinary knock, he had made sure that he got there first. He wanted a quieter alternative that didn't announce their presence to everyone within earshot!

A murmur of animated voices had been audible from within, but a sudden silence followed his tap, as if the people inside were somehow hoping to avoid detection. He looked worriedly at Paul and took a step back. Paul immediately stepped forward, waited a few seconds and rapped loudly on the door.

Barnabas rolled his eyes. So much for arriving quietly!

A window shutter opened next door and a woman looked out at them suspiciously. "Who are you?"

"We are followers of Jesus, the Christ," announced Paul, "and we have come to meet our fellow believers."

A transforming smile spread across the woman's face, and her eager voice was no longer suspicious as she asked, "Are you Paul and Barnabas?"

"Yes," answered Barnabas. "This is Paul, and I am Barnabas. Who are you?"

"I'm Chrysanthe, and I too am a follower of Jesus Christ – although only a very new one. I'd be meeting with the other believers next door if my brother and his wife weren't arriving this morning."

"So how did you become a believer? We didn't meet you when we were in Lystra."

"No, we didn't hear about Jesus until after you left, unfortunately. My husband just heard a report that some 'troublemaking Jews'," she smiled again to take the edge of her words, "were got rid of by a mob." She stopped and looked sympathetically at Paul. "Have you recovered from your injuries? The crowd was sure they'd killed you, but our neighbours said you were still alive – that they'd talked to you afterwards."

"Yes, I'm much better," said Paul.

"He took weeks to recover from the cuts and bruises," offered Barnabas, "but with God's blessing he kept walking and preaching. He's tough."

"And now you've both come back here! Well, we'll do our best to look after you and keep your visit quiet."

"I wish you every success, Chrysanthe, but don't count on it too much," grinned Barnabas. "Paul doesn't 'keep quiet' very well!"

"I don't know why I'm talking through the window like this," said Chrysanthe, suddenly. "I'll come outside to talk." She pulled in her head and they heard her moving towards the door.

"I thought you were meant to be encouraging people," muttered Paul reproachfully as they waited for Chrysanthe to reappear, "not telling me off for doing what we came for!"

"Aren't you afraid of being stoned again?" asked Chrysanthe when she joined them.

"Of course," said Paul, "but Jesus warned me that I would suffer because of making his name known. The suffering is worthwhile to please him."

"Paul has a very real debt he wants to repay," said Barnabas. "He persecuted believers up and down Judea and the neighbouring countries, yet Jesus was willing to forgive him. Naturally, he feels a need to tell others about Jesus and take whatever suffering comes as a result."

"I made others suffer for their beliefs, and now I'm suffering for the same beliefs. That feels fair," said Paul. "Anyway, however much I suffer, I can't ever repay Jesus for what he did for me."

"I suppose so," acknowledged Chrysanthe, "but I'm not sure I could face it myself."

"Of course you could," said Barnabas, shrewdly. "After all, you became a follower of Jesus despite knowing exactly what had happened to Paul in your own home town."

"Oh, that's different," she said, waving it aside. "Anyway, Jesus is worth any sacrifice, don't you think? And I'll never be a leader they're trying to get rid of."

"I hope you never have to make such a sacrifice," said Paul seriously, "but if you do, it *is* worth it. Words can't describe how much I admire Jesus, and appreciate his willingness to welcome me as his servant despite my past behaviour. I'm running a race for him and I'm desperate to finish it well – just as he did. Jesus is coming back soon, and everyone in the world needs to know about it. So we've got to tell them!"

"As you see, Chrysanthe, brother Paul doesn't have small goals," laughed Barnabas.

In the joy of explanations and new acquaintance, they had forgotten about the door on which Paul had rapped so insistently. Now it opened silently and a doubtful face peered cautiously out at them. A wordless double take wiped away the doubt and opened the eyes wide, a broad smile transforming the face.

"Paul! I didn't think we'd ever see you again. Welcome! And Barnabas too!"

"Quintus! It's marvellous to see you," said Paul. "We've just been getting to know your neighbour, Chrysanthe. Another new believer, we hear."

"Indeed. Your stoning and sudden departure slowed us down for a while, but they also gave us lots of opportunities to contrast the generosity of God with the viciousness of your enemies. We all talked to our neighbours, and many of them have seen just how attractive the gift of God is."

"We're so glad to hear it," said Barnabas. "I was a little concerned that you might have been frightened, and perhaps..."

"We thought we should come back and visit you," interrupted Paul. "As you know, Barnabas is very good at encouraging, so here we are."

"Why don't you come in?" asked Quintus, opening the door wide.

"Are you coming in too, Chrysanthe?" asked Barnabas. "You don't get to hear a preacher like Paul very often. We'll all try to listen for any knocks on your door should your brother arrive."

"Oh, yes, of course! I wouldn't miss it for the world – and if my brother comes soon, maybe he can join us too."

Back to Antioch in Syria

Acts 14:21b-26

...they returned to Lystra, and to Iconium, and to Antioch, **22** strengthening the souls of the disciples, exhorting them to continue in the faith and that "through many tribulations it behooves us to enter into the kingdom of God."

23 Now having chosen elders for them in every church, having prayed, with fasting they committed them to the Lord, in whom they had believed.

24 And having passed through Pisidia, they came to Pamphylia, **25** and having spoken the word in Perga, they went down to Attalia.

The Report to the Church at Antioch

26 And from there they sailed to Antioch, from where they had been committed to the grace of God for the work that they had fulfilled.

CR

Acts 14:21-26

It was time to head back to Antioch in Syria. Bravely, Paul and Barnabas returned to each place they had visited in Asia Minor, starting with Lystra, where many disciples welcomed them and the news of the work in Derbe.

Paul reminded them that they could only enter the kingdom of God through much tribulation, but that the reward would make the tribulation worthwhile.

In each town they passed through, they appointed elders and leaders among the disciples, and joined with them in prayer and fasting before committing them to the Lord and moving on.

Lystra, Iconium, Antioch in Pisidia, Perga, Attalia, Antioch in Syria.

The first missionary journey was complete, and the disciples welcomed them back.

PART FIVE
Intermission

- 93 -

Mission Report

Acts 14:27

27 Now having arrived and having gathered together the church, they began declaring all that God had done with them, and that He had opened a door of faith to the Gentiles.

☙

Acts 14:27

Paul and Barnabas were glad to be back, and as soon as they arrived, the believers met together to hear a report.

They told of the ears God had opened, the Gentile hearts touched through their words, and everyone rejoiced.

A door of faith had been opened to the Gentiles.

☙

Sketch 19 – Missionary evening

It was the largest room the believers had in Antioch in Syria, yet the room was crowded and a buzz of anticipation filled the air. Men and women sat waiting and every face wore a smile of anticipation.

Once everyone had arrived, a well-known brother with a loud voice stood up at the front.

"Our beloved brothers Barnabas and Saul – ah, sorry, *Paul* I believe it is now – will tell us this evening about their work in Cyprus, Pisidia, Galatia and Lycaonia. If you would both come forward, I hope you will carry us along with you on your journeys."

Paul and Barnabas stood and made their way to the front: Barnabas purposeful and smiling, picking his way carefully through the crowd; Paul almost bounding forward, full of energy and eager to tell everyone about the astonishing work he had been a part of – and nearly tripping over several people on the way!

The two reached their destination at much the same time, and Barnabas smilingly waved to Paul to begin. He knew his friend's eagerness – which at times almost bordered on desperation. Paul would not be able to relax until he had told everyone all of the amazing things he had seen, of the new believers born through baptism, the miracles of healing and preaching, the transformed lives he had experienced. In short, he couldn't wait to do exactly what Jesus had chosen him to do – talk about his faith!

"Brethren," began Paul, eyes intense as he scanned the audience, "most of you will know that Barnabas and I were set apart to preach at the command of the Holy Spirit. On our journey through Cyprus and beyond, we saw God's hand in many things: blinding a false magician, healing a cripple, and countless examples of guiding us to meet people in unexpected ways and places. These and many other wonderful things, big and small, showed us that we were working with the help of God and Jesus Christ his son."

As Paul stopped to take a breath, Barnabas put in, "One of those amazing things was when Paul was stoned in Lystra and walked away alive. The people stoning him were sure he was dead, and so was I, but then he stood up. Had he been dead? I'm not certain, because he stood up before we could examine him. You can make up your own mind and give thanks to God as we did."

He signalled to Paul to continue.

"Thanks, Barnabas. I can tell you all that, while I may have been miraculously protected or whatever it was that happened, that didn't heal the bruises from the stones! I still bear the marks of my suffering for Jesus, and they remind me every day of his suffering for me and also of the believers I persecuted.

"There were other miracles too, particularly the gift we need all the time when preaching in different areas – understanding languages. Barnabas and I know Greek, but Greek is a second language for most of the people we preached to, and being able to speak in their mother tongue makes all the difference.

"When there was a synagogue in a town, we normally attended for as long as we could, but it got harder as we kept doing it. You see, we preached in the synagogue until they threw us out and then preached to the Gentiles – often men and women who had previously attended the synagogue because they already worshipped the God of Israel. When they learned about Jesus Christ, many left the synagogue to follow us.

But the Jews didn't like us stealing their proselytes – as they saw it – so they did their best to cause trouble, which often forced us to move on to another town. Then, somewhere along the line they started to follow and cause trouble in other towns too.

"As a result, we tried some variations in our preaching method. All up, we visited many towns and spoke to many thousands of people, telling them the good news of the kingdom of God and the name of Jesus Christ, and warning that people can only be saved through Jesus Christ. Of course, that's another reason why the Jews hated us, since they won't believe in the Lord Jesus."

Paul continued to speak passionately about the people who had received the word of truth about the Lord Jesus with joy. Some analysed the prophecies in the Hebrew scriptures and traced in intricate detail their fulfilment through Jesus' crucifixion. Others were convinced simply by the miracles performed by Paul and Barnabas. Still others knew very little about God, but saw his creation and had open hearts and a willingness to learn.

Each individual was different, and their natural responses to the preaching varied widely. Yet Jesus was bringing them individually to his saving name in a way that suited each one. Paul marvelled at this and gave a few specific examples that made his audience marvel with him.

Everyone present was persuaded that Jesus was working powerfully as head of his body – the body of believers.

Paul also drew a powerful lesson from this observation: since Jesus Christ is the head of the body, the believers must concentrate on working as one body under Jesus' control.

Leaders among the believers must lead as slaves of Jesus Christ.

Elders must show that their wisdom is built on the wisdom of the Lord Jesus.

Young men must use their strength in Jesus' work and not get distracted by the temptations of youth.

Young women must love their husbands and children.

Older women must show reverence and never end up as gossips or addicted to wine.

Each believer, whatever their position in life, must fill their time with the work their head wanted to guide them into.

After all, had not the Lord Jesus Christ said that he, himself, was sent as a servant? If the son of God was to be a servant, how much more those who wanted to follow him?

By the time Paul finished, it was clear to everyone that Barnabas was no longer the leader of the duo. Paul had taken over as the energetic, imaginative and passionate leader of a successful preaching machine, and Barnabas obviously was not resisting. His was the attitude of John the Baptist, who had said of Jesus that he must increase while John would decrease. Barnabas continued exercising his special skill as a son of encouragement, and when he spoke it was all about the benefits to the Way of adding such large numbers of new believers.

Barnabas told stories of the courage and commitment of the new Gentile followers of Jesus, and the stories were inspiring. He told of people who had been forced to choose between their family and Jesus and had bravely made the right choice, only to have their family later follow their lead.

He spoke of others who had made the same choice but were still enduring their family's rejection, reminding the group that they needed strong support from fellow believers, in prayer and perhaps in other practical ways.

He spoke of some more academically-minded believers who were minutely studying the Hebrew scriptures to help others discover more of the prophecies of Jesus that filled them.

He spoke of widows who had found a place working hard to help the poor and needy, presenting them as further examples of the burgeoning fellowship of which they were all a part.

Last of all, he commented on the number of new believers he had already met in Antioch, and rejoiced that the work of preaching was continuing apace in the town.

"You are all taking up the responsibility of talking to your neighbours and your families, working hard in the same task of preaching that Paul and I have been doing in faraway lands.

"With God's guidance and blessing and our enthusiasm for the work," concluded Barnabas, "the Way will soon be transforming the entire world. Keep it up!"

Need and Generosity

<table>
<tr><td align="center">Acts 14:28; 11:29</td></tr>
</table>

Paul and Barnabas stayed for a long time with the believers in Antioch.

By that time, the famine predicted by Agabus had spread over the Roman empire and believers in various places were in need. Eager believers in Antioch saw opportunities to help. Collections were taken and everyone gave as much as they could – or even more.

❧

Acts 14:28; 11:29

[28] And they remained no little time with the disciples.

[Acts 11:29-30 moved here into probable chronological order]

[29] And the disciples, as anyone was prospered, each of them determined to send for ministry to the brothers dwelling in Judea,

❧

Sketch 20 – Collecting

"Can you really afford to give that much, widow Chloe?"

"I think so. I still have a few corners I can cut."

"Just don't cut too many! We don't want you starving too."

"No danger of that yet – just look at me, Jason," she said, almost giggling as she prodded her substantial middle. "You can see I'm not starving!"

"No comment, sister," said Jason, smiling but prudent. "Anyway, this money will be a real help for our brothers and sisters in Jerusalem."

"I hope so. I can't bear the idea of anyone starving, particularly fellow believers."

"I know what you mean. Joanna and I have some believing relatives in Jerusalem and they're not doing well. We've already sent them some money, but it's not enough to help all the people we hear are suffering – and the situation keeps getting worse."

"How will the money be delivered?"

"Barnabas and Saul will be able to take it."

"A good pair. Brother Barnabas is so inspiring, and I think brother Saul could develop into a real asset, particularly if he follows Barnabas' example."

"Yes, they're both good preachers and hard workers for the Lord Jesus. They're also completely trustworthy, which is what we need for this job. We want to send at least two brothers, both for security and so that everyone can see that the handling of the gift is all above-board."

"How soon will they be leaving? I'd like to know that our money is helping straight away."

"In a few days, I believe. Early in the morning after our time of worship on the first day of the week. That way we can send them on their way with prayer. Some other brothers may be able to travel with them too."

"That sounds ideal. Thanks for coming to explain everything and collect the money. I'm glad to be able to help."

To Jerusalem

Acts 11:29-30; 15:1-2

[Acts 11:29-30 moved here into probable chronological order]

[29] And the disciples, as anyone was prospered, each of them determined to send for ministry to the brothers dwelling in Judea, [30] which also they did, having sent it to the elders by the hand of Barnabas and Saul.[a]

Acts 15

The Dispute over Circumcision
(Genesis 17:9-27; Leviticus 12:1-8; Joshua 5:1-9)

[1] But certain ones having come down from Judea were teaching the brothers, "Unless you are circumcised according to the custom of Moses, you are not able to be saved." [2] Having been brought about, then, no small commotion and discussion by Paul and Barnabas with them, they appointed Paul and Barnabas and certain others out from them to go up to Jerusalem, to the apostles and elders, about this question.

Acts 11:30; Acts 15:1-2; Galatians 2:1

Soon the believers in Antioch and surrounding areas had collected enough money for it to be useful for needy believers in Jerusalem.

At the same time, however, some visitors from Jerusalem brought trouble with them. They were convinced that circumcision was essential for salvation – whether believers were Jews or Gentiles – and they were insistent that others must obey their demands.

Paul and Barnabas knew that this ultimatum did not match the doctrine of Jesus, and the discussions were long and heated.

---

a   Acts 11:27-30 – The visit of prophets and Agabus' prophecy in verses 27-28 are probably in chronological order with the rest of the chapter, but the fulfilment of it happened later and Barnabas and Saul's resulting visit to Jerusalem is probably best located at the start of Acts 15 when Paul and Barnabas and others were sent to Jerusalem.

As the conflict continued, Paul was told by revelation to go to Jerusalem and discuss the gospel with the apostles and elders. In this way, he could confirm that these important doctrines he was proclaiming were truly part of the gospel of Jesus Christ.

Paul didn't keep this instruction to himself, and it wasn't long before the idea of visiting Jerusalem caught on. The believers in Antioch decided to send a delegation to discuss this issue with the leaders of the faith in Jerusalem.

Barnabas and Paul were obvious choices, and their journey could kill two birds with one stone: they were also asked to deliver the generous donations to the elders in Jerusalem. Others, including Titus, travelled with them.

Sketch 21 – Dispatching the Money

"Today we are sending our brothers Barnabas and Saul to Jerusalem. They have been chosen to carry relief to our brothers and sisters suffering in the current famine. They will be leaving early in the morning, carrying the money we've all donated – money that we all know is desperately needed. If any of you have brought more with you today, please pass it to Jason and Reuben. They will be finalising our gift shortly after we finish our worship, so get your gift to them quickly.

"Several other brothers will be travelling with Barnabas and Saul, including Titus, and they will also be carrying various other gifts that are not money. Our brothers will pass on our greetings to the believers in Jerusalem and deliver the money to the elders there.

"We hope that they will bring back good news from Jerusalem about the situation of the believers, and also some advice from the apostles and elders.

"I'm sure that you all want me to express our thanks to these brothers who are giving up five or six weeks of their time to travel to Jerusalem and return. I know that I will be with them in spirit as they travel the Via Maris and will be praying for God to protect them from robbers.

"Let's pray together for God's blessing on their work."

Acts 15:3-4

³ Therefore indeed having been sent forward by the church, they were passing through both Phoenicia and Samaria, relating in detail the conversion of the Gentiles, and they were bringing great joy to all the brothers. ⁴ And having come to Jerusalem, they were welcomed by the church and the apostles and the elders. And they declared all that God had done with them.

Acts 15:3

It was no small journey to Jerusalem, extended by Paul's eagerness to tell of the amazing growth of the gospel. They stopped in a few towns on the way to Jerusalem, describing their experiences in preaching to the Gentiles and reporting the joy of salvation among these new believers. Everyone rejoiced at the news.

Sketch 22 – On the way

"Now that we've crossed the Valley of Jezreel, how far is it to Jerusalem?" asked Titus.

"About four more days. We'll stay close to the sea on the Via Maris until we turn to go up to Jerusalem. There are more people around on this road and fewer bandits."

"So these Roman roads *are* an advantage, then?"

"Yes, especially during the rainy season. They're so well made and well drained that they rarely become impassable."

"Would the roads over the hills be shorter?"

"Yes – we'd probably get there in three days if we went that way. Normally I would, but it's not my money we're carrying!"

"Ah, well. At least this way we meet lots of travellers to talk to."

"You're right. I've been thinking about that myself. It seems to me that we should be able to do a lot more preaching if we followed these

Roman roads. As you say, lots of travellers use them, and they lead to all sorts of places all over the empire. I've been very happy to be with the assembly of believers in Antioch, but I'm hoping to go travelling sometime. However, I want to talk to the apostles first to make sure I've got everything straightened out about Jesus Christ. I've spent a lot of time mulling over what he told me, and now I think I should be ready to do something more concrete."

"See that group up ahead, Saul? Can we catch them up and see if they've heard of Jesus Christ?"

"Good idea. Let's walk a bit faster."

Acts 15:4; Galatians 2:2-3

As instructed by revelation, Paul discussed with the apostles the gospel he had been preaching and was very pleased to receive confirmation that their teachings all matched. The apostles had received the teachings during their time spent as disciples of Jesus, while Paul had received them by a special appearance from Jesus, but they matched exactly.

One detail the apostles emphasised: don't forget the poor. Paul was very eager to agree – after all, hadn't they come to Jerusalem with a gift for the poor?

The apostles offered the right hand of fellowship to Paul and Barnabas, and when they parted it was not only as brothers, but as fast friends.

Titus, who had travelled with Barnabas and Paul, was a Greek, so some problems could be anticipated. As a Greek, he was not circumcised – a major problem for most Jews, even those who were believers in Jesus. The apostles, however, knew Jesus' plans to include Gentiles in God's salvation, and they welcomed Titus along with his companions.

Conference in Jerusalem

Many other believers in Jerusalem welcomed them too, and most heard their reports with unalloyed delight. Others, however, were more guarded in their reactions. Perhaps it was the presence of Titus, a Greek, or perhaps the reports themselves were enough to raise their hackles. Whatever the reason, their old ways of life and beliefs obscured the truth they had accepted and they insisted that it was necessary to circumcise Gentiles and teach them to obey the law.

This, then, was the nub of the matter. It was the very question which had brought Paul, Barnabas and the others to Jerusalem and it must be sorted out.

The apostles and elders gathered together and there was plenty of discussion. After a while, Peter told of the initial preaching to the Gentiles which God had done through him. He insisted that God had shown clearly then that he made no distinction between Jews and Gentiles, but that both were offered salvation through faith in Jesus.

Next it was Paul and Barnabas' turn to report on their first missionary journey, and they described the miracles God had done through them and the many who had believed. You could have heard a pin drop all through their report – everyone was amazed and thrilled by the astonishing harvest of Gentiles.

At this critical time in the discussions, James, the Lord's brother, spoke up. He pulled the threads together and came up with some practical suggestions as to how the current conflict could be resolved if there was a desire for unity. There was, and it was agreed that the Gentiles should not be forced to keep the law, but rather that they should be encouraged to pay attention to some of the more fundamental rules of the law of Moses, which most Gentiles knew anyway.

He suggested that the Gentiles be instructed to keep four related things:
- Abstain from anything contaminated by idols,
- Abstain from fornication,
- Abstain from eating what is strangled, and
- Abstain from eating blood.

All the assembled believers agreed, and a letter was duly written to be distributed to every group of believers, whether it included Gentiles or not. Everyone needed to know about this agreement.

The letter included an apology for the trouble caused by those believers who had travelled out from Jerusalem without authorisation and insisted on rules which were not part of the truth of the Way at all. Paul and Barnabas were vindicated.

Acts 15:5-29

The Council at Jerusalem

5 Now certain of those who believed, from the sect of the Pharisees, rose up, saying, "It is necessary to circumcise them, and to command them to keep the Law of Moses." **6** And both the apostles and the elders were gathered together to see about this matter.

7 And much discussion having taken place, Peter having risen up, said to them, "Men, brothers, you know that from the early days God chose among you for the Gentiles to hear by my mouth the word of the gospel, and to believe. **8** And the heart-knowing God bore witness to them, having given them the Holy Spirit, as also to us. **9** And He made no distinction between both us and them, having purified their hearts by the faith.

10 Now therefore, why are you testing God, to put upon the neck of the disciples a yoke that neither our fathers nor we have been able to bear? **11** But we believe ourselves to be saved by the grace of the Lord Jesus, in the same manner as they also are."

12 Now the whole multitude kept silent and were listening to Barnabas and Paul relating what signs and wonders God had done among the Gentiles by them. **13** And after they were silent, James answered, saying, "Men, brothers, hear me. **14** Simeon[a] has related how God first visited to take out of the Gentiles a people for His name. **15** And the words of the prophets agree with this, as it is written:

16 'After these things I will return
and will rebuild the tabernacle of David which has fallen,
and its ruins I will rebuild,
and I will set it upright,
17 so that the remnant of men may seek out the Lord,
and all the Gentiles, upon whom has been called My name, upon them,

---

a   BLB: Acts 15:14 – Greek Simeon is a variant of Simon

says the Lord, doing these things,
18 known from eternity.'[a]

19 Therefore I judge not to trouble those from the Gentiles turning to God, **20** but to write to them to abstain from the pollutions of idols, and sexual immorality, and that which is strangled, and from blood. **21** For Moses has ones proclaiming him in every city from generations of old, being read in the synagogues on every Sabbath."

The Letter to the Gentile Believers

22 Then it seemed good to the apostles and to the elders, with the whole church, having chosen out from them, to send men to Antioch with Paul and Barnabas: Judas called Barsabbas and Silas, leading men among the brothers, **23** having written by their hand:

"The apostles and the elders, brothers,

To those brothers among the Gentiles in Antioch and Syria and Cilicia:[b]

Greetings.

24 Inasmuch as we have heard that some went out from us, to whom we had given no instructions,[c] and troubled you by words, upsetting your minds, **25** it seemed good to us, having come with one accord, having chosen men to send to you with our beloved Barnabas and Paul, **26** men having handed over their lives for the name of our Lord Jesus Christ. **27** Therefore we have sent Judas and Silas, and they are telling you the same things by word of mouth.

28 For it seemed good to the Holy Spirit and to us, to lay upon you no further burden, except these necessary things: **29** to abstain from things sacrificed to idols, and from blood, and from what is strangled, and from sexual immorality. Keeping yourselves from these, you will do well.

Farewell."

---

a   BLB: Acts 15:16-18 – Amos 9:11,12. BYZ and TR says the Lord, who does all these things.
      18 Known unto God are all his works from the beginning of the world.
b   Acts 15:23 – Tarsus, Paul's home town, was in Cilicia
c   BLB: Acts 15:24 – BYZ and TR include saying you must be circumcised and keep the law

In Antioch Again

Acts 15:30-35

Returning from the conference in Jerusalem, Paul and Barnabas took with them the letter and two representatives sent by the elders, one of whom was a prophet named Silas.

Once again, the believers in Antioch were gathered together to hear a report, and once again they were wonderfully pleased with the letter's encouraging message. It was confirmed: Gentiles were welcome, circumcision was not required, and keeping away from idols was a good thing anyway.

Silas was an interesting speaker who easily held the believers' attention throughout what ended up quite a lengthy message.

Paul and Barnabas stayed for some time in Antioch, teaching the believers and preaching to any who were not yet believers.

Acts 12:25; Acts 15:30-35

[Acts 12:25 moved here into probable chronological order]

[25] And Barnabas and Saul returned, having fulfilled the mission to Jerusalem,[d] having taken with them John the one having been called Mark.[e]

Acts 15

The Believers at Antioch Rejoice

[30] Therefore indeed having been sent off, they went to Antioch, and having gathered the multitude, they delivered the letter. [31] And having read it, they rejoiced at the encouragement.

---

d   BLB: Acts 12:25 – NE and TR had fulfilled their mission, they returned from Jerusalem,

e   Acts 12:25 – This verse comes at the end of a section (verses 20-24) where Luke leaves his chronological path to look ahead and report Agrippa's well-deserved death and the subsequent spread of the gospel (including during Paul's first missionary journey). Chronologically, it probably refers to the time when Barnabas and Saul returned to Antioch after the Jerusalem conference, as described in Acts 15:30.

32 Both Judas and Silas, also being prophets themselves, exhorted and strengthened the brothers by much talk. **33** And having continued a time, they were sent away in peace from the brothers to those having sent them.[a] **35** But Paul and Barnabas stayed in Antioch, teaching and proclaiming the good news, the word of the Lord, with many others also.

Galatians 2:11-14

After a while, Peter came to visit Antioch, and joined in the fellowship of the believers, including meeting with the believing Gentiles. Trouble came when some believers came from Jerusalem. These were very strict, very Jewish believers, who, while they could accept the decision of the apostles and elders in Jerusalem that Gentiles did not need to be circumcised, could not completely abandon their bias against the Gentiles. They would not eat with them.

Peter tried to keep them happy, and, after a while, even Barnabas was led down the same path, but Paul did not believe in appeasement when truth and salvation were at stake. Although Peter was one of the twelve disciples and still an important leader among the believers, Paul felt that he had to tell him off in front of everyone. His words convinced Barnabas that a stand must be made and he joined Paul, but the stand-off was rather upsetting.

---

a   BLB: Acts 15:33 – TR includes **34** Silas, however, decided to remain there.

PART SIX
The Second Missionary Journey

Arguments and Separation

Acts 15:36-38

There was plenty of work to do in Antioch, but after a while both Paul and Barnabas felt it was time to leave. They wanted to revisit the believers in all the places they had visited on their first missionary journey.

But there was a hitch. John Mark was back in Antioch again, and Barnabas wanted to take him with them. Paul disagreed, strongly, arguing that it was not wise to take with them someone who had let them down before. His argument was good – they needed helpers they could rely on. Yet Barnabas was sure that John Mark had changed and grown spiritually.

℞

Acts 15:36-40

Paul's Second Missionary Journey (Acts 15:36-18:22)
(First: Acts 13:1-3; Third: Acts 18:23-28)

36 Now after some days, Paul said to Barnabas, "Indeed, having turned back, let us look after the brothers, how they are, in every city in which we have announced the word of the Lord." 37 Now Barnabas purposed also to take along John, called Mark.[a] 38 But Paul thought fit not to take him along, the one having withdrawn from them from Pamphylia and not having gone with them to the work.[b]

39 Therefore a sharp disagreement arose, so that they separated from one another. And Barnabas having taken Mark, sailed to Cyprus. 40 But Paul, having chosen Silas, went forth, having been committed to the grace of the Lord by the brothers.

---

a   Acts 15:37 – John Mark was Barnabas' cousin (Colossians 4:10)
b   Acts 15:38 – See Acts 13:13

CR

Sketch 23 – Dispute

"I know that Mark let us down in Pamphylia, but he's only young."

"That's all very well, Barnabas, but we can't afford to have someone we can't depend on."

"I think you'll find we can depend on him now. I've talked to him a lot about this."

"You talked to him a lot before we left last time. You explained exactly what we could expect on the journey, yet he gave up before we even got to anything difficult. If he couldn't cope with the minor troubles we had in Cyprus, how would he cope with a situation like we met in Lystra where they tried to kill us?"

"I think he'd do better now."

"Better, perhaps, but what does that mean? That he'd last a bit longer before he gave up and went home?"

Barnabas sighed. "I don't think you've got a very forgiving attitude towards Mark."

Paul shook his head. "This is nothing to do with forgiveness. I've forgiven him for what happened – that's easy. But that doesn't mean I'm ready to rely on him again. I'm happy to trust him with all sorts of work among the believers, but not on this sort of mission. We need someone who can cope with the danger, the possibility that they might get badly hurt or even killed."

"So how will you ever know you can trust him again?"

"Perhaps if he went on a less important journey and proved that he can cope."

"But if everyone took your attitude, he could never go on *any* journey because no-one would take him! I didn't like it when he abandoned us, but was it really so disastrous?"

"Remember how he really hit it off with… ah, Jabin, I think – in Salamis? They talked and talked and John Mark did a really good job of preaching – but just imagine if he'd chosen that time to give up and go home. How could we have convinced Jabin of the importance of the truth when the man preaching to him had lost confidence himself?"

"I agree that would be a problem, but I don't believe it will happen. I'm sure he's grown up and we won't have a problem like that again. He already knows how we work: he'll be a great help for us, not a hindrance."

"You might be right, Barnabas, but I think the risk is too great. We need helpers we can rely on."

"Indeed we do, but how can you tell whether you can rely on someone if you're asking them to do something they've never done before? John Mark *has* done the job before, and now he wants to join us again. He knows the difficulties, he knows his own problems, and he's sure he can stay with us this time."

"I believe that Silas will be reliable and won't leave us in the lurch."

"Silas may be completely reliable, I'm not questioning that, but I don't want to abandon Mark when he's acknowledged his fault – repented, if you like – and is ready to try again."

"I can't take the risk."

"Is that your final word?"

"I'm afraid it is."

"So you won't give him the second chance you had? Remember how people didn't dare to let you join their fellowship?"

"And you stood up for me. I'll never forget that, nor the way you came looking for me. You're a wonderful brother, Barnabas. I've never met anyone as good as you at encouraging people to walk higher, to climb above themselves."

"But *you* won't give Mark a second chance. Don't you remember how hard it was for you when people doubted you?"

"I remember it well, but I don't blame them for doubting me, Barnabas. And you know, that doubt could easily be part of the reason why Jesus sent us away to new places where I wasn't known at all. I've had to prove myself over many years. Now, most brethren are finally convinced."

"I suppose that's true, but I'm very disappointed that we can't come to an agreement on this."

"So am I. You know I'd always want to have you as a travelling companion. I know I can rely on you to keep working for God however dangerous it may be."

"Thanks, Paul. We've always got along well, other than that disagreement when I let myself be swayed by Peter's suggestion that we appease those brothers from Jerusalem who were insisting on Gentiles being circumcised. Is that incident why you don't trust my judgement now?"

"No, not at all. You know that we've worked together in the most difficult situations, and I'm always willing to trust you. That matter of circumcision was a difficult situation for everyone, and I've made enough mistakes of my own to understand when others make them too."

"Well, this time I'll have to make the choice myself. I really believe that God guides me to encourage, and helps me choose who to encourage when no-one else will."

"I can't disagree with you, but..."

"Don't get too upset about it, Paul, because I'm sure God will bless your work, whether you go with me or Silas. However, I believe God wants me to encourage Mark by accepting his offer to try preaching again. Perhaps it's because he's my cousin that I feel so confident that I understand him and can give him the support he needs."

"So you believe you should go with him?"

"I do," said Barnabas resolutely.

"To Cyprus?"

"Yes."

"Very well," sighed Paul. "I'll see if Silas will come with me and we can visit the congregations in Asia."

"Don't worry about it too much, Paul," said Barnabas, patting him on the shoulder. "Everything will work out. Jesus will guide us to do the work as he wants it done."

"You're right, he will. Perhaps it'll all work out for the best just because two groups are going out to preach instead of only one: you with John Mark and me with Silas."

"And you'll be able to find new places to visit, Paul. Imagine preaching further and further across Asia! New towns, new audiences, new converts. Perhaps you could even cross over into Macedonia or Achaia."

Excitement sparkled in Paul's eyes, the words filling him with anticipation. He hugged Barnabas. "Thanks again, Barnabas. Let's get on with it, then. I genuinely hope I'm wrong about John Mark and you're right, but it's true, two groups of preachers should be better than one."

☙

Acts 15:39-40

The argument was fierce and no path of agreement could be found. In the end, Barnabas took John Mark with him and went home to Cyprus[a] to preach, convinced that this would be a good way to encourage Mark, since he already knew what to expect there.

Paul took Silas and they walked north together, having been committed by the believers to the grace of God.

Paul's second missionary journey had begun.

a   Acts 4:36

Through Syria and Cilicia

Acts 15:41

Paul and Silas travelled north through Syria and Cilicia, past Tarsus and on towards the towns where Paul and Barnabas had preached before.

Along the way, they met groups of believers and shared with them the letter sent with the conclusions of the conference in Jerusalem. Paul's wonderful ways of expressing the truths of the Bible strengthened the faith of the believers.

Acts 15:41

| [41] And he was passing through Syria and Cilicia,[a] strengthening the churches. |

Sketch 24 – Hearing the letter

"So I *don't* need to be circumcised?" asked Zenas, a Gentile believer in Soli, a town on the coast of Cilicia.

"Exactly," said Paul, emphatically. "Circumcision was for the Jews, just as the law of Moses was for the Jews."

"That's a relief!" laughed Zenas. "I would've done it if I had to, but…"

"If you are circumcised according to the law, then you need to keep the rest of the law as well: sacrifices, washings, feasts, tithing, Sabbaths, and all the rest. In Antioch when this question arose, I had a brother with me called Titus who was Greek. Some of the believers wanted him to be circumcised, but I used these arguments and they accepted that he didn't need to be circumcised."[b]

---

a   Acts 15:41 – Tarsus, Paul's home town, was in Cilicia
b   Galatians 2:3

"That sounds sensible to me. Getting circumcised didn't seem to fit with the idea that Jesus had fulfilled the law and become the High Priest of a better covenant."

"You're right again," said Paul. "We've been called to freedom in Christ, not to go back to the law of Moses."

"What exactly do you mean by 'freedom in Christ'? After all, the letter you brought gave us rules to keep."

"True, and the Lord Jesus gave us many rules for our thoughts and behaviour, but our freedom in Christ saves us from the slavery of the law that leads only to death. Of course, the law itself wasn't bad – it was the people who were bad in not keeping the law. But nobody except Jesus has ever kept the law completely. Instead, people have turned the law into a checklist of rules and completely missed the *intention* behind it. Jesus showed us how God wanted us to keep the law – what it meant."

"So, freedom in Christ is freedom to follow a living Jesus instead of… a law that kills." Zenas thought for a moment, then laughed. "It's freedom to carry a cross!"

"Yes. Freedom to serve; freedom to suffer; freedom to endure. And then freedom to live forever."

"I'm glad you've brought us this news. Some brothers visited us and told us that we had to be circumcised. They convinced some of us to be circumcised, but I was a bit doubtful. I wanted time to think."

"You made the right choice, Zenas. The disciples and elders apologised for the wrong message that some people have brought. Now that it's been straightened out, all believers will know not to be taken in by things like that. We aren't going back! Not back to the law – back to slavery. We're going *forward* with Jesus, forward to his kingdom."

"I'm pleased to hear it. But I've got a question about one of the rules we were sent," said Zenas. "The one about keeping away from things offered to idols. Since idols are… are just lumps of wood or stone, surely they're not worth worrying about. Why do we need to worry about things offered to them? Isn't that saying they really are important?"

"That's a really good question, Zenas," answered Paul, a delighted gleam in his eye. He was always happy when people pondered their religion. "You're right that idols are nothing. A lump of metal or some carved piece of wood has no power, and making them look beautiful doesn't give them any power that would make us fear them. If you buy food in the market, don't ask any questions about whether it's been offered to idols or not. Some will have been, some won't – don't go looking for problems. You only have to avoid things offered to idols when you *know* they've been offered. Imagine you're in the market and someone tells you that this piece of meat has been offered to some idol; in that case, don't buy it. Choose another piece that hasn't been offered. Avoid the things offered to idols."

"I can do that, but I don't understand why it matters. Does *knowing* that it's been offered to an idol change anything for me?"

"No, not at all," said Paul, animated as ever when presenting complex logic, "not for *you*. But it's for the person who told you. The idol is important to *them*, so you are refusing to honour their idol because you want to honour God instead. Tell them why you are refusing. Explain your conscience and how important it is to you. Perhaps it'll convince them to leave their love of idols and learn to worship a true and living God."

"Ah, I think I understand. I'll have to think about it more, but I suppose it makes sense that the conscience of the person I'm talking to is important and that I should take any opportunity I can to honour our God. After all, if they have a conscience already, they're more likely to be fertile ground for the truth about God."

Paul stopped for a moment, deep in thought, then looked at Zenas. "You know, I'd never thought about it quite that way," he said, "but you're right. That makes the point even stronger, doesn't it? I get so much joy out of learning to understand God's truth better. Thanks for that idea, Zenas."

"It seemed to come directly from what you said," said Zenas, pleased to be able to help the apostle from whom he had learned so much, but a little surprised that his response should be considered novel. "Thank you for explaining the letter to me, Paul. I have so much to learn. I'm glad I didn't get circumcised."

"I'm glad too," said Paul. "The brothers who've been teaching this have caused a lot of trouble, but hopefully this letter will stop it. It needs to be stopped," he added grimly, "before it takes people away from salvation and back to Judaism."

"And then we'd be just another sect of Judaism like the Pharisees and Sadducees, without the freedom to follow Christ."

"Exactly. Now you seem to be a bit of a thinker, Zenas, so I'll mention a special case. There is one situation in which I would consider circumcising a brother, and that would be when he was already Jewish or partly Jewish and wanted to come preaching with me. In my preaching, I always visit the local synagogue first if there is one, and a Jew who wasn't circumcised couldn't go with me. That would limit the work they could do. However, the brother would have to agree to do it – I would never try to force it."[a]

"Hmm," answered Zenas. "I'd have to think more about that one."

---

a   See Acts 16:1-3. The explanation included here is one possible explanation of Paul's thinking with regard to the circumcision of Timothy.

Derbe and Lystra: Timothy

Acts 16:1-5

When Paul and Silas came to Derbe and then to Lystra, they met a believer called Timothy. He was a marvellous young man, very popular with all the believers in Lystra and Iconium.

His mother was a Jew, but his father was a Greek, so he was not circumcised. With Timothy's agreement, Paul circumcised him because of the unbelieving Jews in the area, since they would not allow any contact with him if he was not circumcised. That would badly limit his opportunities of working with Paul and Silas, and his later chances of preaching to Jews, so it was the best answer.

Acts 16:1-5

Acts 16

Timothy Joins Paul and Silas

[1] And he came also to Derbe and to Lystra. And behold, a certain disciple was there, named Timothy, the son of a believing Jewish woman and a Greek father, [2] who was well spoken of by the brothers in Lystra and Iconium. [3] Paul wanted this one to go forth with him, and having taken him, he circumcised him on account of the Jews being in those parts; for they all knew that his father was a Greek.

[4] And while they were passing through the cities, they were delivering to them to keep the decrees decided on by the apostles and elders who were in Jerusalem. [5] So indeed the churches were strengthened in the faith and were increasing in number every day.

CR

Sketch 25 – Timothy

"You know, Silas, I think it would be good to have some extra helpers travelling with us," said Paul. "The work we do keeps getting bigger and bigger."

"It does," nodded Silas. "When you suggested visiting the believers in the towns you and Barnabas had visited, that sounded fine. But when we get to a town, there's not just the existing believers to talk to, there are lots of others too. Almost all the believers have someone they want us to speak to, whether it's a neighbour, a friend or someone in their family."

"Exactly," said Paul, pleased that Silas shared his concerns. "And yet I still want to have time to talk to others as well – people in the market-place, or on the streets."

"We'll always have to be the ones who pass on the message from the apostles in Jerusalem, but having extra men helping with the preaching would be great."

"Some mature, experienced helpers would be just ideal. Spiritual men with a deep knowledge of scripture."

"Men of the circumcision[a] are most likely to fit your requirements," said Silas.

"That's true – more of them have been immersed in scripture since childhood. There aren't many believing Jews here in Asia, though."

"No, but I think we need some anyway. I doubt that many Jews would listen to a Greek explaining the Hebrew scriptures to them!"

Paul laughed. "You're right about that! Most of our countrymen view Greeks with disdain."

"Why don't we tell the believers here in Derbe that we're looking for helpers, then wait and see what God provides?"

Paul agreed, and as soon as they could, they told the believers their need.

Then they waited expectantly for a response.

---

a   God made a covenant with Abraham that all his male descendants were to be circum-
     cised (Genesis 17:10). The expression, "the circumcised", is sometimes used to refer to
     Jews in the New Testament (e.g., Ephesians 2:11; Colossians 4:11). A related expression
     is "the circumcision party", a group of believers who insisted that Gentile believers
     should be circumcised (Acts 11:2; Titus 1:10). Paul strongly resisted this demand.

In Derbe, however, there was no response. Gradually Paul and Silas resigned themselves to carrying on the work alone, and soon it was time to move on to Lystra.

Paul couldn't forget the terrifying result of his first visit to Lystra, but he didn't let it stop him. He approached the gates with an enthusiastic step, a prayer in his heart and a smile on his face.

Travelling believers had already carried the news that Paul and Silas planned to arrive in Lystra that afternoon, and several believers were waiting eagerly for them at the gate.

Most of them Paul had met previously, but he didn't recognise one young man who stood behind the others. After greeting those he knew and introducing Silas to them all, Paul looked at the young man questioningly and he stepped forward while the others introduced him: "This is brother Timothy."

"Hello, Timothy," said Paul, greeting him in Greek

"Good afternoon, Paul," Timothy replied with a teasing smile.

Paul looked at Timothy in surprise – he had answered in Aramaic!

"You speak Aramaic?" asked Paul.

Timothy nodded and was about to say more when Ampliatus, another of the welcoming party, interrupted, "Let's go back to my house straight away. I hope you'll be staying with me, Paul and Silas. My neighbours are very interested in Jesus now and would like to meet you."

They all agreed and set off – except for Timothy, who had another hour or two of his daily work in the marketplace to complete. Having taken a few minutes off in the now-satisfied hope of meeting Paul and Silas, he returned to work with a big smile on his face.

When Paul and Silas reached Ampliatus' house, they were welcomed warmly. After a while Paul inquired about Timothy, intrigued by his knowledge of Aramaic.

"Ah, Timothy," said Ampliatus. "A good lad. A solid, serious believer." The others in the room agreed. It appeared that no-one had a bad word to say about him.

"How did he learn Aramaic?" asked Paul.

"Mostly from his mother and his grandmother, although his father did speak Aramaic – but only when he had to. He was a Greek from Lystra who spent some time in Israel about twenty years ago and was interested in Judaism for a while. When he came back here, he married Timothy's mother Eunice, whose parents also lived here in Lystra. Eunice was their only child."

"So was Timothy's mother a Jewess?"

"Yes, and his grandmother too. You probably met his grandmother when you were first here. Her name was Lois."

Paul nodded and smiled. "Yes, I remember Lois. A godly, gentle lady with a genuine love of God's word. She was baptised not long before they... before I left Lystra." Paul avoided saying "before they stoned me", but Ampliatus understood.

"She was always very dedicated to Moses' law," continued Ampliatus, "so when she heard about Jesus she saw immediately where he fitted into the law and the prophets. Eunice is also very godly and taught Timothy about God. He knew the Scriptures well from childhood and what they meant – although his father wasn't very pleased with that once he decided Judaism wasn't for him."

"Is the father still alive?"

"No. He died not long after you left here on your way back to Antioch. That left Eunice and Timothy free to pursue their interest in the Way. They were already learning about it, but having his determined opposition removed made it easier for them, particularly for Timothy."

Over the next three weeks, Paul and Silas were very busy. They delivered a copy of the letter from the elders in Jerusalem and all of the other special greetings they had been asked to deliver from Derbe. As requested by the believers in Lystra, they spoke to many neighbours, relatives and friends who were eager to learn more about the Way. They also answered huge numbers of questions from believers, straightening out misunderstandings and explaining difficult scriptures to encourage the believers in their spiritual life.

Yet they could find no time for "green fields" preaching. They seldom walked the streets except to visit yet another believer's home – leaving them no time to touch the ignorant masses who lived in idolatry and barbarism.

"We *must* have more helpers!" said Paul forcefully to Silas one morning.

"Yes," sighed Silas. "The believers are doing a wonderful job of preaching to those close to them, but how can we spread it more widely – and more quickly?"

"All the believers have lives to live, families to care for, careers to develop, education to finish, and even their dead to bury at times."

"And most of those demands on their time are genuinely necessary," agreed Silas.

"They are, and the preaching work they do can only be done by people living where they do."

"Nevertheless, we also need preaching that spreads the word to *new* communities, *new* towns, *new* provinces, *new* countries. That's what you wanted most, wasn't it, Paul? When you started your first missionary journey, there were no existing groups of believers in any of the places you visited. Everywhere was new."

"Until we started retracing our steps from Derbe to Antioch. That was when we started visiting existing groups of believers. That's an important job too, but it's a different job."

"So are you looking for helpers for follow-up work or new preaching?"

"Both. We can't leave all the follow-up work to others because we're the ones who were sent to carry the elders' message to believers, but I can't leave all the new preaching to others either – Jesus made it clear that it was a large part of the work he wanted me to do."

"Shall we ask for volunteers here too?"

"I think we may already have a candidate here, Silas, but I think I'll need to ask him to come with us."

"Who? Ampliatus? I would have thought he was too busy with his..."

"No, not Ampliatus. Timothy."

"But he's a *Greek*. You were talking about one of the circumcision."

"True, I was. I know that Timothy's father was a Greek, and I assume that he's not circumcised."

"He's not," said Silas categorically. "Ampliatus mentioned that the local Jews won't have anything to do with him because of it. They seem to view him as even worse than a Greek."

"I can believe it. Most Jews seem to think that an uncircumcised half-Jew is worse than an uncircumcised Greek."

"Doesn't that mean Timothy wouldn't be much help to us? He couldn't talk to Jews in the synagogue, and isn't your first step in preaching in a new town always to go to the synagogue? Timothy couldn't do it.

Apparently Timothy travels around quite a lot with his trading, so all the Jews in this district know he's not circumcised."

Paul pursed his lips and thought for a while, then shook his head, sighed and said, "I suppose you're right. Maybe this is a case where it might be best to circumcise a believer."

"How could we do that when we've been so loud in our opposition to the circumcision party?"

"We've been opposing the circumcision of *Gentiles*."

"Isn't Timothy a Gentile? His father was Greek and he made sure his son wasn't circumcised."

"His mother also made sure he knew the law of Moses, and everyone agrees that he followed it very carefully from an early age – until he learned about Jesus and was baptised to follow the Way."

"I just wonder whether it would weaken our case against the circumcision party."

"I don't think so…. You see, Timothy has always been dedicated to the law, and he knows he doesn't need to be circumcised to follow Jesus. And it's important that he wouldn't be getting circumcised for that reason. He'd be getting circumcised so he could go into Jewish synagogues and preach to Jews."

"So you'd ask him to come with us on the condition that he's circumcised first?"

"Yes. Otherwise, he won't be able to help much in any of the towns around here. If he wants to preach but doesn't think getting circumcised is a good idea, then he can travel around this area by himself, preaching as he wants to. I'm sure that God would bless his work."

Later that night, the believers gathered together to listen to Paul's teaching. Afterwards, he made an opportunity to take Timothy aside to discuss this request.

"Timothy," said Paul, "I would like you to come with Silas and me as we continue our preaching. However, since you're known throughout the district to be the son of a Greek and thus uncircumcised, there's one important condition. You would need to be circumcised first. We intend to leave next week, so if you want to come with us, you'd need to be circumcised in the next few days. What do you think?"

"I'll come," answered Timothy. "I'll be circumcised tomorrow and tell my boss I'm leaving."

It was as simple as that. Paul was filled with joy, feeling that the young man's reaction was much the same as that of the twelve disciples when Jesus had called them to follow him. Clearly Timothy was made of the right stuff.

Limitations

Sketch 26 – What next?

It was early in the morning. Silas and Timothy were sitting at a table talking to Luke while the lady of the house prepared breakfast for them.

The perplexing subject under discussion was where Paul and Silas should go next. Paul's second missionary journey had been outstandingly successful – until suddenly every door seemed to slam shut in their faces. Syria, Cilicia, Lycaonia, Phrygia and Galatia had all been thoroughly traversed and they had presented each congregation with the letter to Gentile believers written by the apostles and elders in Jerusalem. As they went, new believers sprang up everywhere and Paul and his companions felt God's blessings every day.

It all came to an abrupt end when they prepared to go into the province of Asia.

Quite simply, the Holy Spirit forbade them to do so.

Obediently, they looked for other options. First, they headed west toward Mysia, but preaching was forbidden there also. Still eager, they began to travel northwest into Bithynia, but once more the answer was no. Turning south again, they skirted Mysia and made their way to Troas, still unsure what to do.

In Troas, they met Luke, a Gentile doctor who was also a believer – and very interested in the history of Jesus and The Way. He was an eager traveller and clearly liked the idea of a preaching tour.

A delicious smell filled the room and wafted out the door, but Silas, Timothy and Luke were too engrossed in their discussion to notice. What should they do? Every choice seemed forbidden, but surely the preaching Jesus had commissioned must continue! Where should they preach next?

Suddenly Paul rushed into the room, banging the door against the wall in his haste.

"Oh, sorry," he said, then continued excitedly, "I've got the answer!"

No-one asked what he was talking about: it was obvious.

"Where do we go?" asked Silas.

"Macedonia," breathed Paul, his eyes shining as they always did when an opportunity for preaching offered.

"Macedonia?" queried Timothy. "That's a long way away. What language do they speak there?"

"I'm not sure," said Paul, "but Greek will probably see you through."

"Why Macedonia?" asked Silas.

"During the night, I saw a vision. A man from Macedonia was standing there begging me to come over and help them."

"How did you know the man was from Macedonia?" asked Luke.

Paul smiled. "I'm not sure, but I didn't have any doubt. Maybe he told me so – I don't remember."

"Well, it sounds like we have an answer to our prayers," said Silas. "Macedonia it is."

"Do any of you know anything about Macedonia?" asked Timothy, still looking unsure.

"I do," said Luke. "It's a Roman province and Thessalonica is the capital. There's a wonderful road called the Via Egnatia which passes through Neapolis on the coast and continues to Thessalonica and a long way beyond. There are various important towns on the way, like Philippi and Amphipolis."

The man of the house, also a believer, entered the room as Luke finished.

"Ah, that smells good," he said, smiling at his wife. She smiled back as she stirred the steaming contents of a pot.

"Good morning, Crescens," greeted Paul. "We've found out where we are to go: Macedonia!"

"From what I hear, that's a very big area," answered Crescens.

"What do you know about it?" asked Silas. "I know nothing about Macedonia."

"Well, for a start, you can catch a boat here and cross over to Neapolis. That's probably the best place to start. The voyage should only take a few days."

Paul nodded approvingly at Luke. "That's what Luke suggested too. He mentioned the Via Egnatia."

"That's the road I would take," agreed their host, promptly. "I don't think you'll find much to work with in Neapolis, but Philippi would make a solid starting point. It's a Roman colony and I'm sure you'll find some listening ears there."

"Is there a synagogue in Philippi?" asked Silas.

"I have no idea," answered Crescens.

"It could easily have one," said Paul. "It's amazing how many towns have synagogues, even Roman colonies."

"When are we leaving?" asked Timothy.

"Tomorrow," said Paul, confidently. "Now that we know where to go, we need to start straight away. In fact, I'll go down to the docks now and find out if there's a boat we could catch today."

Paul turned around ready to hurry down to the docks, but Silas grabbed him by the arm.

"Hey, slow down a bit, Paul," he laughed. "It smells like our hostess has a delightful breakfast ready for us, so let's wait until we've done justice to it."

"Oh, yes," said Paul. "Of course."

Silas was right. Their hostess had just begun to serve their meal and, after a blessing, they were soon enjoying a delicious meal of fish and bread.

In the middle of the meal, Luke paused to ask, "Can I come with you to Macedonia?"

Silas and Paul exchanged glances and smiled. They had discussed this very possibility, wondering if Luke would be willing to join them in their work wherever God might send them, and now he was asking them himself. Not only had God shown them where to go, he had also provided another helper!

"Yes, come over and help us," said Paul, echoing the words of the Macedonian he had seen in his vision.

"Are you going to start in Philippi?"

"Yes, that seems to be what God wants."

"I'd like to see how you start preaching in a new city," said Luke. "And then, when you leave, I'd like to stay there and see if I can help The Way progress in a town after the first preachers have to move on."

"That sounds like you have everything planned," said Paul.

"I've thought about it quite a lot while studying the development of The Way. Call it research, if you want. I hope to write a detailed history."

The meal was soon finished, and once again Paul was eager to hurry down to the docks.

"Can I come with you, Paul?" asked Luke.

"Yes, please do. As we walk, you can tell me what you know about Philippi."

Acts 16:6-10

Paul and Silas took Timothy and visited Phrygia and Galatia next, but they were forbidden by the Holy Spirit from going into Asia. Jesus was controlling the preaching of the good news, and Bithynia was excluded too. Arriving at Troas, Paul saw a vision in the night. A man, appealing to him, "Come over to Macedonia and help us." How could they refuse what was so obviously a sign?

The other areas could wait.

Macedonia must be visited next.

Acts 16:6-10

Paul's Vision of the Macedonian

[6] And having passed through Phrygia and the Galatian region, having been forbidden by the Holy Spirit to speak the word in Asia, [7] and having come down to Mysia, they were attempting to go into Bithynia, and the Spirit of Jesus did not allow them. [8] And having passed by Mysia, they came down to Troas.

[9] And a vision appeared to Paul during the night: A certain man of Macedonia was standing and beseeching him and saying, "Having passed over into Macedonia, help us." [10] Now when he had seen the vision, immediately

we[a] sought to go forth to Macedonia, concluding that God had called us to preach the gospel to them.

---

a   Acts 16:10 – The use of "we" and "us" indicates that the writer, believed to be Luke, was with Paul (until Acts 16:17). See also Acts 20:5-15; 21:1-18; 27:1-28:16.

Philippi

Acts 16:11-23a

Lydia's Conversion in Philippi
(Revelation 2:18-29)

[11] And having sailed from Troas, we made a straight course to Samothrace, and on the following day to Neapolis,[b] [12] and from there to Philippi, which is the leading city of the district of Macedonia, a colony. Now we were staying some days in this city.

[13] And on the day of the Sabbaths, we went forth outside the city gate, by a river, where there was customary to be a place of prayer. And having sat down, we began speaking to the women having gathered.

[14] And a certain woman named Lydia, a seller of purple of the city of Thyatira, worshiping God, was listening. The Lord opened her heart to attend to the things being spoken by Paul. [15] And when she was baptized, and her house, she begged, saying, "If you have judged me to be faithful to the Lord, having entered into my house, abide." And she persuaded us.

Paul and Silas Imprisoned

[16] Now it happened of us going to the place of prayer, a certain girl, having a spirit of Python,[c] met us, who was bringing her masters much gain by fortune-telling. [17] Having followed Paul and us, she was crying out, saying, "These men are servants of the Most High God, who proclaim to you the way of salvation."

[18] And she continued this for many days. And Paul having been distressed and having turned, said to the spirit, "I command you in the name of Jesus Christ to come out from her." And it came out that hour.

[19] Now her masters having seen that their hope of profit was gone, having taken hold of Paul and Silas, dragged them into the marketplace before the rulers. [20] And having brought them up to the magistrates, they said, "These men, being Jews, exceedingly trouble our city [21] and preach customs that it is not lawful for us, being Romans, to accept nor to practice."

---

b   Acts 16:11 – 2 days' travel compared with 5 in the opposite direction in Acts 20:6
c   BLB: Acts 16:16 – Greek Python, a spirit of divination named after the mythical serpent slain by Apollo

²² And the crowd rose up together against them, and the magistrates having torn off their garments, were commanding that they be beaten with rods. ²³ And having laid many blows on them...ᵃ

Acts 16:11-23

Paul and Silas caught a boat sailing to Neapolis, the port nearest to the Roman colony of Philippi. It was a very quick trip, confirming for them that this was indeed the will of God. From Neapolis, they walked along the Egnatian Way to Philippi, a Roman colony and a leading city in the area. Since there was no synagogue in the city, Paul had to use a different preaching plan.

From several enquiries, it seemed that some believers in the God of Israel met down by the river outside the city to pray. When Paul and Silas went there on the Sabbath, they found that the reports were true. Surprisingly, however, there were no men present, and Paul and Silas were asked to speak to the women assembled. One, a woman called Lydia from Thyatira, listened very carefully to everything they said. The Lord opened her heart and she learned the gospel of Jesus. Once she had been baptised, she invited Paul and Silas, and those who were travelling with them, to stay at her house. She was very eager to hear as much as she could about this new hope.

But problems are never far away when people want to exploit others. A young slave-girl who had a sickness of her mind was being used to make money for her masters. They called her sickness a "spirit of divination" and had her tell people's fortunes. Every time Paul and his associates went to the place of prayer by the riverside, they passed her, and each time she shouted out to any who would listen that these men were telling people the way to be saved. Paul found this frustrating and irritating. Surely people could listen and work things out for themselves and if this girl knew they spoke truth, why didn't she come and listen herself? At last, he healed her in the name of Jesus. With her mind working properly, she could no longer tell fortunes in her former intriguing, ambiguous and obscure style. Her masters were furious and dragged Paul and Silas before the authorities. Of course, there were no genuine charges they could bring, so they tried to link their complaint with a religious objection to Paul's teachings. They worked up the crowd, and the magistrates too, and soon Paul and Silas had their outer clothes torn off and were beaten with rods. Many blows fell.

After that, they were thrown into prison to think it over.

ᵃ   Acts 16:23 – See 1 Thessalonians 2:2

The Jailer

Acts 16:23b-34

...they cast them into prison, having charged the jailer to keep them securely,[b] **24** who having received such an order, threw them into the inner prison and fastened their feet in the stocks.

The Conversion of the Jailer

25 Now toward midnight, Paul and Silas praying, were singing praises to God. And the prisoners were listening to them. **26** And suddenly there was a great earthquake, so that foundations of the prison house were shaken, and immediately all the doors were opened, and the chains of all were loosed.

27 And the jailer having been awoken and having seen the doors of the prison open, having drawn his sword was about to kill himself, supposing the prisoners to have escaped. **28** But Paul called out in a loud voice saying, "Do not harm yourself, for we are all here!"

29 And having called for lights, he rushed in, and having become terrified, he fell down before Paul and Silas. **30** And having brought them out, he was saying, "Sirs, what is necessary of me to do, that I may be saved?"

31 And they said, "Believe on the Lord Jesus and you will be saved, you and your household." **32** And they spoke the word of the Lord to him along with all those in his house. **33** And having taken them in that hour of the night, he washed them from the wounds, and immediately he was baptized, and all his household. **34** And having brought them into the house, he laid a table for them and rejoiced with all his household, having believed in God.

---

b   Acts 16:23 – See 1 Thessalonians 2:2

Acts 16:24-34

Paul and Silas found themselves in the inner prison, feet held in the stocks and nothing to do but wait for the next morning.

With lacerated backs and feet locked in place, the idea of lying down held no attraction. Lying on their backs would have been the only option, and the pain was just too great. As midnight crawled around, they were praying and singing hymns while the other prisoners listened. A sudden earthquake, sent to do God's work, and they were free to leave. All the other prisoners were likewise freed, their chains having miraculously come undone. But one man's advantage is often another man's problem, and the jailer was far from happy. These prisoners were his responsibility. He rushed in, saw the situation at a glance and snatched out his sword, planning to kill himself before the magistrates did.

Paul had a loud voice when he needed it, and he used all its power that night, shouting to the jailer that he did not need to kill himself since all the prisoners were still there.

God's work is done by earthquakes, visions and many other means. A vision had brought Paul and Silas to Philippi, and now an earthquake had given salvation to the jailer and his family. The jailer was baptised that night.

Sketch 27 – Other prisoners

The damp, foul-smelling cell held eight prisoners, chained together and chained to the wall. There was no light, no ventilation, no drainage, little space and no creature comforts whatever. No beds, no chairs, no cupboards, no bathroom and no privacy – except that supplied by the ever-present darkness.

"What was all that about?" asked Alexander, one of the prisoners, as the door clanged shut.

"Neptune was angry," answered Quintus. "We should be glad we survived."

"That's not what that Jew said," replied Alexander. "What was his name?"

"Paul, I think," said Drusus, another of the eight.

"Yes, it was Paul. He said it was the God of Israel," said Alexander.

"Who would you trust?" asked Quintus. "Our honourable ancestors or some random Jew you met in a prison?"

"Well, he seems to have got out of prison, while we're still stuck in this stinking hole," observed Emilius.

"We should've taken the opportunity to escape," said Faustus. "We'll never get another chance so good."

"You're right," responded Gaius. "We should've ignored him when he told us all to stay."

"And now he's gone himself!" said Faustus.

"But how long would you have stayed free, Gaius, before you got caught again?" asked Drusus.

"It would've been worth it," retorted Gaius.

"Do you know what they do to escaped prisoners when they catch them?" interjected Alexander.

"And not only to the prisoners!" said Brutus. "What they do to their families, too."

"Yes, I've heard terrible stories of what can happen if they know your family – like they do mine," said Quintus. "I wouldn't dare escape unless I could move my family somewhere else first. Some other country, in fact."

"I reckon Paul's advice was good, though I'd probably have taken the opportunity to escape if he hadn't said what he did," said Brutus.

No-one spoke for a while. The men were settling down for what was left of the night, each trying to find a comfortable place to lie on the stone floor.

"I miss the singing," said Alexander. "It helped to pass the time in this hell-hole."

"How can you say that? Didn't you understand what they were singing? It was all Jewish heresies," said Quintus. "I worship the gods of my fathers – I don't have time for Jewish myths."

"If you worship your father's gods, why did you rob that temple?" asked Alexander.

"I didn't!" objected Quintus. "It was Julius."

"Come on!" said Lucius in the darkness. "You can't fool me, Quintus. Don't forget, I was there when you and Julius brought the incense bowls to Tertius looking for some money. I heard what you said, too."

Quintus didn't reply.

"The fact is, we're all in here for some crime or other," continued Lucius. "That's why we don't sing songs like Paul and his friend did. Two weeks ago, a couple of days before they threw me in here, I heard a servant girl shouting out that they were telling the ways of salvation. Now I wish I'd paid more attention. I don't know if she's right, but I know that I've spent far too much time in prisons on and off, and I've never heard anything like that singing, nor heard of an earthquake that opened all the doors in a prison and freed everyone without falling stones hurting anyone."

"You could be right," said Alexander, cautiously.

"They still ended up in prison," said Quintus. "So they can't be too good!"

"But they're not here now," said Emilius. "Lucius is right – it's been a funny night and no mistake."

"And the floor is still hard, the stench is still unbearable, and we're still locked up," said Faustus bitterly. "I wish I'd taken the chance to escape. I wouldn't have cared if they caught me. Execution sounds better than the endless stifling darkness of this cell."

"Anyone know any religious songs?" asked Lucius.

"Huh!" said Quintus. "Do you expect another earthquake?"

"Maybe it'd just be a good thing to do. It could be time for us to do something good."

"It's time to go to sleep," said Drusus.

Sometimes the fact that we cease to notice a smell we are exposed to for a long time is a real blessing. It was for those eight unfortunates, since without it there would have been no sleep in the cell that night. As it was, it wasn't long before all were asleep.

Leaving Philippi

Morning came and the magistrates reviewed Paul and Silas' case. In the cold light of day, it seemed that enough punishment had been meted out – some even suggested it might have been too much. They sent a terse message to the jailer to let the two men go.

Paul refused to leave.

Now, he felt, was the time to play the citizenship card, using it to protect the small group of new believers from persecution. Legally, the magistrates had made a bad error of judgement in beating Paul and Silas – both of whom were Roman citizens. When the magistrates heard this, they hurried to the jail and tried to placate the men who could cause them a lot of trouble should they choose to do so.

Paul was quite happy to go and had no wish to cause trouble, as long as he could be confident that the believers would be left alone also.

Paul could have used his citizenship to protect himself on the previous day. Instead, he used it to protect his new children in the faith.

After a short meeting of encouragement with the believers, Paul and Silas walked out of Philippi.

Acts 16:35-40

An Official Apology

[35] And day having come, the magistrates sent the officers, saying, "Release those men."

[36] And the jailer reported these words to Paul: "The captains have sent that you may be let go. Now therefore having gone out, depart in peace."

[37] But Paul was saying to them, "Having beaten us publicly, uncondemned men being Romans, they cast us into prison, and now do they throw us out secretly? No indeed! Instead, having come themselves, let them bring us out."

38 And the officers reported these words to the captains, and they were afraid, having heard that they are Romans. **39** And having come, they appealed to them, and having brought them out, they were asking them to go out of the city. **40** And having gone forth out of the prison, they came to Lydia, and having seen them, they exhorted the brothers and departed.

Thessalonica

From Philippi through Amphipolis and Apollonia to Thessalonica went Paul and Silas. At Thessalonica they found a synagogue, so Paul could follow his normal custom of visiting the synagogue on the Sabbath.

For three Sabbaths he discussed the scriptures with all who attended, explaining that Jesus had to die and rise again and that he was the Christ, the anointed king.

Some Jews, some God-fearing Greeks and some leading women were persuaded and joined Paul and Silas, but others were jealous. Troublemakers helped them form a mob and an uproar began.

In the end, everything calmed down, but not before one of the new believers, Jason by name, had been compelled to give a pledge of good conduct – in this case, a pledge that Paul would leave and not come back.

Paul and Silas left by night.

Acts 17:1-10a

Acts 17

Paul Preaches at Thessalonica

¹ And having passed through Amphipolis and Apollonia, they came to Thessalonica, where there was a synagogue of the Jews. ² And according to the custom with Paul, he went in to them and for three Sabbaths reasoned with them from the Scriptures, ³ opening and setting forth that it behooved the Christ to have suffered and to have risen out from the dead, and that "this Jesus whom I preach to you is the Christ." ⁴ And some of them were obedient and joined themselves to Paul and to Silas, along with a great multitude of the worshipping Greeks, and not a few of the leading women.

The Uproar in Thessalonica

5 Now the Jews having become jealous, and having taken to them certain wicked men of the market-loungers, and having collected a crowd, set the city in uproar. And having assailed the house of Jason, they were seeking them to bring out to the people. **6** But not having found them, they dragged Jason and certain brothers before the city authorities, crying out, "These ones having upset the world come here also, **7** whom Jason has received. And these all do contrary to the decrees of Caesar, proclaiming another to be king, Jesus."

8 And they stirred up the crowd and the city authorities, hearing these things. **9** And having taken security from Jason and the rest, they let go them.[a]

10 And the brothers sent away both Paul and Silas immediately by night...

---

a   Acts 17:9 – See 1 Thessalonians 2:18

Berea

Acts 17:10-14

Berea was their next haven, and it proved to be a nice safe haven – for a while. Many people in Berea wanted to hear Paul's message and check whether it was true or not. This noble attitude made Paul's job much easier, until the Jews of Thessalonica heard that Paul was in Berea.

They came at once, agitating and stirring up the crowds, and once again, Paul moved on. He was taken straight to the sea, where he boarded a ship bound for Athens.

Silas and Timothy remained in Berea.

Sketch 28 – Checkers

"Why do you say that, Paul?" asked Nahum.

Paul leaned forward, intense and enthusiastic as ever. "In the second Psalm, God said, 'You are my son, today I have begotten you', and in another Psalm, he said, 'You will not let your Holy One see corruption.' Both passages talk about the resurrection of Jesus. In fact, in each case, the whole Psalm prophesies about Jesus. And there are other passages in Isaiah and other prophets."

The two were talking in the market where Paul had set up a small stall, as he often did when visiting a new town or when there was a need for money! Travellers were always on the move throughout the empire, so the skills of tentmakers like Paul were always in demand. He was also skilled with other forms of leatherwork, and could even mend sandals at a pinch. Best of all, though the casual observer would never discern it, Paul's stall gave him the perfect opportunity to talk to customers about the subject dearest to his heart: Jesus, as the saviour of the world.

Nahum had approached him with a leather pouch that was developing a hole in one corner, the result of constant use rather than carelessness.

Paul admired the exquisite softness of the leather and skilfully stitched a supporting gusset within that would add years to the life of the beloved wallet.

As he worked, Paul began to chat. He was not surprised to discover that Nahum was a Hebrew and pleased to find that he was devout. By the time he completed the final stitch, Paul had not only mentioned Jesus, but had described his position in God's plan, his life in Judea, his rejection by the leaders, his crucifixion and his resurrection. It was the mention of Jesus' resurrection that had caused Paul to refer to the Psalms, and Nahum was keen to follow it up.

"Why don't we go to the synagogue now and read them?" suggested Nahum. "It's not that I don't believe you, but I'd like to see them in context."

"That's a good idea," smiled Paul. "Will there be anyone at the synagogue at this time of morning?"

"Oh, yes. A few of us like to read the scriptures frequently. One is a leader of the synagogue, and he keeps the synagogue open every day for anyone who wants to read the scriptures."

"That's a wonderful idea," said Paul. "Let's go now."

Nahum paid his bill and Paul quickly packed up his tools and followed him towards the synagogue.

"Do you often read the scriptures?" asked Paul.

"Oh yes! There are so many fascinating bits of scripture that I often go to the synagogue to re-read some part or other, or to find a new part to read."

"I think you're doing just what God would want his people to do," commented Paul.

"Sometimes travellers visit the synagogue on the Sabbath and are asked to speak," said Nahum. "They often explain what some part of scripture means, and afterwards I try to check that the scripture really means what the speaker said it did."

"And that's what you're doing with me!" smiled Paul.

"True. We don't always get our facts straight, do we? So when I hear new ideas about scripture, I try to check them. It isn't always easy to find the passages people refer to, though, so having you here will be a great help."

They found the synagogue open as expected and Nahum led Paul in. The leader of the synagogue greeted them and Nahum introduced Paul. "Here's a Hebrew I just met in the marketplace. He's a tentmaker and leatherworker, but he's also got some unusual ideas about prophecies in our scriptures. I want to read the passages he's referring to."

"Are these prophecies about the Messiah? Those are always the most popular."

"Yes," answered Paul. "Prophecies of the Messiah in the Psalms. And these particular prophecies have been fulfilled in Jesus of Nazareth."

"Jesus of Nazareth?" asked the leader blankly. "Who's he?"

"It still amazes me how few people have heard of him," said Paul ruefully. "Jesus is a descendant of King David of the tribe of Judah. He was born in the time of the census and executed by our leaders when Pontius Pilate was governor."

"Executed? I thought you said he's the Messiah!"

"Paul says that his execution..."

"And resurrection!" interjected Paul.

"...and subsequent resurrection were just what the scriptures foretold," said Nahum. "So I wanted to check the details."

"Let's get out the scroll of Psalms, then," said the leader. "That's the best way to check it. Shall we get the Greek version?"

"That's the one I can understand," answered Nahum. "Is that alright, Paul?"

"What matters is that you understand it," said Paul. "Let's use the Greek."

Carefully lifting the Greek scroll of the Psalms from its home, the leader placed it on a table where all three of them would be able to read it. Removing the protective covers, he put them to one side and the scroll lay ready.

"Let's start with the second psalm," said Paul. "That's easy to find."

It was quickly found and Paul pointed to the passage, roughly halfway through the psalm.

Nahum began to read out loud, " '*I will tell of the decree: The Lord said to me, You are my Son; today I have begotten you.*'[a] Is '*me*' the writer of the psalm? And is who is '*the Lord*'?"

"Our Hebrew scroll uses the word '*Yahweh*' there," answered the synagogue leader, "so God is claiming a son."

"Exactly!" cried Paul. "And '*me*' is the son speaking – the king, the Messiah mentioned earlier in the Psalm."

Nahum began again, this time reading from the beginning of the psalm and trying to understand the context. After some time, he said, "The psalm seems to describe all the kings of the earth plotting against God and his Messiah – who God also calls *his son*. That doesn't seem likely to be successful! Hmm. I can't remember having noticed this Psalm much before. But now I see that it could be a... a... a powerful component of Paul's argument in favour of God actually having a son."

"And notice the way it finishes," added Paul, pointing.

"It says, '*Kiss the son, lest he be angry, and you perish in the way, for his wrath is quickly kindled. Blessed are all who take refuge in him.*'[b] '*Son*' again. Well, Paul, you certainly weren't making this up! And you believe that Jesus of Nazareth is this '*son*'?"

"I do. And when you take it in conjunction with the words of Isaiah: '*A virgin shall conceive and bear a son...*', we can understand how the birth of Jesus came about, born as he was to a virgin mother and also a son of God."

"That's a big claim," said the leader, frowning. He shook his head for a few moments, then laughed. "In fact, I imagine making a claim like that in Jerusalem could get you stoned! They're not as open-minded as we are here in Macedonia."

"And what about the other psalm you mentioned?" asked Nahum.

"Ah, yes," said Paul, all enthusiasm once more. "It's a miktam of David. Can I...?" he asked the synagogue leader, who responded with a nod. Paul quickly found the object of his search and smoothed out the scroll. Resting his finger near the end of the psalm, he said, "From there to the end."

Nahum began to read. " '*For you will not abandon my soul to Sheol, or let your holy one see corruption. You make known to me the path of life; in your presence there is fullness of joy; at your right hand are pleasures forevermore.*' There's quite a bit in that passage, isn't there? And '*pleasures forevermore*' sounds like living forever, doesn't it?"[c]

---

a   Psalm 2:7
b   Psalm 2:12
c   Psalm 16:10-11

"It does," nodded the synagogue leader.

Paul beamed. "You're absolutely right. And when David writes, '*you will not abandon my soul to Sheol*', he's not writing from his own point of view – after all, David is dead and buried and his tomb is still in Jerusalem. Instead, he's speaking of his descendant, Jesus, who died but was not abandoned to the grave nor left to rot. Instead, as David wrote, he was raised to God's right hand and lives forever."

More questions followed, for the unexpected work of Jesus takes time to understand, but with the scriptures to guide them and Paul to describe the life and works of Jesus, Nahum and his friend gradually came to believe the good news of the kingdom of God and the name of Jesus Christ. And they weren't alone.

Acts 17:10-14

The Character of the Bereans

10 And the brothers sent away both Paul and Silas immediately by night to Berea, who having arrived, went into the synagogue of the Jews. **11** Now these, who were more noble than those in Thessalonica, received the word with all readiness, on every day examining the Scriptures, whether these things were so. **12** Therefore many of them indeed believed, and not a few of the prominent Grecian women and men.

13 But when the Jews from Thessalonica learned that the word of God also was proclaimed by Paul in Berea, they came there also, stirring up and agitating the crowds. **14** And then immediately the brothers sent away Paul to go as to the sea. And both Silas and Timothy remained there.

Paul in Athens

Acts 17:15-34

Brothers accompanied Paul to Athens, then returned to Berea with orders for Silas and Timothy to join him in Athens as soon as they could. He had intended to stay quiet until they came, but it just wasn't possible. How could he say nothing when the city was full of idols?

He could reason with the people at the synagogue – and did so – but what about all the others? How would they hear?

He began talking to people in the market places, speaking to any who would listen. Some were philosophers who revelled in disputation, and they soon brought him to the Areopagus to speak before many others – important people all.

Paul chose to speak about an altar he had seen marked "To An Unknown God", a sort of catch-all dedication to make sure no deities felt left out.

He used the opportunity to tell them about the God they didn't know, an all-powerful God who does not live in temples and does not need anyone to make offerings to keep him well fed. Paul presented the creator of heaven and earth, maker of mankind, and his son Jesus Christ, once dead but raised again to life.

Some sneered – but others listened.

Paul left them, but one of the members of the Areopagus followed him, along with some others.

Acts 17:15-34

15 Now those escorting Paul brought him unto Athens, and having received a command unto Silas and Timothy that as quickly as possible they should come to him, they departed.

Paul in Athens

16 Now of Paul in Athens waiting for them, his spirit was provoked in him, seeing the city to be utterly idolatrous. **17** So indeed he was reasoning in the synagogue with the Jews and those worshiping, and in the marketplace on every day with those meeting him.

18 And also some of the Epicureans and Stoics, philosophers, encountered him, and some were saying, "What may this babbler desire to say?" but others, "He seems to be a proclaimer of foreign gods," because he was proclaiming the gospel of Jesus and the resurrection.

19 And having taken hold of him they brought him to the Areopagus, saying, "Are we able to know what is this new teaching which is spoken by you. **20** For you are bringing some strange things to our ears. We resolve therefore to know what these things wish to be." **21** Now all the Athenians and the visiting strangers spent their time in nothing else than to tell something and to hear something new.

Paul Before the Areopagus

22 And Paul, having stood in the midst of the Areopagus, was saying, "Men, Athenians, I behold that in all things you are very religious. **23** For passing through and beholding your objects of worship, I even found an altar on which had been inscribed:

TO AN UNKNOWN GOD.

Therefore whom you worship not knowing, Him I proclaim to you.

24 The God having made the world and all things that are in it, He being Lord of heaven and earth, does not dwell in hand-made temples, **25** nor is He served by hands of men as needing anything, Himself giving to all life and breath and everything. **26** And He made from one man every nation of men, to dwell upon all the face of the earth, having determined the appointed times and the boundaries of their habitation, **27** to seek God, if perhaps indeed they might palpate for Him, and might find Him. And indeed, He is not far from each one of us.

28 'For in Him we live and move and are.'[a] As also some of the poets among you have said, 'For we are also His offspring.'[b] **29** Therefore, being offspring of God, we ought not to consider the Divine Being to be like to gold or to silver or to stone, a graven thing of man's craft and imagination.

30 So indeed God, having overlooked the times of ignorance, now commands all men everywhere to repent, **31** because He set a day in which He is about to judge the world in righteousness by a man whom He appointed, having provided a guarantee to all, having raised Him out from the dead."

---

a   BLB: Acts 17:28 – Probably a quote from the Cretan philosopher Epimenides
b   BLB: Acts 17:28 – Probably from the poem 'Phainomena' by the Cilician philosopher Aratus

32 Now having heard of a resurrection of the dead, some indeed began to mock him, but some said, "We will hear you concerning this again also." **33** Thus Paul went out from their midst. **34** But some men, having joined themselves to him, believed, among whom also were Dionysius the Areopagite, and a woman named Damaris, and others with them.

Corinth

Acts 18:1-3

Paul went next to Corinth, where he met a couple – Aquila and his wife Priscilla – with whom he became close friends. Like Paul, they were Jews and tentmakers.

❧

Sketch 29 – Aquila & Priscilla

"Thanks for your work, Paul," said the customer, stroking the new patch Paul had expertly sewn in place. "That's just what I need." He rolled up the tent flap and gave Paul some coins.

Paul took the money with a nod of thanks and put it in his purse. It was good to have a satisfied customer, and this would help to cover his living costs. Corinth was an expensive place to live!

The man paused, then said diffidently, "Can I ask a question?"

Paul nodded.

"I… I haven't met very many Jews, but … are you all tent makers?"

"No," answered Paul, surprised. "Why do you ask?"

"Yesterday I found another couple who were tent makers, but they were too busy to fix my tent. They were Jews too."

"Jewish tent makers? I don't know of any in Corinth apart from me. Where were they?" asked Paul eagerly.

"I can show you where they were, if you want."

"Thanks. I'll come straight away." Turning to the tradesman sitting next to him, Paul said, "Gaius, could you keep an eye on my tools? I'll be back soon."

Paul followed his customer out of the market, through a residential area and finally into another market area. After looking around for a few moments, the man seemed to find what he was looking for and led Paul to a quiet area where a man and woman sat cross-legged on a stone bench, their eyes fixed on the material spread across their laps. The needles in their hands moved swiftly and smoothly, adding neat stitches to straight seams.

"Excuse me," said Paul's companion apologetically as he stopped in front of them. "This man wanted to meet you."

The man and his wife looked up quickly, concern on their faces.

"I believe that you two are Jews!" said Paul, smiling.

"Y-e-s," replied the man slowly, eyes alert. "What of it?"

"Well, I'm a Jew too," said Paul, "and I'm also a tentmaker!"

The concern fell away from their faces, replaced by smiles of relief and pleasure.

"A tentmaker?" responded the man. "We don't meet many of them, and to meet one who is of the circumcision, well, that's an unexpected pleasure. I'm Aquila and this is my wife Priscilla, who is an expert tent-maker too."

"Latin names?" prompted Paul. "Do you live here in Corinth?"

"At the moment we do, but we were both born in Rome, although we're of Jewish stock."

"Did you get caught up in Caesar's recent expulsion of the Jews from Rome, then?"

"Yes, and that's why we were a little cautious when you asked if we were Jews. You never know where Jew-hatred will pop up next."

"You're right, Aquila, and I'm sorry to have worried you. It's good to meet you and Priscilla, too. As for me, people call me Paul."

Aquila smiled. "It seems appropriate: you're not very tall."

"No," agreed Paul. "It's certainly much more appropriate than my given name – Saul!"

Aquila guffawed at the incongruity of a small man like Paul being named after the ancient king Saul, famous for being head and shoulders taller than anyone else in Israel at the time when he was chosen to be king. "Was your father an incurable optimist, or just a big man looking for a son to outgrow him?"

"My father was a giant of a man, and my mother was very tall for a woman, too," smiled Paul. "They had reason for the grand name, but I was always small, so my new name fits better."

"How long have you been in Corinth?" asked Aquila.

"Three days. I came from Athens."

"Is the faith of our fathers important to you? Will we see you in the synagogue on the Sabbath?"

"It is indeed. And you will, if the Lord permits," answered Paul.

Suddenly remembering the man who had brought him to meet Aquila and Priscilla, Paul turned back to him. "Thank you very much for bringing me to meet these countrymen of mine. I'm sure the patch I put on will work well, but if it doesn't, make sure you come back and let me know."

"I'm not likely to have a chance. I'm leaving for Athens this afternoon, which is why I needed it fixed this morning."

"It's a pity you're going so soon. I was hoping to be able to talk to you about some good news that everyone needs to hear."

"What sort of good news?"

"Good news about Jesus of Nazareth, sent by God to be the saviour of the world."

"Jesus of Nazareth? I don't know the name."

"He was also a Jew, but the good news is that he can save you from sin and death."

"Death is natural. Everyone dies."

"That's true, and even Jesus died, but he didn't stay dead. God raised Jesus from the dead and now he lives forever."

"Let me guess, I have to become a Jew to join in?"

"No, no, not at all. All you need to do is believe in him, be baptised and live a life of righteousness and faith."

"Tell me more about him."

"Jesus came to direct us away from evil behaviour and the worship of dead idols that can't do anything for us. You must notice all the idols around here, and in Athens you might even see one I noticed while I was there, dedicated to 'An Unknown God'. So many idols, but they never do anything for anyone."

"Are you trying to convince me to worship the God of the Hebrews?"

"Yes. The God who led his people out of Egypt and gave them their Promised Land. Now that's really doing something. That's power! And now he's raised Jesus from the dead after he was crucified by the Romans and Jewish leaders."

"Crucified? Was he a criminal?"

"No, quite the opposite. But you know how things can go – the leaders were jealous of him because crowds went to listen to him instead of them, and he also healed lots of sick people."

"Yes, I can imagine that happening, but could a saviour of the world really be crucified? It's a pretty... humiliating death."

"True, but Jesus believed that being humiliated was worthwhile if it could save people like us."

"Doesn't sound like much of a hero to me!"

"Wouldn't you call someone who was willing to die for others a hero?"

The man inclined his head doubtfully. "Maybe... but, look, I really must go. I'd like to hear more, but I haven't got enough time before I leave for Athens."

"If you want to know more, go to the Jewish synagogue in Athens and find two men, Silas and Timothy. They'll be able to help you."

"Silas and Timothy, hey? I'll try to remember those names. Silas and Timothy. I suppose they're both Jews?"

"Silas is, but Timothy has a Greek father and a Jewish mother."

"Well, I'm a Greek, so maybe he can explain the differences between this Jesus and the religion we grew up with."

"I'm sure he'll do his best," smiled Paul. "He's a wonderful lad, is Timothy. Everyone loves him, and he loves the truth."

The man hurried off and Paul turned back to Aquila and Priscilla.

"Who is this Jesus you're talking about?" asked Aquila.

"He is the Messiah spoken of in our scriptures. Are you familiar with the picture of a suffering servant in Isaiah, where the prophet speaks about one who would carry our iniquities and suffer for others?"

"Y-e-s," said Aquila, "but isn't that talking about Israel as a nation?"

"No, I don't believe so. Isaiah wrote, 'He was despised and rejected by men; a man of sorrows, and acquainted with grief; and as one from whom men hide their faces he was despised, and we esteemed him not. Surely he has borne our griefs and carried our sorrows; yet we esteemed him stricken, smitten by God, and afflicted.'[a] The subject is spoken of as a man, and Israel the nation is included in the 'we' – the audience who esteemed him not. So it couldn't make sense for Israel to be both the man and the audience."

"That's logical," admitted Aquila, and Priscilla nodded.

Paul continued to explain how this passage applied to Jesus, before moving on to other passages from Isaiah and then the other prophets. Aquila and Priscilla continued to nod often, occasionally making comments or asking for clarification. Paul's eyes were full of excitement and he was utterly immersed in his subject. For the moment, he was heedless of anything beyond his need to present Jesus Christ as the saviour of the world.

After a while, Priscilla rolled up the material she and her husband had been working on so that she could concentrate better on Paul's words. With each passage he quoted and then explained her eyes seemed to brighten a little and sometimes a little smile would cross her lips. True, from time to time the pair exchanged puzzled glances, but each time Paul took the hint and tried to explain further or take a different tack in his commentary.

An hour passed, then two; yet neither Paul nor his audience appeared to notice. At last, Paul stopped abruptly, looked down at his hands and said, "I'm afraid that when I start talking to anyone who is interested in God's word like you are, I find it hard to stop talking about it and the amazing news about Jesus the Christ."

"We're fascinated by all you say, and it really does make sense," said Aquila, glancing at Priscilla, who nodded her agreement. "Since you are a tentmaker and so are we, why don't we work together for a while – if that would suit you? Then we could talk more about this as we work."

Paul beamed. "That would be marvellous," he said, eyes gleaming. Suddenly he looked dismayed. "Oh no! I left my tools in the other market and told Gaius I'd be back soon. I hope it hasn't caused him too much trouble!"

---

a   Isaiah 53:3-4

ↂ

> *Acts 18:4-8*

Every Saturday, Paul went to the synagogue as usual, and after a while Silas and Timothy arrived in Corinth too. From that time on, Paul devoted himself entirely to preaching, no longer trying to fit in his work as a tentmaker as well. Some in the synagogue believed and joined Paul. Others resisted. Paul withdrew and went again to the Gentiles.

Crispus, the leader of the synagogue, believed Paul, and his replacement Sosthenes later did the same. Many were believing and being baptised, but even so, it was there in Corinth that Paul reached one of his lowest ebbs. Fear within and fear without – Paul was finding it hard to keep going.

ↂ

Sketch 30 – Fear...

When would it happen here in Corinth?

Paul shivered and rolled over in bed.

He could hear gentle snoring through the wall. Perhaps that was what had woken him. Any sound could wake him nowadays. And any unexpected sound was *guaranteed* to wake him – often dripping with sweat. Constant tension. Fear. He couldn't relax in the face of the ever-present threat that loomed in his mind and set his nerves jangling.

In Iconium, he'd heard of the danger in time. Barnabas and he had escaped without injury.

In Lystra, though, he'd misjudged the danger. He couldn't forget how quickly the argument had escalated from angry words to open violence: the terror he had felt; the stones; the pain; the blackness that enveloped him. One stoning. And three times now the Jews had given him the "forty lashes less one". It wasn't legal, but that didn't stop it happening. In Philippi, Silas and he had been beaten and thrown into prison.

Wherever he went, it was a balancing act. He *had* to preach about Jesus Christ, but whenever he did, people wanted to kill him – as they had killed his Lord. Would they kill him in Corinth?

He couldn't teach people The Way in a day, but if he spent too long in a place... well, death seemed within touching-distance most of the time.

How long had he been in Corinth – three months? He was well into the danger zone. Any day the situation might explode. Either jealous Jews or pagan enemies could attack him. They might even work together against him, however contradictory that was.

Paul stopped for a moment, consciously trying to relax. How ironic that pagans and Jews – people who hated each other – were willing to cooperate together against him! He managed a small smile in the darkness.

A sudden creak made him instantly alert. Was that the front door? Were they attacking at night this time? Creeping towards his room with knives in hand; moving towards his door, ready to burst in... No, no, No! It was only the innocent sound of wooden beams creaking as they adjusted to the cool of night. No-one was out there. Through the wall, his host was still snoring.

There was nothing to worry about.

Surely God would protect him as he preached the salvation God offered through his son? Yet Jesus had not been protected from violence. His death had been even worse than the horror of stoning. And had not Jesus warned Paul that he would suffer for the sake of his name?

Paul fell into desperate, urgent prayer, and for a time the overmastering fear was pushed back. Calm and confidence trickled slowly into his mind and his jerky breathing slowed. God was there. God was good. And everything worked together for good for those who love God. Slowly he relaxed and drifted off into an exhausted sleep.

But there it was again. Or was it? What had woken him? Was it another creak or were they really coming for him this time? Terror constricted his throat, sweat broke out on his forehead and he couldn't lie still. Up on one elbow, he listened to the quiet of the night. No snoring. That was it. The snoring through the wall had stopped and been replaced by a few deep breaths.

He couldn't go on like this. Any attempt he made to relax lasted only moments before his nerves were on edge again.

Meeting Aquila and Priscilla had helped, there was no doubt about that. And they still did their best to help him. Being with fellow-Jews who shared an unfeigned love of God's word tempered his fear. Teaching them of Jesus had been a joy, and their response had been so uplifting.

But the oppressive fear was still there. Day and night.

Sometimes Paul even longed for the easier times when he was not a marked man. Yet back then *he* had been the hunter, making others feel as he felt now. There could be nothing good about that!

His work now was good, worthwhile, essential. If he went home to Tarsus and kept silent, or fled to Arabia to hide, how would people like Aquila and Priscilla hear about Jesus?

His work *must* go on.

Yet at times he felt like young David as he was continually chased by King Saul, constantly in danger with eventual capture and death seeming inevitable.

And despite his monumental faith, David had eventually run away to Gath.

A scraping noise. That must be out in the street. Were they coming...?

Calm down, Paul, he told himself. There's nothing to worry about.

Yet the temptation to leap up, pack his goods and run away was almost irresistible. He could board a ship at Cenchrea in the morning and sail away. Away from this fear.

Paul stilled his galloping thoughts. Flight was not an option. Jesus had died for him and forgiven him. How could he ever betray him by running away?

He took several deep breaths. Closed his eyes. Relaxed again. And again. Finally he prepared himself for prayer, but as he did so, he felt a sudden change.

His fear began to subside.

Jesus was there. Paul could see him and recognise him. Yet his eyes were closed, so it must be a vision. Nevertheless, it was Jesus. Paul knew that voice.

"Paul, do not fear," said Jesus. His voice was full of love and compassion, of sympathy for a troubled child, yet there was also a sense of command. "Continue speaking, and do not be silent, because I am with you, and no one will lay a hand on you to harm you. I have many people in this city."

The voice faded and soon the presence could no longer be felt, but fear had melted away.

Within moments, Paul fell into a deep restful sleep. The worst was over.

Acts 18:9-18

Jesus spoke to him in a vision by night and told him not to be afraid, but to keep speaking to everyone. He gave Paul a guarantee that no-one would harm him and that many in the city would believe.

Paul took hold of his courage and kept going.

He stayed for a year and six months before there was any attempt to attack him, but the attempt was unsuccessful and Paul was able to stay safely for many days longer.

The promise of protection had been fulfilled, but it was time to move on again.

Acts 18:1-18a

Acts 18

Paul's Ministry in Corinth

[1] And after these things, having departed from Athens, he came to Corinth. [2] And having found a certain Jew named Aquila, a native of Pontus, and Priscilla his wife, recently having come from Italy because of Claudius having commanded all the Jews to depart out of Rome, he came to them, [3] and because of being of the same trade, he stayed with them and worked. For they were tentmakers by the trade.

[4] And he was reasoning in the synagogue on every Sabbath, persuading both Jews and Greeks. [5] Now when both Silas and Timothy came down from Macedonia, Paul was occupied with the word, earnestly testifying to the Jews Jesus to be the Christ. [6] But of them opposing and reviling him, having shaken out the garments, he said to them, "Your blood be upon your head; I am clean. From now on I will go to the Gentiles."

[7] And having departed from there, he came to the house of a certain one named Titius Justus, worshiping God, whose house was adjoining the synagogue. [8] And Crispus,[a] the ruler of the synagogue, believed in the Lord, with his all household. And many of the Corinthians hearing believed and were baptized.

---

a   Acts 18:8 – See 1 Corinthians 1:14

9 Now the Lord said to Paul through a vision in the night, "Do not fear,[a] but continue speaking, and do not be silent, **10** because I am with you, and no one will lay a hand on you to harm you, because there are many people to me in this city." **11** And he remained a year and six months, teaching the word of God among them.

Paul Before Gallio

12 But Gallio[b] being proconsul of Achaia, the Jews with one accord rose up against Paul and led him to the judgment seat, **13** saying, "This man persuades men to worship God contrary to the Law."

14 Now Paul being about to open the mouth, Gallio said to the Jews, "If indeed it was some unrighteousness or wicked crime, O Jews, according to reason I would have endured with you. **15** But if it is a question about a word, and names, and in reference to your law, you will see to it yourselves. I resolve not to be a judge of these things." **16** And he drove them from the judgment seat.

17 Then all of them, having seized Sosthenes[c] the ruler of the synagogue, began to beat him before the judgment seat. And it mattered nothing to Gallio about these things.

Paul Returns to Antioch

18 Now Paul, having remained many days more, having taken leave of the brothers, sailed away to Syria—and with him Priscilla and Aquila...

---

a   Acts 18:9 – See 1 Corinthians 2:3
b   Acts 18:12 – Believed to be the brother of the writer Seneca
c   Acts 18:17 – See 1 Corinthians 1:1

Cenchrea

<table>
<tr><td align="center">Acts 18:18</td></tr>
</table>

Paul was leaving Corinth, but as he left, he stopped at Cenchrea, one of the ports of Corinth, to cut his hair. It was the fulfilment of a vow.

But it was time to leave and he was eager to get home to Antioch. He had been away for several years.

Acts 18:18

18 Now Paul, having remained many days more, having taken leave of the brothers, sailed away to Syria—and with him Priscilla and Aquila—having shaved the head in Cenchrea, for he had a vow.

Back to Antioch

Acts 18:18-22

Cenchrea, Ephesus, Caesarea, Antioch.

Paul was in a hurry. When they asked him to stay longer in Ephesus, he refused.

At Caesarea he greeted the believers, then went to Antioch.

Paul's second missionary journey was complete.

Acts 18:18-22

18 Now Paul, having remained many days more, having taken leave of the brothers, sailed away to Syria—and with him Priscilla and Aquila—having shaved the head in Cenchrea, for he had a vow.

19 Now they came to Ephesus, and left them there. And he himself having entered into the synagogue, reasoned with the Jews. **20** Now of them asking him to remain for a longer time, he did not consent, **21** but having taken leave and having said,[a] "I will return to you again, God willing," he sailed from Ephesus, **22** and having landed at Caesarea, having gone up and having greeted the church, he went down to Antioch.

---

a   BLB: Acts 18:21 – BYZ and TR include I must by all means keep this feast that comes in Jerusalem, but

PART SEVEN
Intermission

Time in Antioch in Syria

Sketch 31 – I wonder...

"It's great to back in Antioch," said Paul to Andronicus, "and the situation among the believers looks good."

"Oh yes," agreed Andronicus. "The brethren are always eager to worship God and preach the gospel. They work together as a good family should."

"That takes a great weight off my mind," breathed Paul. He sighed. "Perhaps I didn't need to be in such a hurry to come back, but I was worried about what I might find here."

Andronicus laughed. "You don't need to worry, Paul. I don't see any failing in our enthusiasm, or any reduction in our dedication to prayer. Instead, the church continues to grow!"

"I'm so pleased to hear it. The fervour in your voice warms my heart, cousin."

"And we're glad to hear your news, too," said Andronicus. "Your reports of new believers joining our fellowship everywhere you go are just what we need."

Paul nodded and sat for a while in silence. Finally he said, "This mutual encouragement is really important to us all as believers. My news inspires you, and your reports fill me with confidence. With God's help, the Way really is turning the world upside down."

"And look at how it genuinely changes people," marvelled Andronicus. "You're a prime example, of course, cousin, but I constantly marvel at the joy and godliness that shines through so many believers."

"And we need to make sure that we keep going. All sorts of things can destroy our momentum. But we mustn't start worrying that the fellowship is getting too big, or fear that things can't keep growing as they are. If we hold our nerve, cling to our faith, keep preaching and continue to seek God's kingdom first, this seismic change in the empire will continue, and even speed up."

"I expect so," said Andronicus confidently. "And why wouldn't it keep going? We've seen how it works: seen the changes faith brings, the altered lives, the joy of godliness. Why would it ever stop?"

"There will always be some people who lose their direction or their conviction," said Paul, carefully, "but I fear there will come a time when *many* believers will fall away and lose their faith."

Andronicus shook his head with a puzzled frown. "Why would that happen, cousin? It doesn't make sense. The truth is so good, so valuable for everyone."

"Look at history, cousin. Did Israel keep obeying Moses' commands? Did the kingdom continue to follow David's leadership? No, it split up only one generation later. How long did Hezekiah's revival last? Or Josiah's? There is always resistance to righteousness, and such new starts will only continue or remain healthy if you can get rid of human nature. Unfortunately, people are the consistent problem."

"But Jesus is greater than Moses," insisted Andronicus. "Greater than David, or Hezekiah, or Josiah. Surely the new kingdom he has built in people's hearts can endure and spread? He is so much *better* than the kings and prophets of old, and so is his kingdom."

"True, but the problem is still people. There are people who want to tear down the temple Jesus is building. Some want to go back to Judaism. Others just want to be leaders and don't care much about the Way – or the believers. Some are even trying to mix Jesus' teachings with Greek mythology or fanciful Roman ideas, and if we aren't careful, these… these errors and wrong ideas will spread like a deadly disease."

"Is that why you came back to Antioch?" asked Andronicus shrewdly. "Were you worried about us?"

"Partly, yes. I'm always concerned about my brothers and sisters, and you are always in my prayers. Recently I've even taken to writing letters to various congregations I've preached to. I remember their initial eagerness and their joy in salvation through Jesus, so when I hear reports from travellers of troubles in doctrine or life or fellowship, I feel compelled to do something. If I can't go back to visit immediately, I write letters to address the problems I've heard of and emphasise ideas that might help them."

"It sounds like an intolerable weight to bear, cousin."

"Oh, I wouldn't say that. It's heavy, yes, but not intolerable. After all, that's the task Jesus gave me. He warned me that it would be hard, but he also said it was essential work and would be very rewarding."

"Has it been?"

"Rewarding beyond words! I can't describe how much better my life has been since I met Jesus and became his servant."

"We – everyone in the family, I mean, cousin – have all noticed the change in you, but it must be very demanding work. Exhausting. And terrifying at times, too."

"It is, but it's still worthwhile. You're right that it's terrifying at times, though. Each time I visit a new town, I know that it won't be long before people are attacking me – and not just with words."

"I suppose it's not really a surprise. After all, that's what you would have done yourself in the past!"

"I know. But it can make it difficult to push on. You see, I know that if I just keep my mouth shut, even a little, I'm less likely to get beaten, or stoned, or arrested, or shouted at, or rioted over."

"We all have that temptation to keep quiet to some extent," said Andronicus.

"I know, but I think it's more extreme for me."

"Of course, Paul! You've been given the greatest ability of all the believers to 'turn the world upside down', and the greatest blessings of the spirit to do this work. Those blessings have kept you alive, but preaching God's truth in the face of every possible form of opposition will always provoke a violent reaction. Vested interests and people accustomed to power will resist anything that threatens to weaken their control over others. Encouraging the ordinary people to have consciences of their own will always anger such people."

"I suppose so – but it still tests my faith at times."

"Tell me more about the churches you've helped form in Asia, Macedonia and Achaia, not to mention Cilicia, Galatia and Bithynia. How are they developing?"

"They're doing well, overall, but they're also proof of my wider problem. You mentioned Galatia – well, I've already had to write a letter to the congregations there because they were listening to travelling teachers who were presenting new teachings, changing the truth Jesus taught me. They were adding new ideas of their own and changing doctrines – which completely defeats the purpose of Jesus' unchanging gospel. Remember: one Lord, one faith, one baptism, one God and father of us all. So I had to write to them and remind them that Jesus' gospel cannot change – ever."

"Did they listen to you?"

"I *think* so, but that concern is always hanging over me. Are they holding onto truth or letting it slip through their fingers? Are people trying to seize leadership positions so that they can drag the believers in their preferred direction, instead of Jesus' direction?"

"I can see that you take it all very seriously," said Andronicus, sympathetically.

"Sometimes I think these new congregations need more support from long-standing believers. Many new converts have little background in the scriptures, so they can easily be led astray. As you know, the town of Corinth is legendary for its immorality, yet we have a group of new believers there who are trying to grasp the truth of Jesus and honestly change their lifestyle. I was there for two years, but what has happened since I left to come here? I don't know, and it worries me. Their faces fill my mind and their names fill my prayers, but I long to do more. I want to be there to help them. But there are so many other places to visit too."

"So you think it would help if believers who have been believers for a long time went to live in such places and joined their congregations?"

"Yes, I'm certain it would."

"I'll keep that in mind, then. A situation has been arising that means it might be better for my business if my wife and I were in Rome now that Jews are allowed to live there again. I hear that there's a small congregation there. We'll pray about it and see what God wants us to do."

Acts 18:23

| ²³ And having stayed some time... |

| Acts 18:23 |

Paul stayed some time in Antioch in Syria, but soon he was back on the road again: north through the interior, then round the corner past Tarsus.

PART EIGHT
The Third Missionary Journey

Galatia and Phrygia

Acts 18:23

Paul travelled into Galatia and Phrygia, doing his best to strengthen the believers. He considered this task vital. Individual believers and groups of believers should never be left to wither on the vine, their faith dying a slow death without support.

Sketch 32 – Encouragement

When a congregation in Galatia learned that the Apostle Paul had arrived in town, they welcomed him and quickly arranged an evening meeting. Everyone was eager to hear what he had to say – they all remembered his inspiring words from previous visits. Not only did they miss his guidance, the truth was that they were finding it hard to keep their eyes on the kingdom. Here was an opportunity not to be missed.

The upper room in which they met was crowded, and everyone was in a festive mood.

One of the local elders welcomed Paul and his companions joyfully, then invited the diminutive preacher to speak. Paul stood in front of everyone and the smile on his face invited many answering smiles from his audience. He no longer looked as young as when he first visited them, but the fire in his eyes was undimmed and his body language spoke volumes about his pleasure in greeting them once more.

He seemed to be in no hurry to begin, but stood looking around for a few moments, catching the eyes of those he recognised and greeting them with a twitch of his lips or a small wave. New converts felt the full force of his personality as his broad smile welcomed them to the worldwide fellowship built around the sacrifice of the Lord Jesus.

After a while, he felt attuned to his audience and began to speak. His words were measured.

"Grace to you, my brothers, and peace from God our Father and the Lord Jesus Christ, who gave himself for our sins to deliver us from the present evil age. This was according to the will of our God and Father, to whom be the glory forever and ever.

"You have been called to freedom, brothers, a freedom that is spreading quickly all over the world. It is freedom from sin, freedom to grow in grace, freedom to serve your neighbours and freedom to offer that freedom to others.

"We have received freedom to be spiritual, but we must always remember that the Lord Jesus Christ did not use his power or his freedom to serve himself. It is not an opportunity for the flesh, to serve it, but an opportunity through love to serve one another.

"Some people still wish to follow the Law of Moses, but they follow it only in a technical way. They worry about keeping special feast days and insist on circumcision or fine details of the law, but they miss the main message of the law. Remember that love is the fulfilling of the law. The Ten Commandments have their basis in love. Loving your neighbour fulfils the law, and Jesus fulfilled both the law and the prophets.

"If we aren't careful, our religion can become very selfish and conceited. We can view ourselves as righteous and look down on others. We can notice everybody else's failings and ignore our own, but that will only lead to us biting and devouring each other as if we were a pack of vicious dogs. But if we do this, we will devour and destroy each other.

"So I say to you, walk by the Spirit, not gratifying the desires of the flesh. You all know that the desires of the flesh are against the Spirit, and the desires of the Spirit are against the flesh. These two things are opposed to each other. And while our freedom in Christ is a freedom from the Law, it is not a freedom to indulge the flesh. Instead, it is an upward call to lead us away from the lusts of the flesh to the spirituality that comes from Jesus Christ.

"You all know the works of the flesh. We see them around us constantly in society and sometimes feel their attraction ourselves. Yet think of the meaningless emptiness of those works of the flesh. The lives ruined, the anger caused, the love destroyed, the fellowship broken by sexual immorality, impurity, sensuality, idolatry and sorcery, hatred, strife, jealousy, fits of anger, rivalries, divisions, factions, envy, drunkenness, orgies, and things like that.

"My brothers, I warn you, as I have warned you before, that those who do such things will not inherit the kingdom of God.

"Yet the value of the kingdom of God is beyond any description. You've already been transferred into his kingdom, so live as if you are there.

"We must all produce the fruit of the Spirit: love, joy, peace, patience, kindness, goodness, faithfulness, gentleness, and self-control. There's no law against things like these.

"If we belong to Christ Jesus, we have crucified the flesh with its passions and desires. We live by the Spirit, and since we live by the Spirit, let us walk in step with the Spirit."

Paul continued speaking with active encouragement, reminding them of their commitments to God and of the faithfulness of God that would reward their service. He ranged widely over the victories and difficulties of faith, hope and love, speaking for a long time. Encouragement flowed from him, and all those present that evening were strengthened. Their determination to take up their cross every day and follow their Lord Jesus to the kingdom of God increased.

Paul's work continued.

❧

Acts 18:23

Paul's Third Missionary Journey (Acts 18:23-21:17 in Jerusalem)

(First: Acts 13:1-3; Second: Acts 15:36-41)

23 And having stayed some time [in Antioch], he went forth, passing successively through the Galatian region and Phrygia, strengthening all the disciples.

Ephesus

Acts 19:1-22

Aquila and Priscilla had been busy in Ephesus, teaching a man named Apollos the truth about Jesus, since he only knew of John the Baptist. After he had learned enough about Jesus, Apollos went on to Corinth and supported the believers there.

Meanwhile, Paul came to Ephesus and found twelve more disciples who believed in the baptism of John, much as Apollos had done. These twelve, however, had not met Aquila and Priscilla, so Paul explained to them that John the Baptist had told people to believe in the one coming after him, that is Jesus. The twelve accepted his teaching and were baptised into the name of Jesus, after which Paul laid his hands on them and they received the Holy Spirit, speaking in tongues and prophesying.

Paul then spent three months speaking in the synagogue, persuading people about the kingdom of God. As usual, some began to speak evil about The Way, so Paul withdrew with those who would listen and they discussed their faith every day for two years in the school of a man called Tyrannus. Everyone in the area heard the message about Jesus.

Yet preaching wasn't all Paul did. God also did extraordinary miracles through him. Not only could he cure the sick people he met, but people could even take handkerchiefs or aprons he had touched to sick people and they would recover.

Some Jewish charlatans wanted to have some of the glory of doing miracles. They took to healing people by pronouncing the "name of Jesus whom Paul preaches". On one occasion, they got what they deserved, when a man admitted to knowing Jesus and Paul, but having no recognition of the fakes. He jumped on them and beat them severely.

Sometimes the results of preaching were as spectacular as they were unexpected. After all of Paul's many miracles and the well-deserved beating of the charlatans, many who practised magic were convinced that Paul was right. They collected their valuable books of magic and started a bonfire in the sight of everyone. Books of magic might sell for a high price, but these men recognised that they had no real value at all.

❧

Sketch 33 – Next steps

"Ephesus has proved a good base for preaching," said Paul to Timothy, contentedly one afternoon.

"I agree. It has kept us really busy."

"I still find it amazing how many people Jesus can call out from among pagans."

"And how many of them are already prepared for our preaching before Jesus leads us to them."

"You're right. It *is* all planned beforehand, isn't it? We aren't the ones who initiate it all or get things organised for preaching. Yet from Apollos meeting Aquila and Priscilla to my meeting of those dozen followers of John the Baptist, Jesus has prepared the ground here for quick conversions that have formed fertile ground for the entire town."

"And with Apollos, he was able to preach here and then go on to Corinth so that there was no need for you to hurry back there," pointed out Timothy.

"Jesus really does work as a powerful general, planning ahead and sending his troops to and fro wherever they are needed most across the empire."

"He sent me here from Corinth, too," said Erastus, another believer who had been listening quietly.

"And we were glad to hear your news from Corinth and enjoyed your help in our preaching as well," said Paul. "But now, I believe that I've spent enough time here."

"Where will you go instead?" asked Timothy.

"Ultimately, I want to go to Rome," said Paul. "The gospel of Jesus must be presented in Rome – the centre of the empire."

"So do you want to go there now?" asked Erastus.

Paul wrinkled his forehead and breathed in as he shook his head slowly. "I don't think so. Right now, I..." He stopped and sighed. I've been praying about it for a few days, going through various options in my mind, but this morning I started to feel some more guidance in the spirit.

Although it seems strange, given that I want to go to Rome, I feel that I need to go to Jerusalem first."

"Now?"

Paul gave an ironic smile. "That leads me to the other unexpected part of this plan of going to Jerusalem. How would you two like to go to Macedonia now? I'll follow you in a while so that I can visit places like Philippi, Amphipolis, Apollonia, Thessalonica and Berea with you before going down to Achaia and visiting Corinth."

"So you'll be going to Jerusalem by heading in the opposite direction?" laughed Timothy.

"Pretty much!" smiled Paul.

"If we didn't have experience with Jesus controlling his forces, it wouldn't make much sense, would it?" asked Erastus.

"No, but he always guides us in ways that convert more people and make the most of unexpected opportunities."

"So I wonder why you are staying here while we get sent to Macedonia?" pondered Timothy.

"Don't try to guess too much detail," said Paul. "Just take the opportunities you're given and fill your time with running the race Jesus wants you to run."

"Have you ever been distracted into concentrating too much on what was about to happen, Paul?"

"In Corinth, it was fear that distracted me. In other places it has been ill-health at times, where I've been forced to slow down and take each day as it comes and even let Jesus deliver the audience to me in my bedroom. What I've learned most, though, is what I said: don't worry about the future, don't try to predict the future or plan for the opportunities I expect – just take the ones I'm actually given."

"Fair enough," nodded Timothy.

"I suppose that we should get ready to travel to Macedonia then," said Erastus.

"We'll go to Troas first," said Timothy, "and then cross over by ship to Neapolis and visit Philippi. I wonder if Luke is still there?"

"I'm already starting to look forward to finding out," said Erastus. "And I wonder how Lydia and her family are going?"

"The jailer and his family too," added Timothy. "I've heard that he has converted quite a few prisoners by telling them about Paul and Silas and that earthquake."

"Yes. I'm not so sure about that," murmured Erastus. "Inviting criminals into our congregations seems a bit risky."

"I know what you mean, Erastus," said Paul, "and I've no doubt you've seen lots of unrepentant criminals and troublemakers as treasurer in Corinth, but don't forget that these aren't criminals any more. They've been cleansed, washed in the blood of Jesus and made pure. We don't need to worry about them as long as they keep their new beliefs."

"I suppose so, but..."

"You'll have to see what you find there," said Paul, "but I'm quite confident you'll like what you see."

"Now if we leave tomorrow," said Timothy, "how long will it be before you follow us? If the Lord wills, we'll take about 2-3 weeks to get to Philippi and I'm sure we'll have a lot to keep us busy."

"I'll follow you when it seems to be the right time. As I said, I can't predict the future, or worry too much about it."

Acts 19:23-20:1

Money and religion are a dangerous mix.

While Paul was in Ephesus, the makers of silver shrines of Artemis became upset because they felt their income was declining. Paul, they said, was to blame, and they got up a mob to prove it.

The objection was couched in religious terms, with great respect being shown to Artemis, but in truth, it was their livelihood that was important to them.

Two hours is a very long time for a massive crowd to keep shouting, "Great is Artemis of the Ephesians", and it was a terrifying time.

Eventually the city clerk was able to get the right mix of threats and cajoling to calm the situation and everything went back to normal.

Once again, it was time for Paul to move on.

∞

Acts 18:24-20:1

24 Now a certain Jew named Apollos, a native of Alexandria, came to Ephesus, being an eloquent man, mighty in the Scriptures. **25** He was instructed in the way of the Lord. And being fervent in spirit, he was speaking and was teaching earnestly the things concerning Jesus, knowing only the baptism of John. **26** And he began to speak boldly in the synagogue. But Priscilla and Aquila having heard him, took him to them and expounded the way of God to him more accurately.

27 And he resolving to pass through into Achaia,[a] the brothers, having encouraged him, wrote to the disciples to welcome him, who having arrived, helped greatly those having believed through grace. **28** For he was powerfully refuting the Jews publicly, showing by the Scriptures Jesus to be the Christ.

Acts 19

The Holy Spirit Received at Ephesus
(Joel 2:28-32; John 14:15-26; John 16:5-16; Acts 2:1-13; Acts 10:44-48)

1 Now it came to pass, while Apollos was in Corinth, Paul having passed through the upper parts[b] to come to Ephesus, and having found certain disciples, **2** he also said to them, "Did you receive the Holy Spirit, having believed?"

And they said to him, "But not even did we hear that there is a Holy Spirit."

3 And he said, "Into what then were you baptized?"

And they said, "Into the baptism of John."

4 Then Paul said, "John baptized a baptism of repentance, telling the people that they should believe in the One coming after him, that is, in Jesus."

5 And having heard, they were baptized into the name of the Lord Jesus. **6** And of Paul having laid the hands on them, the Holy Spirit came upon them, and they were speaking in tongues and prophesying. **7** And there were in all about twelve men.

Paul Ministers in Ephesus
(Revelation 2:1-7)

8 And having entered into the synagogue, he was speaking boldly for three months, reasoning and persuading them concerning the kingdom of God. **9** But when some were hardened and were disbelieving, speaking evil of the Way before the multitude, having departed from them, he took the disciples

---

a   Acts 18:27 – Particularly Corinth (see Acts 19:1)
b   BLB: Acts 19:1 – Or interior

separately, reasoning every day in the lecture hall of Tyrannus. [10] And this continued for two years, so that all those inhabiting Asia heard the word of the Lord, both Jews and Greeks.

[11] And God was performing extraordinary miracles by the hands of Paul, [12] so that even handkerchiefs or aprons from his skin were brought to the ailing, and the diseases departed from them, and the evil spirits left.

The Sons of Sceva

[13] Now some of the itinerant Jews, exorcists, also attempted to invoke the name of the Lord Jesus over those having evil spirits, saying, "I adjure you by Jesus, whom Paul proclaims." [14] And seven sons of Sceva, a Jewish high priest, were doing this. [15] But the evil spirit answering, said to them, "Jesus I know, and Paul I am acquainted with; but you, who are you?" [16] And the man in whom was the evil spirit, having leapt on them, having overpowered them all, prevailed against them so that they fled out of that house naked and wounded.

[17] Now this became known to all those inhabiting Ephesus, both Jews and Greeks. And fear fell upon them all, and the name of the Lord Jesus was being magnified. [18] And many of those having believed were coming, confessing and declaring their deeds, [19] and many of those having practiced the magic arts, having brought the books, burned them before all. And they counted up the prices of them and found it five myriads of silverlings.[c] [20] Thus the word of the Lord continued to increase and prevail with might.

The Riot in Ephesus

[21] Now after these things were fulfilled, Paul purposed in the Spirit to go to Jerusalem, having passed through Macedonia and Achaia, having said, "After my having been there, it behooves me to see Rome also." [22] And having sent two of those ministering to him, Timothy and Erastus, into Macedonia, he remained for a time in Asia.

[23] Now at the same time no small disturbance arose concerning the Way. [24] For a certain silversmith named Demetrius, making silver shrines of Artemis, was bringing no little business to the craftsmen, [25] whom having brought together along with the workmen in such things, he said, "Men, you know that from this business is our wealth. [26] And you see and hear that not only in Ephesus, but almost all of Asia, this Paul, having persuaded them, has turned away a great many people, saying that they are not gods which have been made by hands. [27] Now not only is this business to us endangered to come into disrepute, but also for the temple of the great goddess Artemis to be reckoned for nothing, and also her majesty to be deposed, whom all Asia and the world worship."

---

c   BLB: Acts 19:19 – Or fifty thousand drachmas. A drachma was a silver coin worth about one day's wages.

28 And having heard, and having become full of rage, they were crying out saying, "Great is Artemis of the Ephesians."[a] **29** And the whole city was filled with confusion, and with one accord they rushed to the theatre, having dragged off Gaius and Aristarchus, Macedonians, fellow travelers of Paul.

30 But of Paul intending to go in to the people, the disciples would not allow him. **31** And also some of the Asiarchs[b] being friends to him, having sent to him, were urging him not to venture into the theatre.

32 So some indeed were crying out one thing; others another. For the assembly was confused, and most did not know for what cause they were assembled. **33** Now out of the crowd they put forward Alexander, the Jews having thrust him forward. And Alexander, having motioned with the hand, was wanting to make a defense to the people. **34** But having recognized that he is a Jew, there was one cry from all, ongoing about two hours, crying out, "Great is Artemis of the Ephesians."

35 Then having calmed the crowd, the town clerk says, "Men, Ephesians, what man is there indeed who does not know the city of the Ephesians as being temple-keeper of the great Artemis, and of that fallen from the sky? **36** Therefore these things being undeniable, it is necessary for you to be calm and to do nothing rash. **37** For you brought these men, neither temple plunderers nor blaspheming our goddess.

38 So if indeed Demetrius and the craftsmen with him have a matter against anyone, courts are conducted, and there are proconsuls; let them accuse one another. **39** But if you inquire anything beyond this, it will be solved in the lawful assembly. **40** And indeed, we are in danger of being accused of insurrection in regard to this day, there existing not one cause concerning which we will be able to give a reason for this commotion."

41 And having said these things, he dismissed the assembly.

Acts 20

Paul in Macedonia and Greece

1 Now after the uproar had ceased, Paul, having summoned the disciples and having encouraged them and having said farewell, departed to go to Macedonia.[c]

---

a   Acts 19:28 – A localised form of the Greek goddess Artemis (equivalent to the Roman goddess Diana)

b   Acts 19:31 – High ranking officials in the province of Asia

c   Acts 20:1 – Overall, Paul had spent three years in Ephesus (Acts 20:31)

Macedonia and Greece

Acts 20:1-6

Leaving Ephesus, Paul went on to Macedonia, going though all the districts he had visited before and encouraging any believers he met.

Continuing on to Greece, he spent three months there, but a plot against him forced him to abandon his plan to sail from there to Syria, and instead he walked back through Macedonia. Luke was with him, but his other travelling companions had already travelled to Troas to wait for him there.

After the Feast of Unleavened Bread, Paul and Luke left Philippi for Troas, making a much slower trip than the speedy crossing made after Paul had seen the vision of a man from Macedonia, begging for help.

Acts 20:1b-6a

Acts 20

Paul in Macedonia and Greece

...Paul ...departed to go to Macedonia. **2** And having passed through those districts and having exhorted them with much talk, he came to Greece. **3** And having continued three months, a plot having been made against him by the Jews, he being about to sail into Syria, a purpose arose to return through Macedonia.

4 And he was accompanied by Sopater son of Pyrrhus from Berea, and Aristarchus, and Secundus of the Thessalonians, and Gaius of Derbe, and Timothy, and the Asians Tychicus and Trophimus. **5** But these, having gone ahead, waited for us[d] in Troas. **6** And we sailed away from Philippi after the days of the Unleavened Bread, and within five days we came to them at Troas...[e]

---

d   Acts 20:5 – The use of "us" and "we" indicates that the writer, believed to be Luke, was with Paul (until Acts 20:15). See also Acts 16:10-17; 21:1-18; 27:1-28:16.

e   Acts 20:6 – 5 days' travel compared with 2 in the opposite direction in Acts 16:11

Troas

Arriving at Troas, Paul caught up with his travelling companions: Sopater, and the son of Pyrrhus from Berea; Aristarchus and Secundus the Thessalonians; Gaius of Derbe, and Timothy; as well as Tychicus and Trophimus from Asia. Paul often had several people travelling with him and frequently sent them to do things he could not spare the time to attend to himself.

After seven days in Troas, it was the first day of the week and Paul was to leave the following morning. Everyone was eager to hear as much as they could from him, so whenever he started to slow down, they encouraged him to continue. It was stuffy in the upper room and a young man named Eutychus fell asleep. It must have been an embarrassing memory for the rest of his life, but for a while it was tragic. He fell out of the window, and by the time anyone could get down to him, he was dead. It was a great blessing that Paul was there, for he bent over the lad and embraced him, then reassured the crowd that he was not dead. Not any longer. The believers were so happy that they asked Paul to continue and he did, talking until daybreak.

No-one else fell out of a window!

Sketch 34 – Walking

Paul needed to be alone, and now at last he could be.

He would have two days by himself on the road to Assos before rejoining his travelling companions and proceeding to Jerusalem.

Two days of meditation and thought.

Troas was well behind him now and Paul was enjoying a brisk walk in the spring morning – although he had to admit that he was tired after a night without sleep!

Yet the night had been profoundly uplifting, revealing again Jesus' amazing work among the believers to spread the faith like wildfire across the empire.

Paul thought over his years of missionary travel. What an amazing encourager Barnabas was! And how much that subtle gift had changed Paul's life. It was Barnabas who had travelled to Tarsus to encourage him to travel south again and join the believers in Antioch. Wonderful Barnabas! Then there was the sudden and radical change in his life when Barnabas and he had been sent by the Holy Spirit to preach.

That first journey with Barnabas had taken them around Cyprus, through Pamphylia and up into Galatia. How were the believers in those places progressing now?

Paul mentally revisited the towns where they had preached on that first journey. From time to time they had met believers – people who had been baptised in the name of Jesus many years before on the Day of Pentecost. Peter and the other eleven had presented the truth about Jesus with great power to Jews from all over the empire. That one day of preaching had been astonishingly successful in making the name of Jesus known by one person here, another there, all over the empire. Most of the audience were not gifted preachers able to return home and fill their home towns and provinces with the gospel of Jesus, but their altered lives meant that their neighbours knew the name of Jesus. Not only so, but they had improved their local society along the way.

The congregations Barnabas and he had helped form in Pisidian Antioch, Iconium, Lystra and Derbe – towns in the southern areas of Galatia – were still thriving communities of believers and he received messages and reports from them often. Nevertheless, he couldn't help worrying about them! They weren't new believers any more, but sometimes he still felt that they needed guides to hold their hands. Thankfully, they hadn't been losing their way recently as they had done early on, when he had been forced to write them a stern letter reminding them to hold fast to truth. Paul still remembered the shock he had felt at receiving reports that some visiting preachers had taught them false doctrines, misleading many believers in Galatia.

Why were false doctrines so attractive to so many? That letter had been written and dispatched in haste, reminding them that the good news of Jesus didn't change just because some new preacher had come along! Not only so, but truth doesn't change. Ever. However well a preacher may speak, however smoothly he may present himself, however beautiful his voice may be, it is his message that matters. And if that message contradicted the truth Barnabas and Paul had presented to them, the believers should reject it.

Truth is truth; anything else is lies. Truth saves; everything else kills. Paul had reminded them that Gentiles did not have to become Jews – after all, had not God himself called Abram 'Abraham', the father of many nations? And it was not the law of Moses that had saved Abraham – no, Abraham came before the law of Moses and was saved by his faith.

And now, Jesus had saved both Jews and Gentiles from their sins through his own sacrifice, a much better sacrifice than that of animals under the law.

Of course, it wasn't that everyone in the congregations had been led astray, but it was enough to be worrying. Thankfully, his letter had been enough to damp down the fires of heresy and encourage the believers to revel in the joy of truth once more.

Nevertheless, one letter couldn't solve all the problems of the congregations, and Paul kept wishing that he had more time to visit them all again.

But it just wasn't possible.

There were only so many days in a year, and short visits could do little to help.

It was hard enough to know how best to preach in new areas, but when it came to pastoral care and offering support and guidance to young congregations, that was even harder.

Paul had met many thousands of people while preaching. Many of these had progressed from an initial interest in the gospel to being convinced and converted. Paul had spent countless hours with many of them discussing the Way, and his mind was full of their faces as he walked along the road. Sometimes, individual names escaped him, but most were recovered with a few minutes' thought. He added each of them to his prayers for God's guidance and care and wished he could meet them all again. Fellowship, he thought, was wonderful, and the shared hope of resurrection tied them all together in love.

How astonished he had been when he heard that some believers in Corinth had abandoned their belief in the resurrection. He smiled a wry smile. Another letter he'd had to write, addressing that vital subject and criticising the ignorance of scripture that had allowed them to make such a mistake! The same ignorance had also been shown in various other subjects which he had been forced to include in the letter. How could he convince believers everywhere to spend more time learning scripture and becoming familiar with God's principles?

Paul shook his head as he walked, thinking of the other serious criticisms he had been compelled to include in that letter and praying for those who were meant to be leaders but lacked the knowledge to lead well. Still, following 'the Way' did require a massive change of theology from the religious beliefs most had previously held, so perhaps it wasn't too surprising that some took a wrong turn or two! And at least they had been willing to listen and learn. He mused over the believers who had strayed, including their names in his ongoing prayer for them all. How would they fare when he and other preachers could no longer visit them?

After all, the congregation hadn't only had problems with complex matters of doctrine! That horrible case of a man taking his father's wife would not have been acceptable in the ordinary society of godless Corinth, so how could it ever have been thought acceptable among followers of Jesus? It was as if they thought following Jesus Christ absolved them from obeying any laws of the land or meeting societal expectations of morality. Perhaps some thought God's grace and forgiveness allowed them to do anything.

Nevertheless, they had listened to his instruction in that matter also, and after a bit of heartfelt communication back and forth, the situation had been straightened out. He loved the Corinthians for their eager faith, but sometimes guiding the believers was like looking after little children and trying to help them grow up!

Paul continued his prayer for the brothers and sisters in Corinth, listing them each by name and rejoicing in the growth each had shown and was showing. True, there were still some matters to straighten out after his latest visit; perhaps he should write them another letter.

Paul found this sort of time spent alone in contemplation and prayer invaluable – essential, really – and he made the most of it in those two days on the road. When he arrived in Assos he found his companions waiting for him, and they sailed on together.

Acts 20:6b-13

...and within five days we came to them at Troas, where we stayed seven days.

Eutychus Revived at Troas
(John 11:38-44)

[7] And on the first day of the week, of us having come together to break bread, Paul, about to depart on the next day, talked to them and continued the talk until midnight.

⁸ Now there were many lamps in the upper room where we were assembled. ⁹ And a certain young man named Eutychus was sitting by the window, over-powered by deep sleep as Paul talked on longer. Having been overpowered by sleep, he fell down from the third story and was picked up dead. ¹⁰ But Paul having descended, fell upon him, and having embraced him, he said, "Do not be alarmed, for his life is in him!"

¹¹ And having gone up, and having broken the bread, and having eaten, and having talked at length until daybreak, so he departed. ¹² Then they brought the boy alive, and were not just a little comforted.

From Troas to Miletus

¹³ But we, having gone ahead to the ship, sailed to Assos, being about to take in Paul there. For having arranged thus, he was readying himself to go on foot.

Miletus and the Elders of Ephesus

Acts 20:14-38

From Troas, Paul walked to Assos, while the rest of his companions went by ship. From there, they all went to Mitylene and then Miletus.

Paul did not want to stop at Ephesus because it would slow him down and he was eager to get to Jerusalem by Passover if possible.

Instead, he sent for the elders of Ephesus to come to him at Miletus, where he gave them a message of sober warning, reinforcing his attitude to them over the three years he had spent with them and reminding them that they must now stand on their own. None of them, he warned, would see his face again. He also warned them about false believers, people from their own community who would behave like savage wolves among a flock of defenceless sheep. A sobering message indeed.

There was plenty of weeping and embracing, and finally they accompanied Paul to the ship. He sailed away and they returned to Ephesus.

Sketch 35 – Farewell
(Written by Luke)

Paul's farewell to the elders of Ephesus was deeply touching – a scene none of us will soon forget.

I've spent a lot of time with Paul now and I really admire him, both for his courage and his abilities. I first met him in Troas when he and his companions were trying to figure out where they should go next to preach.

He was nothing like some leaders I've met – those who are determined to pursue their own path and drag others along willy-nilly. From the first moment I met Paul, Silas and Timothy, it was clear that they were all keen to find out what *God* wanted them to do. They had opinions of their own and had already tried a few different ideas, but all had proved to be false starts – and they accepted that.

I found their dedication to finding out God's will so inspiring that I included it in my diary, and it encourages me every time I read it.

Since then, I've seen time and again that this attitude is no pretence. Paul met Jesus on the way to Damascus and has committed the rest of his life, however long that may be, to doing what God and his son want him to do.

He shows very little sign of fear, despite the fact that the enemies of truth – both political and religious – are willing to use any amount of violence against him to achieve their ends. He really is in constant danger.

And that concerns all of us who know him, because we love him deeply. We've listened to his preaching and encouragement and we all want to hear more. If his enemies are ever successful in their attempts to kill him, I'm not sure what we'll do without him. He's like an immoveable rock for us, with his incisive mind and deep scriptural background.

When questions arise, he has the answers. When false prophets turn up, he confronts them and defeats them with God's word.

He makes The Way seem an ordinary part of everyday life – almost inevitable, in fact. He follows it every hour and makes it feel completely natural. As I said before, it's not a performance, it's the way of life that is Paul.

Most believers find that inspiring. I do myself.

Paul spent quite a few hours with the elders from Ephesus, reminding them that leaders are there to look after the flock, not their own egos. Their job is to serve God and their congregation just as Paul has done, despite the plots of unbelievers and false brothers.

The thing that really got their attention was when he told them that they wouldn't see him again. In fact, there wasn't a dry eye among them as they subsequently said their thanks and goodbyes to him and walked with him to the ship.

I've heard some people criticise Paul as being hard and unemotional – but only ever people who don't know him. Those who do know him are glad they do.

It was very clear that those elders felt the same concern as I feel: if Paul is taken away from us, how will we continue with The Way? Particularly when he warned us that there will be people from inside our own congregations who will act like wolves. His words to the elders gave me a sudden mind-picture of new believers, young lambs just learning about the truth, being attacked by callous, uncaring teachers interested only in their own importance. And that is exactly the opposite of how Paul has worked.

I think we need more written records of his work to share around, but perhaps it would be even better if Paul could write down his Jesus-given thoughts on important subjects. They could be distributed among the congregations just like that letter from the elders and apostles in Jerusalem was passed around to all the Gentile congregations. It was an excellent foundation for us Gentiles, showing us what parts of Judaism we should adopt and what parts of idolatry we need to avoid. Simple, but compelling. Perhaps Paul could write a lot more letters like that, or even books like the prophets of old.

We all expect Jesus to return soon, but over time we're losing many witnesses to the work of Jesus and the apostles due to old age or persecution. I don't think we stand to lose anything if Jesus returns to earth and finds us busily writing down his words and his tremendous work.

Perhaps that's something I can help with.

Acts 20:14-38

14 Now when [Paul] met with us at Assos, having taken him in, we came to Mitylene. **15** And having sailed away from there, on the following day we arrived opposite Chios, and the next day we arrived at Samos,[a] and the following day we came to Miletus.

16 For Paul had decided to sail by Ephesus, so that it might not come upon him to spend time in Asia; for he was hastened, if it was possible for him, to be in Jerusalem on the day of Pentecost.

Paul's Farewell to the Ephesians

17 And from Miletus, having sent to Ephesus, he called for the elders of the church.

18 And when they had come to him, he said to them, "You know from the first day on which I arrived in Asia, how I was with you the whole time, **19** serving the Lord with all humility and tears, and trials having befallen me in the plots of the Jews; **20** how I did not shrink back from declaring to you anything being profitable, and teaching you publicly and from house to house, **21** earnestly testifying both to the Jewish and to Greeks repentance

---

a   BLB: Acts 20:15 – BYZ and TR include after remaining at Trogyllium

in God and faith in our Lord Jesus.[a]

22 And now behold, bound in the Spirit I go to Jerusalem, not knowing what will happen to me in it, **23** except that the Holy Spirit fully testifies to me in every city, saying that chains and tribulations await me. **24** But I make my life neither dear nor any account to myself, so as to finish my course and the ministry that I received from the Lord Jesus: to testify fully the gospel of the grace of God.

25 And now, behold, I know that all of you among whom I have gone about proclaiming the kingdom will see my face no more. **26** Therefore I testify to you in this day that I am innocent of the blood of all. **27** For I did not shrink back from proclaiming to you the whole counsel of God.

28 Take heed to yourselves and to all the flock, among which the Holy Spirit has set you overseers, to shepherd the church of God,[b] which He purchased with the own blood.[c] **29** I know that after my departure, grievous wolves will come in among you, not sparing the flock, **30** and out from your own selves, men will rise up, speaking perverse things to draw away disciples after them. **31** Therefore stay awake, remembering that three years night and day I never ceased admonishing each one with tears.

32 And now I commit you to God and to the word of His grace, being able to build you up and to give you an inheritance among all those having been sanctified.

33 I coveted nobody's silver or gold or clothing. **34** You yourselves know that these hands ministered to my needs and to those being with me. **35** In everything I showed you that by thus straining, it behooves us to aid those being weak, and also to remember the words of the Lord Jesus, how He Himself said, 'It is more Blessed to give than to receive.'"

36 And having said these things, having bowed his knee, he prayed with them all. **37** Then there was much weeping among all, and having fallen upon the neck of Paul, they were kissing him, **38** sorrowing especially over the word that he had spoken, that they are about to see his face no more. Then they accompanied him to the ship.

---

a   BLB: Acts 20:21 – TR the Lord Jesus Christ
b   BLB: Acts 20:28 – BYZ and Tischendorf of the Lord
c   BLB: Acts 20:28 – Or with the blood of his own Son.

On to Jerusalem

Acts 21:1-16

Acts 21

Paul's Journey to Jerusalem

1 And it happened that after having drawn away from them, having run directly in our[d] sailing, we came to Cos, and the next day to Rhodes, and from there to Patara. **2** And having found a boat passing over into Phoenicia, having gone on board, we set sail. **3** And having sighted Cyprus and having left it on the left, we kept sailing to Syria and landed at Tyre, for the ship was unloading the cargo there.

4 And we remained there seven days, having sought out the disciples, who kept telling Paul through the Spirit not to go up to Jerusalem. **5** And it happened that when we had completed the days, having set out, we journeyed, all accompanying us with wives and children as far as outside the city. And having bowed the knees on the shore, having prayed, **6** having said farewell to one another, we then went up into the boat, and they returned to the own.

7 And having completed the voyage from Tyre, we came down to Ptolemais, and having greeted the brothers, we stayed one day with them.

Paul Visits Philip the Evangelist

8 And having gone forth on the next day, we came to Caesarea, and having entered into the house of Philip the evangelist, being of the seven,[e] we stayed with him. **9** And with this man there were four daughters, virgins prophesying.

10 And remaining many days, a certain prophet named Agabus came down from Judea. **11** And having come to us and having taken Paul's belt, having bound his feet and hands, he said, "Thus the Holy Spirit says, 'In this way the Jews in Jerusalem will bind the man whose belt this is, and will deliver him into the hands of the Gentiles.'" **12** And when we had heard these things, both we and those of that place began begging him not to go up to Jerusalem.

13 Then Paul answered, "What are you doing, weeping and breaking my heart? For I have readiness not only to be bound, but also to die at Jeru-

---

d   Acts 21:1 – The use of "our", "we" and "us" indicates that the writer, believed to be Luke, was with Paul (until Acts 21:18). See also Acts 16:10-17; 20:5-15; 27:1-28:16.

e   Acts 21:8 – See Acts 6:3-6

salem for the name of the Lord Jesus." **14** And of him not being persuaded, we were silent, having said, "The will of the Lord be done."

15 Now after these days, having packed the baggage, we started on our way up to Jerusalem. **16** And some of the disciples from Caesarea also went with us, bringing a certain Mnason, a Cypriot, an early disciple with whom we would lodge.

CR

Acts 21:1-16

Changing ships at Patara, Paul and his companions landed at Tyre and stayed there seven days with the disciples.

While there, Paul was given a warning that trouble awaited him in Jerusalem. Paul had already told the Ephesian elders that he had no choice about going to Jerusalem – he was bound in the Spirit to do so. Nevertheless, it was concerning.

At the end of the allotted time, Paul left, after all the believers had gathered on the beach and knelt in prayer.

Back on the ship, the company travelled to Ptolemais and the next day to Caesarea, where a prophet named Agabus gave an inspired warning that Paul would be bound and handed over to the Gentiles. Many tried to discourage him from continuing, but Paul was immovable.

Eventually, the believers acknowledged: "The Lord's will be done."

From Caesarea to Jerusalem, and the third missionary journey was complete. What awaited Paul in Jerusalem?

CR

Sketch 36 – Philip and his Daughters

"Brother Paul has left, then, daughters," commented Philip the Evangelist, leaning back in his chair and stretching out his legs. "He's on his way to Jerusalem and we know that trouble awaits him there. I wonder what it will be?" His four daughters sat on stools around a table at the other end of the small room.

"Agabus said he would be bound by the Jews and handed over to the Gentiles," observed Anna, the oldest.

"Is that meant to be literal?" asked Philip. "You all know how God's prophecies work."

"It could be literal. It could be exactly literal," said Zoe, the youngest, leaning forward with a worried expression on her face. Her eyes appeared to focus far away, possibly immersed in a scene in far-off Jerusalem.

"Poor Paul," breathed Chloe. "Imagine being tied up with your own belt and delivered to the Romans as a prisoner." Chloe was second oldest, with the dark, mobile, expressive eyes of the mother she could hardly remember, the mother who had died when she was just four years old. The look in her eyes at that moment was one of horror.

"That's about what happened to Jesus, isn't it?" responded Philip. "The High Priest and his cronies condemned him and used the Sanhedrin as a rubber stamp, then handed him over to Pilate, who they manipulated into doing what they wanted."

"Do you think Paul will die as Jesus did?" asked Miriam in alarm. Miriam was third of the girls, the quietest of them all.

There was silence for a while as the family considered her suggestion.

"Perhaps," said Philip finally. "You know Jesus told him in Damascus that he would have to suffer persecution in many places."

"Hasn't he already suffered enough?" asked Anna, who had always had a soft spot in her heart for the energetic, courageous, outspoken preacher.

"No," said Philip.

"Why do you say that, father?"

"Because Agabus said he had some more suffering coming in Jerusalem, didn't he?"

"I suppose so, but it seems so... unfair...? No, that can't be the right word – Jesus wouldn't be unfair. So... concentrated. Perhaps that is a better word. Paul seems to suffer more than any other believer."

"That's true," said Chloe. Zoe nodded. Miriam looked thoughtful.

Philip smiled at them. "You're all kind and gentle young women, and you're right too. Paul does suffer a lot. But don't forget that God made Paul as he needed him. I'm not suggesting that all of this suffering doesn't hurt Paul at all, or that he finds it easy to endure, but I know that he can endure it with the character God has given him and the help God provides. God has led him slowly through many lessons of suffering that he had to learn. He does the same with all of us. God has worked as a potter, first making Paul what he had to be and then shaping him as necessary to accomplish the work he had to do. Could any of you do the work Paul does?"

"No!" chorused the girls.

It wasn't an empty answer, nor one given to satisfy their father's expectations. Paul's unceasing determination and astonishing achievements were already legendary, and anyone who met him quickly recognised that he was a very unusual person. Paul had a drive and perseverance that stood out in any crowd. From when people first met him, his personality – and, yes, that amazing determination – was immediately visible.

Others might get burnt out, but Paul kept finding new, extraordinary ways to work harder. When others were worn down, Paul kept persevering. When others were tempted by the pleasures of the world, Paul kept his focus on Jesus' coming kingdom, dismissing the world's much-vaunted benefits as nothing but short-lived rubbish – a poison distilled by a self-deluded dystopia and presented to the masses as ambrosia.

Among the believers, Paul was universally famous but not always popular, often becoming unpopular for the very characteristics that made him famous. Many who didn't know him considered him superhuman and spoke of him in an awed wonder that could border on worship. Often, they dismissed his attainments as entirely God-driven, almost as if he was an automaton with no freedom to choose his way of life.

Recently, however, reports of his time of utter despair and fear in Corinth had begun circulating, a time when he had required Jesus' direct encouragement to enable him to keep going under that crushing, overwhelming workload.[a] Paul the unstoppable had been proven human after all, and the sympathy he received had grown astronomically as a result.

"We must always include him in our prayers," said Philip, "and we might as well start now, as a family. Let us pray together."

He began to pray, asking that Paul would be given the strength he needed to endure the difficulties he was facing in Jerusalem. Philip also recalled in his prayer many examples of God's care in the past, particularly those where Paul had survived attempts to kill him or endured despite brutal mistreatment from his enemies. The fervent prayer of Philip and his family revealed their love for Paul and for the saviour he proclaimed so bravely. It also acknowledged our human need for the love, care and help of God who has given us life and everything.

When Philip finished, the family looked at each other and Chloe and Zoe smiled.

"I feel much better now, father," said Zoe. "Handing over my worries to God always feels better."

---

a   1 Corinthians 2:3; Acts 18:9-11

"Yes, but I'd still like to know what will happen to brother Paul," said Chloe. "I'm content that God will care for him as he has planned, but I'm still curious!"

"Inquisitive Chloe," smiled Anna. "But I have to admit that I feel the same. I have pictures in my mind of Paul in the temple being attacked by a mob," she finished, soberly.

"I imagine soldiers coming into the temple," said Miriam. "Paul could be caught between a Jewish mob and the Roman soldiers. There could be a major reaction across Judea – even a rebellion – if soldiers entered the temple."

"Hush, hush," said Philip as his daughters became increasingly upset again by the turmoil of their thoughts. "We agreed that God is in control, didn't we? As to what happens and how, we'll just have to wait and see, however hard that is to do."

PART NINE
Jerusalem and Caesarea

Attacked in Jerusalem

Acts 21:17-22:29

Paul's Arrival at Jerusalem

17 Now of our having arrived at Jerusalem, the brothers received us gladly. **18** And on the following day, Paul went in with us unto James, and all the elders arrived. **19** And having greeted them, he began to relate, one by each, the things God had done among the Gentiles through his ministry.

20 And those having heard began glorifying God, and they said to him, "You see, brother, how many myriads there are among the Jews having believed, and are all zealous ones for the Law. **21** Now they have been informed about you, that you teach all Jews among the Gentiles apostasy from Moses, telling them not to circumcise the children nor to walk in the customs. **22** What then is it? Certainly they will hear that you have come.

23 Therefore do this that we say to you. With us there are four men, having a vow on themselves. **24** Having taken these men, be purified with them and bear expense for them, so that they will shave the head, and all will know that of which they have been informed about you is nothing, but you yourself also walk orderly, keeping the Law.

25 Now concerning those of the Gentiles having believed, we wrote, having adjudged them to keep from both the things offered to idols, and blood, and what is strangled, and sexual immorality."

26 Then Paul, having taken the men on the following day, having been purified with them, entered into the temple, declaring the fulfillment of the days of the purification until the sacrifice was offered for each one of them.

Paul Seized in the Temple

27 Now when the seven days were about to be completed, the Jews from Asia, having seen him in the temple, began stirring up the whole crowd and laid the hands upon him, **28** crying out, "Men, Israelites, help! This is the man teaching all those everywhere against the people and the Law and this place. And besides, he has also brought Greeks into the temple and defiled this holy place." **29** For it was they having previously seen Trophimus the Ephesian in the city with him, whom they were supposing that Paul had brought into the temple.

30 And the whole city was provoked, and there was a rushing together of the people. And having laid hold of Paul, they dragged him outside the temple, and immediately the doors were shut. **31** And of them seeking to kill him, a report came to the commander of the cohort that all Jerusalem was in an uproar, **32** who at once, having taken with him soldiers and centurions, ran down upon them. And having seen the commander and the soldiers, they stopped beating Paul.

33 Then having drawn near, the commander laid hold of him and commanded him to be bound with two chains, and began inquiring who he might be and what it is he has been doing.

34 They were crying out in the crowd one thing, but others another. And he being unable to know the facts on account of the uproar, ordered him to be brought into the barracks. **35** Now when he came to the stairs, it happened that he was carried by the soldiers because of the violence of the crowd. **36** For the multitude of the people were following, crying out, "Away with him!"

Paul Speaks to the People

37 And being about to be brought into the barracks, Paul says to the commander, "Is it permitted to me to say something to you?"

Then he was saying, "Do you know Greek? **38** Are you not, then, the Egyptian, the one before these days having led a revolt and having led out into the wilderness the four thousand men of the 'Assassins?'"

39 But Paul said, "I am indeed a Jew, a man of Tarsus of Cilicia, a citizen of no insignificant city. Now I implore you, allow me to speak to the people." **40** And he having allowed him, Paul, having stood on the stairs, made a sign with the hand to the people. And great silence having taken place, he spoke to them in the Hebrew language,[a] saying:

Acts 22

Paul's Defense to the Crowd
(Acts 9:1-9; Acts 26:1-23)

1 "Men, brothers, and fathers, hear now my defense to you." **2** And having heard that he was addressing them in the Hebrew language,[b] they became even more quiet.

And he says, **3** "I am a Jew, a man born in Tarsus of Cilicia and brought up in this city at the feet of Gamaliel, having been instructed according to the exactness of the Law of our Fathers, being a zealous one of God, even as you all are this day, **4** who persecuted this Way as far as death, binding and betraying to prisons both men and women, **5** as also the high priest and the whole elderhood bears witness to me, from whom also having received

---

a   BLB: Acts 21:40 – Or Aramaic
b   BLB: Acts 22:2 – Or Aramaic

letters to the brothers, I was on my way to Damascus to bring also those being there, bound to Jerusalem, in order that they might be punished.

[6] But it happened to me, journeying and drawing near to Damascus about noon, that suddenly a great light out of heaven shone around me, [7] and I fell to the ground and heard a voice saying to me, 'Saul, Saul, why do you persecute Me?'

[8] And I answered, 'Who are You, Lord?'

And He said to me, 'I am Jesus of Nazareth, whom you are persecuting.' [9] And those being with me indeed beheld the light, but they did not hear the voice of the One speaking to me.

[10] Then I said, 'What shall I do, Lord?'

And the Lord said to me, 'Having risen up, go to Damascus, and there it will be told you concerning all things that it has been appointed you to do.'

[11] And while I could not see from the brightness of that light, I came to Damascus, being led by the hand by those being with me. [12] And a certain Ananias, a devout man according to the Law, borne witness to by all the Jews dwelling there, [13] having come to me and having stood by me, said to me, 'Brother Saul, receive your sight.' And the same hour I looked up at him.

[14] Then he said, 'The God of our fathers has appointed you to know His will, and to see the Righteous One, and to hear the voice out of His mouth. [15] For you will be a witness for Him to all men of what you have seen and heard. [16] And now why do you delay? Having arisen, be baptized, and wash away your sins, calling on His name.'

[17] And it happened to me, having returned to Jerusalem and of my praying in the temple, I fell into a trance [18] and saw Him saying to me, 'Make haste and go away with speed out of Jerusalem, because they will not receive your testimony about Me.'

[19] And I said, 'Lord, they themselves know that in each of those synagogues I was imprisoning and beating those believing on You. [20] And when the blood of Your witness of Stephen was poured out, I myself also was standing by and consenting and watching over the garments of those killing him.'

[21] And He said to me, 'Go, for I will send you far away to the Gentiles.'"

Paul the Roman Citizen

[22] Now they were listening to him until this word. Then they lifted up their voice, saying, "Away with such from the earth. For he is not fit to live!"

[23] And they were crying out and casting off the garments and throwing dust into the air. [24] The commander ordered him to be brought into the barracks, having directed him to be examined by flogging, so that he might know for

what cause they were crying out against him like this.

25 But as he stretched him forward with the straps, Paul said to the centurion standing by, "Is it lawful to you to flog a man who is a Roman and uncondemned?"

26 And the centurion having heard it, having gone to the commander, reported it saying, "What are you going to do? For this man is a Roman."

27 And having come near, the commander said to him, "Tell me, are you a Roman?"

And he was saying, "Yes."

28 Then the commander answered, "I bought this citizenship with a great sum."

But Paul was saying, "But I even was born so."

29 So immediately those being about to examine him departed from him, and the commander also was afraid, having ascertained that he is a Roman, and because he had bound him.

CR

Acts 21:17-22:29

Paul was back in Jerusalem. Since his conversion, he had spent very little time there – in the centre of Jewish life. His busy life had been spent in travelling, preaching, teaching and supporting, but now his freedom was coming to an end.

All the leaders of the believers were glad to see him, and eager to hear the news of his latest work across the empire. But they were also a little concerned that there could be trouble due to reports among believers that Paul had abandoned the Jewish law. A plan was put in place to show the doubters that Paul was just as much a follower of the law as anyone else. Some of the brethren at the time required rites of purification, and the idea was to have Paul join them and pay their expenses. This was to take seven days.

The seven days were almost completed when trouble broke like a storm. Some visiting Jews from Asia recognised Paul as a hated enemy. Having seen Trophimus from Ephesus in the city with Paul, they jumped to the completely baseless conclusion that Paul had taken Trophimus into the temple. They rushed around and shouted and caused all the trouble they could until the whole temple area was in an uproar.

Their main hope was to kill Paul quickly, but the commander of the Roman garrison heard the uproar and hurried into the temple court, snatching Paul from their clutches before they could kill him.

Instead of rejoicing that he was still alive, Paul saw an opportunity to speak to the crowd, so he asked the commander for permission to do so. It was granted and Paul spoke. He told of his conversion, explaining how there could be no doubt that Jesus was alive, and the crowd listened enraptured. Then he repeated Jesus' momentous words, "Go! For I will send you far away to the Gentiles." That did it. Cloaks and dust filled the air along with shouts demanding his immediate death. If the Roman soldiers had not hurriedly carried Paul up the stairs into the barracks, it is unlikely he would have remained in one piece.

The commander wanted to find out the cause of the disturbance, so he had Paul stretched out with ropes in preparation for scourging. Paul enquired politely whether it was lawful to scourge a Roman citizen. It wasn't, of course, and the supervisor quickly spoke to his commander in forceful terms, "Be careful what you do! He is a Roman citizen." After some to-ing and fro-ing Paul was released from the ropes, but kept in custody overnight.

Before the Council

Acts 22:30-23:11

30 And on the next day, desiring to know for certain why he is accused by the Jews, he unbound him and commanded the chief priests and the whole council to assemble. And having brought down Paul, he set him among them.

Acts 23

Paul Before the Sanhedrin

1 And having looked intently at the Council, Paul said, "Men, brothers, I have lived as a citizen in all good conscience to God unto this day." **2** Then the high priest Ananias commanded those standing by him to strike his mouth.

3 Then Paul said to him, "God is about to strike you, whitewashed wall! And you, do you sit judging me according to the Law, and, violating law, command me to be struck?"

4 Now those who stood by said, "Do you insult the high priest of God?"

5 And Paul was saying, "I was not aware, brothers, that he is high priest; for it has been written: 'You shall not speak evil of the ruler of your people.'[a]"

6 Then Paul, having known that the one part consists of Sadducees, but the other of Pharisees, began crying out in the Council, "Men, brothers, I am a Pharisee, the son of a Pharisee; I am judged concerning the hope and resurrection of the dead."

7 And of him saying this, a dissension arose between the Pharisees and Sadducees, and the crowd was divided. **8** For indeed Sadducees say there to be no resurrection, nor angel, nor spirit; but Pharisees confess both.

9 Then a great clamor arose, and some of the scribes of the party of the Pharisees, having risen up, were contending saying, "We find nothing evil in this man. And what if a spirit or an angel has spoken to him?" **10** And great dissension arising, the commander, having feared lest Paul should be torn to pieces by them, commanded the troop, having gone down, to take him by force from their midst and to bring him into the barracks.

---

a   BLB: Acts 23:5 – Exodus 22:28

[11] But the following night the Lord, having stood by him, said, "Take courage, for as you have fully testified about Me at Jerusalem, so also it behooves you to testify in Rome."

❧

Acts 22:30-23:11

Next day, the chief priests and all the council were gathered to hear Paul. After Paul publicly claimed to have a clear conscience before God, the angry high priest ordered him to be struck on the mouth.

Paul weighed up the options and quickly recognised that the easiest way to handle the council was to divide it in two. And the easiest way to divide it was to use the ancient quarrel: resurrection. Pharisees accepted the doctrine of resurrection, while Sadducees did not. Paul's ruse worked dramatically, and the council stopped examining him and fell to arguing among themselves.

As voices rose and the argument grew hotter and hotter, the commander was afraid it would escalate out of control. He sent in his troops and they carried off Paul to the barracks.

On the following night, Jesus stood at Paul's side and told him that he must be a witness to Jesus in Rome.

To Caesarea by Night

Acts 23:12-33

The Plot to Kill Paul
(John 16:1-4)

12 Then when it was day, the Jews having made a conspiracy, put them-selves under an oath, declaring neither to eat nor to drink until they should kill Paul. **13** Now there were more than forty having made this conspiracy, **14** who, having come to the chief priests and the elders, said, "We have bound ourselves with an oath to eat nothing until we should kill Paul. **15** Now therefore you with the Council make a report to the commander, so that he might bring him down to you, as being about to examine more earnestly the things about him. And we are ready to kill him before his drawing near."

16 But the son of Paul's sister, having heard of the ambush, having come near and having entered into the barracks, reported it to Paul. **17** Then Paul, having summoned one of the centurions, was saying, "Take this young man to the commander, for he has something to report to him."

18 So indeed the one having taken him brought him to the commander, and he says, "Paul the prisoner, having called to me, asked me to lead this young man to you, having something to say to you."

19 Then the commander, having taken hold of his hand and having withdrawn in private, began to inquire, "What is it that you have to report to me?"

20 And he said, "The Jews have agreed to ask you that you might bring down Paul into the Council tomorrow, as being about to inquire something more earnestly about him. **21** You therefore should not be persuaded by them. For more than forty of their men lie in wait for him, who have put themselves under an oath neither to eat nor to drink until they have killed him; and now they are ready, awaiting the promise from you."

22 So indeed the commander dismissed the young man, having instructed him, "Tell no one that you have reported these things to me."

Paul Sent to Felix

23 And having summoned certain two of the centurions, he said, "Prepare for the third hour of the night[a] two hundred soldiers and seventy horsemen

---

a   Acts 23:23 – ie. 9pm

and two hundred spearmen, so that they might go as far as Caesarea, **24** and provide mounts, so that having set Paul upon them, they might bring him safely to Felix the governor," **25** having written a letter having this form:

26 "Claudius Lysias,

To the most excellent, governor Felix:

Greetings.

27 This man having been seized by the Jews and being about to be killed by them, having come up with the troop, I rescued him, having learned that he is a Roman. **28** And resolving to know the charge on account of which they were accusing him, I brought him down to their council, **29** whom I found being accused concerning questions of their Law, but having no accusation worthy of death or of chains.

30 And it having been disclosed to me of a plot that would be against the man, I sent him to you at once, also having instructed the accusers to speak these things against him before you."

31 Therefore indeed the soldiers, according to that having been ordered them, having taken Paul, brought him to Antipatris by night. **32** And on the next day, having allowed the horsemen to go with him, they returned to the barracks, **33** who having entered into Caesarea and having delivered the letter to the governor, also presented Paul to him.

Acts 23:12-33

Next day, the Jews came up with a plot. Clever and simple, but doomed to failure, nevertheless.

The scheme was to notify the commander that the council wanted to examine Paul again, but when he was sent to the council, the plotters would murder him on the way.

More than forty men committed themselves to the plot, vowing to refuse all food and drink until they had killed Paul.

Somehow, the son of Paul's sister heard of the plan and passed it on to Paul, who asked a centurion to take the young man to the commander. After hearing of the plot, the commander made some quick plans. Perhaps it was a massive overreaction, but it worked.

Two hundred soldiers, seventy horsemen and two hundred spearmen were dispatched that night to rush Paul to the governor in Caesarea. They also carried a note whose message was almost true, but claimed a little more credit for the commander than was really justified.

> That night, they went to Antipatris, and the following day the horsemen continued with Paul to Caesarea, while the rest returned to Jerusalem.
>
> This story cannot tell whether the plotters kept their vows. If they did, then they surely died before Paul, for he was safely in Caesarea and would not leave Roman custody there for two years.

❧

Sketch 37 – Overkill

Just received orders. We're heading off at 9 o'clock tonight. Not sure who's going or what for, but from the stir in the barracks, it looks like a big deal.

And, joy of joys, they've warned us to make sure we're topped up with food for the night. It can't be all bad if they're giving us more food!

Could it be a training drill just to keep us on our toes? Or are the Jews planning some sort of rebellion?

★ ★ ★ ★

It was a long night.

A long, hard night – even for us Roman soldiers.

After my last diary note, we were told to quieten down. Too much noise, too much excitement: the Jews would be suspicious, they said. I asked if they wanted us to walk around whistling happily and singing unconcerned songs, but the centurion told me to shut up and get ready quietly. So I went to the mess and topped up with rations. Couldn't forget that!

It had been dark for more than an hour when we set off.

And no wonder there had been a big stir – we took half the troops in Jerusalem with us! Would you believe it? Two hundred of us soldiers armed with swords, seventy horsemen following us, and two hundred spearmen bringing up the rear.

Despite the heat of the summer night, we were told to hurry – and be on the alert for any groups of Jews that might look suspicious. Personally, I've always reckoned that they all look suspicious!

Anyway, we poured out of the gates of the fortress and marched at a fast clip towards the Fish Gate. I was in the vanguard, carrying torches to clear the way through the darkened streets. We were all a bit on edge, and some shouted out in Aramaic to any we met to Make way for Caesar's army! They all know what happens if they don't, so they scuttled away into side streets and we hurried on.

I was glad when we reached the gate without any drama. The Jews know their city streets better than we do, and when ten of them disappear down a side street, you can never be sure a hundred won't come out of the next side street! I've never seen it personally, of course, but one hears stories.

We got through the gate without trouble and soon joined the main road heading north. It's a good road – built by us Romans, of course. The sky was clear and the moon perfect for our journey. The centurion told me that's why the tribune instructed us to set off at 9pm, just as the moon rose. He said it would be a "waning gibbous moon", but it just looked like an ordinary sort of three-quarters moon to me.

So the light was almost as good as it gets at night, and we marched off as the moon rose in the east.

Marching at night is a bit of an art. It works better if the ranks can spread out a bit to minimise the shadows, but the tribune had warned the centurions to stay close together for at least the first hour. So we stumbled a bit, but it really wasn't too bad. I was just glad I wasn't one of the horsemen. I've never trusted horses to keep their feet at all, let alone in the dark! Not since that old nag fell under me riding down a hill at home when I was about ten. Nevertheless, there were no disasters last night, and the shadows grew less of a problem as the moon climbed up in the sky.

After an hour or two, we were marching easily, in a good rhythm, and our centurion seemed to relax a bit. He didn't seem to mind us chatting, and the news went up and down the line that all this great troop movement was to deliver one man – just one! – to Felix the governor in Caesarea.

Well, then I had to know just who this mega-important man was! With no fewer than 470 of Rome's superlative fighting men assigned to protect him, he must at least be someone from the senate, maybe even a relative of the emperor!

"It must be one of Nero's friends," said my friend Gaius. "Otherwise, he'd let him travel without protection."

"And probably tell his enemies where he was going," I laughed.

In the dark, I couldn't be sure, but I think it was the centurion who answered from a few ranks back at the head of the main body of troops, "Or have us deliver him to them."

That was a new thought. Perhaps the centurion was right and this was one of the emperor's powerful enemies in the senate – another enemy to be dealt with in the dead of night!

We left the high country as the night grew older and colder and finally saw Antipatris in the distance as the light spread over the plains.

I was tired as we marched into the town – almost too tired to appreciate its beauty and the grand architecture which shows clearly whose hand constructed it. Herod the Great was a great builder alright, but another of these dangerous tyrants. As the emperor Augustus is said to have observed, "I'd rather be Herod's pig than his son."

But I digress.

With 470 men, our contingent greatly outnumbered the town garrison, but I still hoped to be able to get some food from them while we rested for a while. And that's how it turned out. So now, we're having a little rest. Then the next challenge begins. You see, we'd barely arrived before we were told that we soldiers and spearman are to return to Jerusalem today while the horsemen take our special charge on to Caesarea.

I'm not looking forward to that! Walking down from the heights of Jerusalem in a night wasn't too bad, but the thought of climbing back up again in the heat of a summer's day without proper sleep and nowhere near enough food is daunting.

However, we can't leave Jerusalem with half of her troops missing. It wouldn't be long before the Jews tried to take advantage of our weakness. So we have to get back there quickly.

I still haven't found out who our mysterious mega-important charge is, though.

✳ ✳ ✳ ✳

It was a long day's walk, but we made it back to Jerusalem after all. True, it was well and truly dark before we arrived, but it was an amazing achievement. And we've had plenty of extra rations as a reward!

It's been a tough 24 hours – after all, we spent almost 20 of those hours marching.

70 miles[a] we marched, and my feet are reminding me of every one of them. Hopefully we can have a few days' rest now!

But we are Roman soldiers: we fulfilled our task, and that's what matters. The man we were protecting was delivered safely to Antipatris.

---

a   70 Roman miles is about 104 kilometres

Now we catch up on sleep.

But who was that mega-important man? Royalty? Aristocracy? Patrician? Tomorrow I must find out...

Tried by Felix

Acts 23:34-24:27

[34] And having read it and having asked what province he is from, and having learned that he is from Cilicia, [35] he was saying "I will hear you fully when your accusers may have arrived also," having commanded him to be guarded in the Praetorium of Herod.

Acts 24

Tertullus Prosecutes Paul

[1] And after five days, the high priest Ananias came down with some elders and a certain orator, Tertullus, who made a representation against Paul to the governor.

[2] And of him having been called, Tertullus began to accuse, saying, "We are attaining great peace through you, and excellent measures are being done to this nation through your foresight. [3] Both in every way and everywhere, we gladly accept it, most excellent Felix, with all thankfulness. [4] But in order that I should not be a hindrance you to any longer, I implore you to hear us briefly, in your kindness.

[5] For we are having found this man a pest, and stirring insurrection among all the Jews in the world, and a leader of the sect of the Nazarenes [6] who even attempted to profane the temple, whom also we seized.[a] [8] Having examined him yourself, you will be able to know from him concerning all these things of which we accuse him."

[9] And the Jews also agreed, declaring these things to be so.

Paul's Defense to Felix

[10] And the governor having made a sign to him to speak, Paul answered: "Knowing you as being judge to this nation for many years, I make a defense cheerfully to the things concerning myself. [11] You are able to know that there are to me not more than twelve days since I went up to worship in Jerusalem. [12] And neither did they find me reasoning with anyone or making a tumultuous gathering of a crowd in the temple, nor in the synagogues,

---

a   BLB: Acts 24:6 – BYZ and TR include and we would have judged him according to our law. [7] But Lysias the commander came with great force and took him out of our hands, [8] ordering his accusers to come before you.

nor in the city. ¹³ Nor are they able to prove to you concerning the things of which now they accuse me.

¹⁴ But I confess this to you, that according to the Way which they call a sect, so I serve the God of our fathers, believing all things throughout the Law and that have been written in the Prophets, ¹⁵ having a hope in God, which they themselves also await, that there is about to be a resurrection, both of the just and of the unjust. ¹⁶ In this also I myself strive to have a conscience without offense toward God and men through everything.

¹⁷ Now after many years, I arrived to bring alms to my nation, and offerings, ¹⁸ during which they found me purified in the temple, not with a crowd nor in tumult. But there are some Jews from Asia ¹⁹ who ought to appear before you and to make accusation if they may have anything against me. ²⁰ Otherwise, let them say themselves any unrighteousness they found in me, having stood before the Council, ²¹ other than concerning this one voice, which I cried out standing among them: 'I am judged by you this day concerning the resurrection of the dead.'"

The Verdict Postponed

²² But Felix, more precisely having knowledge of the things concerning the Way, put them off, having said, "When Lysias the commander might have come down, I will examine the things as to you," ²³ having commanded the centurion to keep him and to let him have ease and not to forbid his own to minister to him.

²⁴ Then after some days, Felix, having arrived with the own wife Drusilla, being a Jewess, sent for Paul and heard him concerning the faith in Christ Jesus. ²⁵ And of him reasoning concerning righteousness and self-control and the coming judgment, Felix, having become frightened, answered, "Go away for the present, and having found opportunity, I will call for you." ²⁶ At the same time also he is hoping that riches will be given him by Paul. So also sending for him often, he was talking with him.

²⁷ But two years having been completed, Felix received Porcius Festus as successor, and wishing to acquire for himself favor with the Jews, Felix left Paul imprisoned.

Acts 23:34-24:27

Felix was the Roman governor, and now the problem of Paul was his to solve. But he didn't.

Five days after the night-time escape from Jerusalem, the high priest Ananias was in Caesarea with some heavyweight officials and a very clever attorney named Tertullus. Although it was almost 25 years since Paul had become a follower of Jesus, they still viewed him as a traitor and couldn't let him go unpunished.

Tertullus tried to butter up the governor and paint Paul as a rabble-rouser, but eventually it was Paul's turn to speak. Paul took the opportunity to preach about The Way, including resurrection and judgement, before concluding that the charges presented were trumped-up nonsense.

Felix put the matter on hold. He refused to give the Jews what they wanted, but didn't want to upset them too much by freeing Paul. And since he also hoped that Paul would pay a bribe, he kept him in prison.

Two years passed and there was still no bribe forthcoming. Paul remained in prison, but Felix's time as governor was up.

Tried by Festus

Sketch 38 – Two years

I've been in prison here for two years now – two years today.

I have some freedom, and at least there's light in my cell, but I can't leave. Local believers and friends visit me and bring things I need, but I can't help thinking how different these two years would have been if I hadn't been locked up.

Another missionary journey with Silas – possibly with Barnabas as well. Imagine visiting all the congregations throughout Syria, Cilicia, Galatia and Asia Minor, Macedonia, Greece and Achaia, and then travelling further afield as well. Spain and even further west.

Instead, I've sat here in prison and have nothing to show for it. Well, other than quite a few letters sent to several congregations. After all, I can't just sit around doing nothing!

However, it might all be coming to an end soon. It seems that the rumours I heard were true and that Felix has been recalled to Rome. It won't have been because he was asking for bribes, but I'm glad he got no money from me.

Accepting bribes is wrong, but offering them isn't much better. Still, two years has been a long time to be stuck in prison because of a corrupt governor under pressure from corrupt priests. But I'll still refuse to pay if the matter comes up again.

If the latest rumours are also right, a man named Festus will soon replace Felix. Will he send me to Rome straight away? Jesus made it clear that I'm going to end up there, but these last two years have made me wonder how long it might take.

Has Felix left Festus a report about me? Or will this be his way of getting back at me for not paying him a bribe? He could leave me locked away here but not tell his replacement. I could languish in this cell for another two years as an undocumented prisoner that only the jailer knows anything about!

Is there anything I can do about it? They already know I'm a Roman citizen, so I can't get their attention by playing that card. The only option might be to appeal to Caesar, but I can't even do that without seeing the governor.

There's no point in going through all this again. I've already asked God to get me out of here every day I've been here, and gone through all the legal possibilities as well. I'm just going round and round in circles and… What's that noise?

✳ ✳ ✳ ✳

Voices could be heard through the cell door and soon the rattle of the jailer's keys were followed by the sliding, scraping sound of a bolt being drawn back.

"Good morning, Paul," called a voice that I recognised as Philip's. "God bless you."

"The Lord keep you," I answered, pleased to hear his voice and see his smiling face. "How are you? And how are your daughters?"

"We are all healthy, physically and spiritually, but we were talking about you last night and wondering how you're coping with being locked up in here for so long."

"Frustrated, but satisfied," I answered. Then I recognised how strange those two ideas sounded together and added, "If that combination is possible!"

"Tell me more," prompted Philip.

"I'm frustrated at being stuck in here instead of travelling around preaching, but satisfied that this is what God wants of me at the moment and willing to wait to see what happens next."

"That sounds like a healthy mix to me, brother," said Philip. "I'm too old and weak to travel around now, and I've had to learn different ways of keeping busy preaching about Jesus and walking 'The Way'."

"I've heard that you're *always* busy, Philip," I said, "and even with your age, you have more freedom to choose what you do with your time than I do at the moment."

"You know, I haven't found it easy to learn to slow down, Paul. I still long to go on the sort of preaching journey I used to take when I travelled through Samaria and many other places. But if I ever start doing too much, I end up with such a bad back that I can't walk and have to spend a week in bed. And that means I can't do anything useful for a week –

except for praying. So I've had to learn to pace myself. Slow down; take it easier. If I do that well, I get more done."

His words surprised me and I was silent for a few moments. I'd never thought of life in quite that way before. True, I'd sometimes had to stop for a day or two to recover from injuries after receiving a beating – but after that, it was straight back to work, working as hard as I could manage! That was my job.

"That would be terribly difficult," I said, slowly. "I really can't imagine *having* to take it easy like that." And I truly couldn't. Whenever something needed doing, I'd always just started it and kept going until it was finished. I suppose being able to do that is a blessing from God that I hadn't recognised.

"Perhaps that's why God has taken it out of your hands at the moment," said Philip wryly. "Maybe he's saving you from complete physical or mental collapse."

"I've never thought of that possibility," I answered, "and it starts a bit of a conflict in my mind. After all, I've found many times that I can do all things through him who gives me strength. And it's not as if I haven't been able to do useful things while I've been stuck here. Hmmm. It's an odd concept: being kept in prison for my own health!"

I thought for a while, and Philip allowed me to think without interruption. I remembered some past occasions when I'd been slowed down by unexpected events – times when I was *forced* to wait. I could almost taste the frustration I'd felt at times, but I also had to admit that I often felt a great revival of energy when the waiting was finally over and I could continue with my plans. Perhaps those delays truly were God slowing me down to prevent me collapsing! Yet, at other times, there was no doubt that he had given me strength to keep going when it had seemed impossible.

"Convinced?" asked Philip.

"It could fit, I suppose," I answered, "but if you're right, when does the time come to an end? Two years is a long time to sit around like this."

"You sound more eager to get out than you did a year ago, brother. Perhaps your wait is coming to an end."

"Oh, I hope you're right!"

"This news may be connected, Paul. I heard yesterday that Festus, the new governor, is arriving in Caesarea tomorrow."

"That's good news, brother. Perhaps I can gain a hearing before him soon. Somehow or another, I need to travel to Rome, so I don't think it's likely that Festus will free me."

"I can't really see how he could justify keeping you here, let alone sending you to Rome. Perhaps you need to quickly appeal to Caesar before he lets you go."

"I'll have to wait and see."

Philip stayed chatting for an hour and enlisted my help in praying for some of the needs of our brothers in Caesarea. When he left, I thought about his ideas again and wondered if I could ever learn to slow down as he had done.

I still couldn't imagine how.

Perhaps Philip was right: that was why God hadn't given me the choice.

∞

Acts 24:27-25:12

27 But two years having been completed, Felix received Porcius Festus as successor, and wishing to acquire for himself favor with the Jews, Felix left Paul imprisoned.

Acts 25

Paul's Trial Before Festus

1 Therefore Festus, having arrived in the province, after three days went up to Jerusalem from Caesarea. **2** And the chief priests and the chiefs of the Jews made a presentation before him against Paul, and they were begging him, **3** asking a favor against him, that he would summon him to Jerusalem, forming an ambush to kill him on the way.

4 So indeed Festus answered that Paul is to be kept in Caesarea, and he himself is about to set out in quickness. **5** He says, "Therefore those among you in power, having gone down together, if there is anything wrong in the man, let them accuse him."

6 And having spent with them not more than eight or ten days, having gone down to Caesarea, on the next day having sat on the judgment seat, he commanded Paul to be brought. **7** And he having arrived, the Jews having come down from Jerusalem stood around him, bringing many and weighty charges, which they were not able to prove.

8 Paul made his defense: "Neither against the law of the Jews, nor against the temple, nor against Caesar, have I sinned in anything."

9 But Festus, wishing to lay a favor on the Jews, answering, said to Paul, "Are you willing, having gone up to Jerusalem, to be judged before me there concerning these things?"

The Appeal to Caesar

10 And Paul said, "I am standing before the judgment seat of Caesar, where it behooves me to be judged. I have done nothing wrong to the Jews, as you also know very well. **11** Therefore if indeed I do wrong and have done anything worthy of death, I do not refuse to die. But if there is nothing of which they can accuse me, no one can give me up to them. I appeal to Caesar!"

12 Then Festus, having conferred with the Council, answered, "You have appealed to Caesar; to Caesar you will go!"

Acts 24:27-25:12

Two years in prison for doing nothing wrong. God's plans are hard to fathom sometimes.

Finally, Festus replaced Felix as the Roman governor, and inherited the problem of Paul.

The Jews hadn't forgotten their hatred for Paul, and when Festus went to Jerusalem, they asked him to send Paul to Jerusalem for trial, planning again to kill him on the way.

Festus refused and after about ten days went back to Caesarea and waited for the Jews to come to him.

They came.

Festus was not really interested in justice. He wanted to do the Jews a favour. In his eyes, Paul was disposable. A mere pawn.

However, a Roman citizen could appeal to have his case heard by Caesar, and in the end, Paul felt compelled to make this appeal. Jesus had already told him that he must travel to Rome, so it was no real surprise.

Tried before Agrippa II

Acts 25:13-27

Festus Consults King Agrippa

13 Now some days having passed, Agrippa the king and Bernice came down to Caesarea, greeting Festus. **14** And as they stayed there many days, Festus laid before the king the things relating to Paul, saying, "There is a certain man left by Felix as a prisoner, **15** concerning whom, on my having been in Jerusalem, the chief priests and the elders of the Jews made a presentation, asking judgment against him, **16** to whom I answered that it is not the custom with Romans to give up any man before that the one being accused may have it to face the accusers, and he may have the opportunity of defense concerning the accusation.

17 Therefore of them having come together here, having made no delay, the next day having sat on the judgment seat, I commanded the man to be brought, **18** concerning whom the accusers, having stood up, were bringing no charge of the crimes of which I was expecting. **19** But they had certain questions against him concerning their own religion and concerning a certain Jesus having been dead, whom Paul was affirming to be alive.

20 Now I, being perplexed concerning this inquiry, was asking if he was willing to go to Jerusalem and there to be judged concerning these things. **21** But of Paul having appealed for himself to be kept for the decision of the Emperor, I commanded him to be kept until that I might send him to Caesar."

22 Then Agrippa said to Festus, "I have been wanting also to hear the man myself."

He says, "Tomorrow you will hear him."

Paul Before Agrippa and Bernice

23 So on the next day Agrippa and Bernice, having come with great pomp and having entered into the audience hall with both the commanders and the men in prominence in the city, and Festus having commanded, Paul was brought in.

24 And Festus says, "King Agrippa and all men being present with us, you see this one concerning whom the whole multitude of the Jews pleaded with me, both in Jerusalem and here, crying out of him that he ought not to live any longer. **25** But I, having understood him to have done nothing worthy of death, of this one himself now having appealed to the Emperor, I determined to send him, **26** concerning whom I have nothing definite to write to my lord. Therefore I have brought him before you all, and especially before you, King Agrippa, so that of the examination having taken place, I might have something to write. **27** For it seems absurd to me, sending a prisoner, not also to specify the charges against him."

Acts 25:13-22

After Paul made his appeal to have his case heard by Caesar, Festus agreed to send him, but important visitors were arriving in a few days and he saw no urgency.

Paul was left in prison.

Sometime, Festus knew, he would have to send Paul to Rome, but he was caught in a dilemma. It didn't seem reasonable to send a prisoner to Caesar without providing any information about the charge against him! No doubt it would also reflect badly on him as governor: just imagine presenting a case to the highest court in the empire with no charges and no particulars!

He would have to hear Paul's case again.

Agrippa was visiting. He was king over various areas in and around the land of Israel, and Bernice was his sister – or maybe his wife, or maybe both. The Roman kings weren't so very particular about this, and Agrippa was happy to agree with them.

Sketch 39 – Festus' visitors

"That was a delicious meal, governor Festus." The king spoke in a rich, oily drawl, burping politely to emphasise his appreciation.

"I'm glad you enjoyed it, O king. It wasn't bad." Festus patted his mouth with a napkin, then turned and held out his hands to a servant, who poured water over them, catching it in a basin. "When I arrived in Caesarea, I was a little concerned about what sort of fare I'd find in an out-of-the-way province like Judea, but Felix seems to have provided himself with a decent chef."

King Agrippa[a] looked sideways at his sister Bernice, rolling his eyes a little. These Roman officials were always quick to dismiss Judea as insignificant, yet for the Herodian dynasty, Judea and the surrounding areas had been a source of power and comfort for a century. The Herods had provided stability, security, permanence and reliability in the face of an ever-changing Roman Empire. Judea might not have the flashy importance of Rome, but his family had maintained a consistency that Rome could never achieve with its constant procession of prefects, governors and procurators.

Bernice gave a slight smile but said nothing. She and her brother understood each other well and she knew exactly what he meant.

Festus was a middle-aged Roman administrator, confident, as they all were, of Rome's excellence, and committed to the goals of the Roman Empire. As the newly-appointed procurator of Judea, he was determined to maintain peace in the province, and, although he would never have said so publicly, to avoid the violence, cruelty and corruption made commonplace by his predecessor Felix. He also knew that, should unrest arise, he would not have the safeguard of a brother to whisper in Nero's ear as Felix did.

Having washed his hands, he sat back in his seat and laced his fingers together over his fair-to-middling paunch. He was comfortably fed, and the wine he had been imbibing filled his mind with a pleasant glow.

He was about to embark on some after-dinner small talk when he suddenly remembered the subject he wanted to discuss with Agrippa.

"Ah, King Agrippa, I have a matter that I want to discuss with you. You are familiar with the conditions of this area and the complexity of the religious situation. There is a man here in Caesarea who was left as a prisoner by Felix. I believe he's been imprisoned here for two years, but no judicial decision has ever been made. In fact, there aren't even any real charges."

"Is this Saul of Tarsus?" asked the king, interested enough to drop his affected drawl.

"Saul? No, I don't think so. This man is called Paul or Paulos."

"I wonder if it's the same man. Is he a religious crackpot?"

Festus laughed a little. "Aren't all you Jews religious crackpots?"

---

a   King Herod Agrippa II ruled from 52AD to about 92 or 100AD. He was the son of King Herod Agrippa I, who ruled over Judea, Iturea and Samaria from 41AD to 44AD and was the 'Herod' referred to in Acts 12. Agrippa II was about 30-35 years old at the time of this story and his sister Bernice about a year younger.

Agrippa laughed in turn, but shook his head. His drawl returned as he replied, "Oh, no, Festus. Religion is certainly important to most of us, but most of us manage to avoid having our need for religion eclipse our love of money and power. This Saul of Tarsus, however, is a polarising character in our religion. Anyway, tell me more – perhaps we can determine whether Saul and Paul are the same person."

"I arrived from Rome a few months ago and went up to Jerusalem after just three days, since I thought it was important to get to know the Jewish leaders as soon as possible. I was amazed when they immediately talked about this Paulos. I didn't know anything about him at the time, but they made it clear that they considered his case the most important one that Felix hadn't finalised – and that they were angry about it."

Agrippa nodded. "This Paulos is definitely Saul of Tarsus. I've just remembered that both names were used in a report I received about that uproar in the temple two years ago. And, yes, the chief priests hate him. They plotted to kill him two years ago. Their first attempt didn't work because the tribune sent his troops into the temple courts and rescued him before they could kill him. So then they made a plot to kill him on the way to a court hearing, but the tribune learned about it and sent him away to Caesarea. Sent him by night, in fact, with hundreds of soldiers to protect him. It caused all sorts of a ruckus at the time. I'm not surprised they're still trying to get him."

"I see. Well, while I was in Jerusalem, the chief priests and the elders of the Jews presented their case against him and asked for a judgement against him. I did my best to put them off by saying that it was not the Roman custom to give up anyone before the accused met the accusers face to face and had an opportunity to make his defence concerning the charge laid against him."

"I'll bet they didn't like that!" said Agrippa, smiling.

"No, they tried to tell me that the hearing had already been carried out in Jerusalem and there was no question of the man's guilt, but I was a bit suspicious that they weren't telling me the whole truth."

"I'm not sure that some of those leaders know what truth is. They just know that they hate any opposition, including Saul," said Bernice.

"Do you know of this man, my lady?" asked Festus, turning to her.

"Only by common report. I'm just making a general observation about the chief priests. However, Agrippa is right, Saul of Tarsus is a religious crackpot. He's travelled all over the world trying to spread his crazy ideas."

"And the leaders hate him particularly because he used to be on their side and now he shows them up for their hypocrisy," said Agrippa.

"Ah, a turncoat?" said Festus, nodding. "Now I understand why they were so insistent – there's no better way to earn someone's undying hatred than to leave them and swap sides. Anyway, when they came here with me, I didn't delay. I sat on the judgement seat the very next day and ordered that the man be brought in. But when his accusers got up to speak, they didn't charge him with any of the crimes I had expected. They only had some contentions with him regarding their own religion and a certain Jesus who had died, but whom Paul affirmed to be alive."

"This conflict has been going on for more than 35 years," said Agrippa. "It started before I was born when the chief priests killed Jesus, the Nazarene carpenter, because he kept showing them up. It sounds like he was a genius at rhetoric and debate. He had thousands of followers – mostly uneducated peasants."

"Paul is no ignorant peasant, though. He's well educated, and a powerful speaker, too."

"True, and that's another reason why they hate him. Originally, the chief priests were sure that if they killed Jesus, that would be the end of the movement he led. But they were wrong. Those ignorant peasants wouldn't back down, and they made the leaders look small-minded and weak."

"How?"

"From the start, they claimed that the carpenter was alive..."

"Wasn't he executed? Did they make a hash of the execution?"

"They? He was crucified by you Romans. Do you think your soldiers would have got it wrong?"

"No," said Festus decisively. "We wouldn't get that wrong. So he was dead. How could his followers say he was alive? Surely all the leaders had to do was produce the bones?"

"You'd think so, but it seems that something happened to the body. The leaders claimed that his followers came and stole the body from the tomb."

"Wait, you said he was crucified. Wasn't the body just thrown into the rubbish tip and burned? That's what we Romans do with the bodies of crucified men."

"Yes, that's what normally happens here too, but two important leaders of the Jews went to Pilate, the governor, and asked to have the body so that they could bury it."

"I thought the leaders all hated him," said Festus, puzzled.

"Not quite all. There were a few who liked his teaching and didn't agree with his execution. I heard that one of those leaders put the body in his own new tomb."

"And then his followers came and took the body? What a mess."

"Well, it wasn't quite that simple. You see, apparently many people had heard the carpenter say that he would be killed and come back to life again, so after he was buried, the leaders went to Pilate and insisted that the tomb be sealed and guarded."

"And Pilate agreed to that?"

"Yes. The tomb was sealed and soldiers were sent to guard it."

"So what happened to the body then?"

"Nobody knows. The leaders say that the carpenter's disciples came and stole the body while the soldiers slept. Does that sound likely to you?"

"If any of my soldiers let that happen now, they wouldn't live long enough to tell the tale." Once more, Festus spoke decisively.

"Of course not," agreed Agrippa. He glanced at Bernice then leaned forward and spoke confidentially. "When I was young, my father[a] was involved with some of the followers of the carpenter. They've formed a sect they call The Way and their enemies call the sect of the Nazarene. My father wanted to please the chief priests, so he executed one of their leaders – one of the original followers of the carpenter. Then he locked up another one and kept him in prison while everyone was celebrating the Passover feast. He planned to kill him too, once the feast was over, but it didn't work."

"What do you mean?"

"The man disappeared," said Bernice, snapping her fingers indicatively.

"Disappeared? What do you mean?"

"Gone; missing; absent," said Bernice, her eyes gleaming.

"In the morning, when our father was about to send for the man, the guards reported that the man had disappeared from his cell," explained Agrippa, triumphantly, sitting back in his seat.

"Were some of the guards on the man's side?" asked Festus, frowning.

---

a   Agrippa I (reigned 41-44AD)

"That's what our father assumed, so he executed them all," said Agrippa.

"Sounds sensible to me."

"Perhaps. But for the conspiracy to work, all of the guards would have had to be involved. It wasn't just a few guards outside his cell, you know. The man was chained between two soldiers in his cell. There were guards outside the door, guards along the corridor, guards at the building entrance, guards in the courtyard. And then there was the locked iron gate leading into the city. There were guards inside and outside." Agrippa leaned forward again, tapping his finger on the table for emphasis. "But none of those guards – not one – admitted to seeing anything unusual."

"Bribery, perhaps? Are the followers of the carpenter rich?"

"If it was bribery, none of them got to enjoy their ill-gotten gains because our father killed them all," said Bernice.

"And not one of them admitted anything before they were executed," repeated Agrippa.

Festus looked thoughtful. "So what do you think happened?"

"I don't know," said Agrippa, simply. "One can't help seeing a similarity between that incident and the disappearance of the carpenter's body. Yet his followers aren't militant, so I can't imagine them taking the body from a guarded tomb. They don't fight."

"Except for that one incident I heard of when the Nazarene was arrested," said Bernice. "They say that one of his followers hacked a man's ear off."

"I've never really believed that story," said Agrippa. "After all, no-one could ever produce the earless man. All they have are stories about the carpenter telling off his follower and then magically putting the man's ear back on. I doubt any of it happened. Just a fantastic story. What is clear is that, to this day, his followers are never violent."

"Then they won't last long as a sect!" laughed Festus grimly.

Agrippa inclined his head. "What if the explanations the carpenter's followers give for those disappearances are true? It's hard to wipe out a group when locking them up doesn't work and they don't stay dead when you kill them."

"The idea's absurd," scoffed Festus.

"They say that hundreds of people saw the carpenter alive after he was crucified, dead and buried. And some say that the follower of his that I mentioned has been seen alive in other countries."

"I suppose it is only ever his followers who see the carpenter!" snorted Festus. "That's not very convincing. Perhaps we should track down that follower your father locked up. We could ask him what happened."

"Why? Would you join their sect if he told you it was a miracle?"

"Of course not."

"Sometimes it's best not to search too deeply. You might find an answer you don't like."

"You could be right. Well, thanks for giving me more background. At the start, I had no idea what it was all about, so since I was at a loss as to how to investigate these matters, I asked Paul if he was willing to go to Jerusalem and be tried there on the charges."

"That would have played right into the chief priests' hands! If you'd sent Saul with a party of soldiers, they'd have been ambushed by a contingent of irregular fighters on the way. Hundreds of them, probably."

"That wouldn't have occurred to me before you gave me some of the background. You've been a great help. I would've liked to let Paul go, but these Jewish leaders have caused previous governors plenty of trouble and I was trying to placate them. But when Paul appealed to be held over for the decision of the Emperor, he took the decision out of my hands. So I ordered that he be held until I could send him to Caesar."

Agrippa leaned forward. "I'd like to hear this man myself," he said.

"Tomorrow you will hear him," declared Festus.

Acts 26:1-32

Acts 26

Paul's Testimony to Agrippa
(Acts 9:1-9; Acts 22:1-21)

[1] And Agrippa was saying to Paul, "It is permitted you to speak for yourself."

Then Paul, having stretched out the hand, began his defense: [2] "Concerning all of which I am accused by the Jews, King Agrippa, I esteem myself fortunate before you, being about to defend myself today, [3] you being especially acquainted with all the customs and also controversies of the Jews. Therefore I implore you to hear me patiently.

4 Then indeed all the Jews know my manner of life which is from youth, having been from its beginning among my own nation and in Jerusalem, **5** knowing me from the first, if they would be willing to testify, that according to the strictest sect of our religion I lived as a Pharisee.

6 And now I stand being judged for the hope of the promise having been made by God to our fathers, **7** to which our twelve tribes hope to attain, serving in earnestness night and day, the hope concerning which I am accused by the Jews, O king. **8** Why is it judged incredible by you if God raises the dead?

9 Therefore I indeed in myself thought I ought to do many things contrary to the name of Jesus of Nazareth, **10** which also I did in Jerusalem. And I also locked up many of the saints in prisons, having received the authority from the chief priests; and they being put to death, I cast against them a vote. **11** And in all the synagogues, punishing them often, I was compelling them to blaspheme. And being exceedingly furious against them, I kept persecuting them even as far as to foreign cities, **12** during which, journeying to Damascus with the authority and commission of the chief priests, **13** at midday on the road, O king, I saw, a light from heaven above, the brightness of the sun, having shone around me and those journeying with me. **14** And of all of us having fallen down to the ground, I heard a voice saying to me in the Hebrew language,[a] 'Saul, Saul, why do you persecute Me? It is hard for you to kick against the goads.'

15 Then I said, 'Who are You, Lord?'

And the Lord said, 'I am Jesus, whom you are persecuting. **16** But rise up and stand on your feet. For I have appeared to you for this purpose, to appoint you a servant and a witness both of that which you have seen of Me, and of the things in which I will appear to you, **17** delivering you out from the people and from the Gentiles to whom I am sending you, **18** to open their eyes, that they may turn from darkness to light, and from the power of Satan to God, that they may receive forgiveness of sins and an inheritance among those having been sanctified by faith in Me.'

19 So then, O king Agrippa, I was not disobedient to the heavenly vision, **20** but both first to those in Damascus and Jerusalem, and all the region of Judea, and to the Gentiles, I kept declaring to repent and to turn to God, doing works worthy of repentance. **21** On account of these things the Jews, having seized me being in the temple, were attempting to kill me.

22 Therefore having obtained help from God unto this day, I have stood bearing witness both to small and to great, saying nothing other than what both the prophets and Moses said was about to happen: **23** that Christ

---

a   BLB: Acts 26:14 – Or Aramaic

would suffer. As first through resurrection from the dead, He is about to preach light both to our people and to the Gentiles."

Festus Interrupts Paul's Defense

24 Now of him saying these things in his defense, Festus said in a loud voice, "You are insane, Paul! The great learning turns you to insanity!"

25 But Paul says, "I am not insane, most excellent Festus, but I speak words of truth and sobriety. **26** For the king understands concerning these things, to whom also I speak using boldness. For I am persuaded none of these things are hidden from him, for none of these things is done in a corner. **27** Do you believe the prophets, King Agrippa? I know that you believe."

28 Then Agrippa said to Paul, "Within so little time do you persuade me to become a Christian?"

29 Then Paul said, "I would wish anyhow to God, both in a little and in much, not only you but also all those hearing me this day to become such as I also am, except these chains."

30 Then the king and the governor rose up, and Bernice and those sitting with them, **31** and having withdrawn, they began speaking to one another, saying, "This man is doing nothing worthy of death or of chains."

32 Then Agrippa was saying to Festus, "This man could have been released if he had not appealed to Caesar."

Acts 25:23-26:32

After discussing Paul's case with King Agrippa and Bernice, Festus invited them to join him in hearing more from Paul.

Paul spoke well, telling yet again the story of his conversion and speaking of repentance, resurrection and hope.

All his hearers agreed that Paul could have been set free – if only he had not appealed to Caesar!

PART TEN
Journey to Rome

Julius

Acts 27:1-4

Acts 27

Paul Sails for Rome

¹ Now when our[a] sailing to Italy was determined, they delivered both Paul and certain other prisoners to a centurion named Julius, of the cohort of Augustus. ² And having boarded a ship of Adramyttium being about to sail to the places along Asia, we set sail—Aristarchus, a Macedonian of Thessalonica, being with us.

³ And the next day we landed at Sidon. And Julius, having treated Paul considerately, allowed him, having gone to his friends, to receive care. ⁴ And having set sail from there, we sailed under Cyprus because of the winds being contrary.

> *Acts 27:1-4*
>
> Paul and some other prisoners bound for Rome were entrusted to a centurion called Julius, who arranged a passage on a ship from Adramyttium which was to sail along the coast of Asia. It was a dangerous time of year for sailing and the first stages of the voyage were very slow.

Sketch 40 – A Centurion named Julius

Festus was seated in the judgement hall when Paul was led in by two guards. He was talking to a soldier – a centurion, based on his uniform.

---

a   Acts 27:1 – The use of "our", "we" and "us" indicates that the writer, believed to be Luke, was with Paul (until Acts 28:16). See also Acts 16:10-17; 20:5-15; 21:1-18.

"Julius, this is Paul of Tarsus," said Festus. "You have your orders regarding him and the details of the charges against him – such as they are – for you to present to the emperor."

"Very well, sir."

"Paul's case is unusual. Had he not appealed to Caesar, I would have let him go, because there is no evidence of him having committed any crime. However, the appeal has been made and cannot be reversed."

"So he is innocent, sir?"

"In a manner of speaking, yes, but that must now be confirmed by the emperor. He must appear before the emperor and gain his approval. Until then, he is a prisoner."

"I see. I've heard a lot about this man, sir."

"Good or bad?"

"Good, sir."

"Well, don't get led astray by rumours, Julius. Do your duty."

"Very well, sir."

"Saul, or Paul, or whatever your name is," said Festus, turning to Paul, "Julius here, one of the centurions of the Augustan cohort, will conduct you to Rome. You will be accompanied by a squad of soldiers and some other prisoners. Julius will arrange transportation, leaving as soon as possible. With ordinary sailing weather and good fortune, you should be able to reach Rome before winter."

"Thank you," answered Paul. "I appreciate your promptness in arranging this matter."

"I don't like leaving uncondemned men in prison any longer than I can help," said Festus. "You will leave immediately once Julius has made the necessary arrangements."

"I have one or two friends here in Caesarea who would like to come with me to Rome," said Paul. "Could I give them details of the ship?"

"Julius will look after that," said Festus, generously.

✱ ✱ ✱ ✱

Julius was a diligent worker. Early the next morning, Paul was taken from his cell by a pair of soldiers who signed him out and led him towards the docks. It was exciting to leave the dark stone room that had been his unwelcome home for more than two years. Julius was already at the dock, watching his squad of soldiers herd several other prisoners up the gangplank – men being transferred to Rome for judgement or punishment.

Paul approached Julius immediately, expressing concern about Luke and Aristarchus, who had both expressed a strong wish to travel with him to Rome. Such a sudden and unexpected departure might make them miss the boat.

"Don't worry," said Julius, "You gave me their names and where they were living, so I sent them details of the vessel and its departure time. In fact, they're already onboard. Look over there at the bow." The centurion waved his arm in their direction.

Paul's eyesight wasn't very good, but when he peered at the front end of the ship, he could just make out Luke standing there with another man close behind him.

"Thanks for your help," he said, waving to Luke, who immediately waved back and began to walk towards the gangplank. The other man turned and, seeing Paul, hurried after Luke. Soon Paul could see that it was Aristarchus, smiling and waving. Paul smiled and returned the waves. Aristarchus was an old friend and a great companion.

"Good morning, Paul," called Luke as he walked down onto the quay, closely followed by Aristarchus. They each gave Paul a hug.

"Greetings in the name of Jesus Christ, brother Paul," said Aristarchus.

"And congratulations!" said Luke. "You're out of that prison and on your way to Rome."

"Rome's not always the safest place to go," observed Julius. "And although it sounds as if your case should be pretty simple, Caesar isn't always predictable."

"Jesus told me that I'm to testify about him to Caesar in Rome," said Paul, "so the sooner we get there, the better!"

"Look, I don't have time to talk to you about this Jesus now," said Julius, "but I'd like to hear more sometime soon. In the meantime, come on board. Make sure you stay near these two soldiers. Once we set sail, you'll be free to roam the deck."

Julius hurried away to make final arrangements with the captain while Luke and Aristarchus climbed back on board, followed by Paul and his two guards.

The three friends stood near the bow looking out to sea, thankful for Julius' kindness and the cooperation of the guards.

"It's good to be on a boat again," said Paul, rubbing his hands together.

"And better for your health too, I think," said Luke. "Spending years in prison isn't what we're designed for."

Paul laughed, "Oh, Luke. You doctors spend too much time thinking about physical health. But I must admit it's wonderful to be outside again with the sea wind blowing my hair. Being out on the open sea will be even better."

"If God wills it, you won't be out at sea for long," said Aristarchus. "The captain says we should put in at Sidon tomorrow."

"That's good news," said Paul. "There are believers in Sidon. Perhaps Julius will let me visit them."

"I wouldn't hold your breath," warned Luke. "You know what would happen to him if you escaped, so he's not likely to give you the chance."

"I've already told him that I have to travel to Rome."

"I'm sure plenty of prisoners have told him plenty of things, but he won't want to risk his life by relying on your word."

"How can I convince him to trust me, then?"

"You might have to hope that he'll let Aristarchus and me go ashore and bring the believers to meet you on the ship. Julius may be willing to take that risk."

It wasn't long before they were ready to sail. The ropes were cast off and the crew eased the ship away from the quay. Sails were quickly hoisted and the ship slowly but steadily left Caesarea behind. Paul stood at the bow, leaning on the rail and breathing in the sea air. As he exchanged hopes and ideas with Luke and Aristarchus, he couldn't keep a smile off his face for long, and his laughter burst out frequently.

Memories of two years of imprisonment were left behind as the ship cut through the gentle waves. Paul was looking forward again, eager to meet the believers in Sidon.

✴ ✴ ✴ ✴

After a calm night of slow sailing, they put in at Sidon the following day. Paul didn't even need to ask Julius for the opportunity to visit the believers there: Julius offered it.

"Now that's faith, isn't it?" marvelled Luke when Paul told him the good news. "He's probably risking his life for you."

"If you left the ship and never came back, he'd lose his job at a minimum, and there's a good chance he'd be executed," agreed Aristarchus.

"It's an honour to be trusted like that," said Paul, "and I'm not yet sure why he'd do it. I hope to have an opportunity to talk to him about it. People who can have such faith in people they've never met have something special. It reminds me of the centurion who went to Jesus asking him to cure his servant, and of Cornelius, the centurion who sent for Peter and was so sure that Peter would come and tell them some vital truth that he gathered his friends and relatives to meet him."

"Inspiring, isn't it?" said Luke. "Shall we go and find the believers now? I hope they're not too busy today."

Aristarchus had never visited Sidon before, so Paul and Luke led the way to the home of one of the elders they knew. By the grace of God, he was at home and full of joy to see them. "Greetings, my beloved brothers – and Paul in particular. We've all been praying for your freedom, but I never expected to hear the news by meeting you at my door! Come in. We'll send messages around to gather all the believers who are available. How long can you stay?"

"Only a few hours," said Paul. "We leave this afternoon, after the sailors have finished loading the new cargo. Then it's on to Rome, so that I can testify to the truth before the emperor!" Excitement shone in Paul's eyes, and Luke marvelled at how quickly the frustration of two years' imprisonment had been replaced by an eagerness to preach once more.

Acts 27:5-13

[5] And having sailed across the sea and along Cilicia and Pamphylia, we came to Myra of Lycia. [6] And there the centurion, having found a ship of Alexandria sailing to Italy, placed us into it.

[7] Now sailing slowly for many days, and with difficulty having arrived off Cnidus, the wind not permitting us, we sailed under Crete, off Salmone. [8] And coasting along it with difficulty, we came to a certain place called Fair Havens, near to which was the city of Lasea.

[9] Now much time having passed, and the voyage being already dangerous because of even the Fast[a] already being over, Paul was admonishing them, [10] saying to them, "Men, I understand that the voyage is about to be filled

a   BLB: Acts 27:9 – That is, Yom Kippur, the Day of Atonement

with disaster and much loss, not only of the cargo and of the ship, but also of our lives."[a]

11 But the centurion was persuaded by the pilot and the ship owner, rather than by the things spoken by Paul. **12** And the harbor being unsuitable to winter in, the majority reached a decision to set sail from there, if somehow they might be able, having arrived at Phoenix—a harbor of Crete looking toward the southwest and toward the northwest—to winter there.

ॐ

Acts 27:5-12

When the ship reached Myra in Lysia, Julius found an Alexandrian ship sailing to Italy and put the soldiers and the prisoners on board.

The ship struggled slowly along the coast towards Cnidus, but when they could sail no farther in the face of steady headwinds, the crew sailed south instead, making their way around the lee of Crete to a harbour called Fair Havens.

By that time, the Day of Atonement had passed. It was a time of year when wise crews found a safe harbour and waited out the winter storms.

But the pilot and the owner of the ship had no wish to sit around for any longer than necessary. An entire crew, sitting idle? A waste indeed! There might be contrary winds, but there were no storms yet. They should at least keep sailing to the end of Crete where there was a better harbour. It was worth the risk to shorten the remaining distance to Italy.

Paul warned them of the dangers, but who would listen to a tentmaker when there were expert seamen at hand?

Julius agreed to sail on.

---

a   Acts 27:10 – It appears that Paul's prayers changed this outcome so that all were saved alive and only the cargo was lost (Acts 28:22-24, 44)

Shipwreck

Acts 27:13-44

The Storm at Sea
(Jeremiah 6:10-21; Jeremiah 25:15-33; Jonah 1:4-10; Romans 1:18-32)

[13] Now a south wind having blown gently, having thought to have obtained the purpose, having weighed anchor, they began coasting along very near Crete. [14] But not long after, there came down from it a tempestuous wind called the Northeaster. [15] And the ship having been caught and not being able to face to the wind, having given way, we were driven along.

[16] And having run under a certain island called Cauda,[b] we were able with difficulty to gain control of the lifeboat, [17] which having taken up, they began using supports, undergirding the ship. And fearing lest they should fall into the sandbars of Syrtis, having lowered the gear,[c] thus they were driven along.

[18] And we being storm-tossed violently, on the next day they began to make a jettison of cargo, [19] and on the third day they cast away the tackle of the ship with the own hands. [20] And neither sun nor stars appearing for many days, and no small tempest lying on us, from then on all hope of our being saved was abandoned.

[21] There being also much time without food, at that time having stood up in their midst, Paul said, "It behooved you indeed, O men, having been obedient to me, not to have set sail from Crete and to have incurred this disaster and loss. [22] And yet now I exhort you to take heart, for there will be no loss of life from among you, only of the ship. [23] For this night an angel of God, whose I am and whom I serve, stood by me, [24] saying, 'Fear not, Paul. It behooves you to stand before Caesar. And behold, God has granted to you all those sailing with you.'[d]

[25] Therefore take heart, men, for I believe God that it will be thus, according to the way it has been said to me. [26] But it behooves us to fall upon a certain island."

---

b   BLB: Acts 27:16 – NE, BYZ, and TR Clauda
c   BLB: Acts 27:17 – Or the sails
d   Acts 27:22-24 – This was a change from Paul's earlier pronouncement (Acts 28:10) and was presumably the result of prayer (see also Acts 28:44).

The Shipwreck

27 And when the fourteenth night had come, of us being driven about in the Adriatic,[a] toward the middle of the night the sailors began sensing some land to be drawing near to them. **28** And having taken soundings, they found twenty fathoms.[b] Then having gone a little farther and having taken soundings again, they found fifteen fathoms.[c] **29** And fearing lest we might fall somewhere on rocky places, having cast four anchors out of the stern, they were praying for day to come.

30 And of the sailors seeking to flee out of the ship and having let down the lifeboat into the sea under pretense as being about to cast out anchors from the bow, **31** Paul said to the centurion and to the soldiers, "Unless these remain in the ship, you are not able to be saved." **32** Then the soldiers cut away the ropes of the lifeboat, and allowed her to fall away.

33 And until that day was about to come, Paul kept urging all to partake of food, saying, "Today is the fourteenth day you continue watching without eating, having taken nothing. **34** Therefore I exhort you to take food, for this is for your preservation; for not one hair of your head will perish."

35 Now having said these things and having taken bread, he gave thanks to God before all; and having broken it, he began to eat. **36** And all, having been encouraged, also took food themselves. **37** And we were altogether two hundred seventy-six[d] souls in the ship. **38** Then having been filled with food, they began to lighten the ship, casting out the wheat into the sea.

39 And when it was day, they did not recognize the land, but they noticed a certain bay, having a shore on which they determined to drive the ship if they should be able. **40** And having cut away the anchors, they left them in the sea, at the same time having loosened the ropes of the rudders. And having hoisted the foresail to the blowing wind, they began making for the shore. **41** But having fallen into a place between two seas, they ran the vessel aground. And indeed the bow, having stuck fast, remained immovable, and the stern was being broken up by the violence of the waves.

42 Now the plan of the soldiers was that they should kill the prisoners, lest anyone, having swum away, should escape. **43** But the centurion, desiring to save Paul, hindered them of the purpose; and he commanded those being able to swim, having cast themselves off first, to go out on the land, **44** and the rest, some indeed on boards, and some on things from the ship. And thus it came to pass that all were brought safely to the land.[e]

---

a   BLB: Acts 27:27 – The Adriatic Sea referred to an area also extending well south of Italy.
b   BLB: Acts 27:28 – About 120 feet or 37 meters
c   BLB: Acts 27:28 – About 90 feet or 27 meters
d   BLB: Acts 27:37 – WH seventy-six
e   Acts 27:44 – This was a different result from that earlier predicted by Paul (Acts 28:10)

Acts 27:13-44

The decision was made and Paul's advice ignored.

When the south wind blew gently, they left Fair Havens and sailed close in to shore, hoping to reach Phoenix and winter there.

Paul's God-given warning caught up with them. A furious storm swept down on them from the land and the ship was tossed about like a cork. Fourteen days the storm raged, and on the fourteenth night the crew began to fear that they were approaching land. Soundings showed the water growing ever shallower as the night dragged on.

Eventually day came, and hope with it: a bay with a beach. The pilot aimed, but his skill could not overcome the savagery of the waves, and the ship was caught on a reef and battered to pieces.

The soldiers had an idea: kill the prisoners and let everyone else make for shore. But Julius had a better idea, and soon everyone was making for safety on pieces of the broken ship.

During the storm, Paul had foretold that no-one would die.

All reached land safely.

---

and was presumably the result of prayer (see Acts 28:22-24).

Malta

Acts 28:1-10

Acts 28

Ashore on Malta

[1] And having been saved, we then found out that the island is called Malta. [2] And the natives were showing not just the ordinary kindness to us. For having kindled a fire, they received all of us, because of the rain coming on and because of the cold.

[3] Now of Paul having gathered a quantity of sticks and having laid them on the fire, a viper, having come out from the heat, fastened on his hand. [4] And when the natives saw the beast hanging from his hand, they began to say to one another, "By all means this man is a murderer whom, having been saved from the sea, Justice[a] has not permitted to live." [5] Then indeed, having shaken off the creature into the fire, he suffered no injury. [6] But they were expecting him to be about to become inflamed or suddenly to fall down dead. But of them waiting a great while and seeing nothing amiss happening to him, having changed their opinion, they began declaring him to be a god.

[7] Now in the parts around that place were lands belonging to the chief of the island, named Publius, who having received us, entertained us hospitably for three days. [8] And it came to pass, the father of Publius was lying, oppressed with fevers and dysentery, toward whom Paul, having entered and having prayed, having laid the hands on him, healed him. [9] And of this having taken place, also the rest in the island having infirmities were coming and were healed, [10] who also honored us with many honors, and on setting sail, they laid on us the things for our needs.

---

a   BLB: Acts 28:4 – Greek Dike, that is, the Greek goddess of justice

Acts 28:1-10

Safely ashore, the ship's company found that the island was called Malta.[a] The people living there looked after them very kindly, lighting a fire and helping to keep them warm in the rain.

Paul was helping to collect sticks when a viper came out because of the heat and bit his hand. He shook the creature into the fire, and thought no more of it. Had not Jesus promised that deadly snakes would not hurt his disciples?

The people of the island had no such faith.

They saw crude justice in the serpent's fangs and waited for Paul to suffer. Then, when nothing happened, they changed their minds and called him a god.

Paul knew the God who was in control, and taught the people of the island as much as he could in the three months they waited for the storms to pass before travelling on in another ship.

---

a   "Melita" in the Greek of the New Testament.

PART ELEVEN
Rome

To the End

Acts 28:11-31

Paul Arrives in Italy

11 Then after three months, we sailed in an Alexandrian ship having wintered in the island, with a figurehead of the Dioscuri.[a] **12** And having put in at Syracuse, we stayed three days, **13** from where having gone around, we arrived at Rhegium. And after one day a south wind having come on, on the second day we came to Puteoli, **14** where having found some brothers, we were entreated to remain with them seven days. And so we came to Rome.

15 And the brothers from there, having heard the things concerning us, came out as far as the market of Appius and the Three Taverns to meet us, whom Paul having seen, having given thanks to God, took courage.

Paul Preaches at Rome

16 Now when we came to Rome,[b] Paul was allowed to stay by himself, with the soldier who was guarding him.

17 And it came to pass after three days, he called together those being leaders of the Jews. And of them having come together, he was saying to them, "Men, brothers, having done nothing against the people or the customs of our fathers, I was delivered from Jerusalem a prisoner into the hands of the Romans, **18** who having examined me, were wanting to let me go, on account of not one cause of death existing in me. **19** But of the Jews objecting, I was compelled to appeal to Caesar, not as having anything to lay against my nation. **20** Therefore for this cause I have called to see you and to speak to you. For because of the hope of Israel, I have around me this chain."

21 Then they said to him, "We received neither letters concerning you from Judea, nor any of the brothers having arrived reported or said anything evil concerning you. **22** But we deem it worthy to hear from you what you think, for truly concerning this sect, it is known to us that it is spoken against everywhere."

---

a   BLB: Acts 28:11 – The Twin Brothers, that is, the Greek gods Castor and Pollux
b   BLB: Acts 28:16 – BYZ and TR include the centurion delivered up the prisoners to the captain of the barrack, but

23 Then having appointed him a day, many came to him to the lodging, to whom he expounded from morning to evening, fully testifying to the kingdom of God and persuading them concerning Jesus from both the Law of Moses and the Prophets.

24 And indeed, some were persuaded of the things he is speaking, but some refused to believe. **25** And being discordant with one another they began to leave, Paul having spoken one word: "The Holy Spirit spoke rightly by the prophet Isaiah to your fathers, **26** saying:

'Go to this people and say,
"In hearing you will hear and never understand;
and in seeing you will see and never perceive."
27 For the heart of this people has grown dull,
and with the ears they barely hear,
and they have closed their eyes,
lest ever they should see with the eyes,
and they should hear with the ears,
and they should understand with the heart,
and should turn,
and I will heal them.'[a]

28 Therefore be it known to you that this salvation of God has been sent to the Gentiles, and they will listen!"[b]

30 And he stayed two whole years in his own rented house, and was welcoming all coming unto him, **31** proclaiming the kingdom of God and teaching the things concerning the Lord Jesus Christ with all boldness, unhinderedly.

Acts 28:11-31

On to Rome to stand before the emperor. Paul spent two years in Rome on this first visit and was allowed to stay in his own hired house.

Sketch 41 – Guards

"Good morning, Paul," the guard greeted him as Paul left his bed chamber early one morning.

---

a   BLB: Acts 28:26-27 – Isaiah 6:9,10
b   BLB: Acts 28:28 – BYZ and TR include **29** When he had said this, the Jews went away, disputing sharply among themselves.

He stood near the door of the house; some guard or other had stood there every day during the 20 months Paul had so far spent waiting for his trial before Caesar. Paul may have the luxury of his own hired house, but the guard was a constant reminder that he was very much a prisoner, unable to come and go as he chose. Still, there was no point in moping or complaining. Another day meant more opportunities.

"Greetings, Crispinus," answered Paul as he went and sat at the table in the spacious room where he frequently welcomed visitors who wanted to hear about the gospel. "You're back on shift again. Have you had a chance to think about my comments – two days ago, was it? – about why you should believe Jesus Christ rose from the dead?"

"Yes, some – and I talked to my wife about it too. We can see why *you* are so convinced about it, if you saw him alive, but we haven't. After about a year of guarding you on and off, I trust you in many things, but this seems a bit of a stretch. The fact is, people don't come back from the dead. I don't know anyone who's died and come back to life."

"You're right, it doesn't happen normally. The Lord Jesus was and is a special case. That's one of the reasons why I call him 'The Lord' or 'Jesus Christ'."

"Our Roman religion has lots of gods and demi-gods and people ascribe all sorts of amazing achievements to them. But I don't know many people who expect any of those sorts of marvels to happen nowadays. Today, life comes and goes. People live and die – and they don't come back to life."

"Jesus Christ did, and I've met him a few times."

"That's all very well, but can *I* meet him?"

"Probably not," smiled Paul, apologetically. "One of the most important things about the Lord Jesus Christ is that he *died on a cross*. He was crucified. He's not being presented as a hero like your heroes or a god like your gods. He was a hero as a sacrifice; a servant."

"Doesn't sound like much of a hero to me. It's criminals who get executed on crosses, and we burn their bodies as rubbish."

"Ah," said Paul, his eyes lighting up. As always, he was eager to convince doubters, and here he sensed an opening. "That's what makes Jesus Christ different. He wasn't a criminal. He was no thief, no liar, no murderer, no adulterer, no brawler. In fact, there's never been a man who was further from being any of those things. Even Pilate the governor realised that he wasn't guilty of any crime. No, the problem was that he was *too good*. The Jewish leaders were jealous of his goodness and his popularity, so they were determined to kill him. Pilate wanted to free him, but didn't dare to do so because of the threats of the Jewish leaders. His enemies were only able to kill him because of his goodness. If he'd been like them, fighting to maintain his own position, he could easily have defeated them. He had power to do miracles! Thousands of people saw that. But God's plan for Jesus was for him to die on a cross, not because he was guilty but because he *wasn't*."

Crispinus looked puzzled. He always felt a little puzzled when Paul began to talk about Jesus. The religion Paul presented had a completely different foundation from anything Crispinus had ever learned. It wasn't that it was impossible or ridiculous, it was just that most of what Paul described was counter-intuitive or paradoxical. He presented a religion of victory through defeat; joy through suffering; mastery through service; life through death; riches through poverty. It had a radically different starting point.

He sighed. "I don't understand how you can expect to be saved by a man who was defeated and killed by his enemies."

"I understand your problem," answered Paul, earnestly, "but this question goes to the root of God's entire plan for salvation. He made us and wants to save us, but it has to be done his way – and that's not through human pride, ability, arrogance or even determination. Jesus Christ won his victory by *obedience* to God, his father, through death on a cross."

"I suppose obeying God makes sense – since you say he created us and having one God as our creator seems reasonable to me. So obeying one's creator really does make sense."

"I'm glad it makes sense to you, because it certainly makes sense to me," said Paul. "Unfortunately, Adam, the first man God made, chose to ignore his creator's instructions. God calls that sin, and Adam died because of his sin. And death was passed on to everyone because we all sin – although in many different ways. Everyone disobeys God's laws, whether by doing things he forbids or by not doing things he requires. Everyone, that is, except for Jesus Christ. And that's why the Jewish leaders were jealous of him."

"I can see how that could happen, and why they would kill him. But resurrection is a different story."

"Yet the resurrection is just another logical part of the whole plan. Sin led to death as God had promised. Does that make sense?"

"Yes, I think so."

"Yet if Jesus Christ never sinned, did he deserve to die?"

"I suppose not."

"So how could he stay dead? Death was a punishment for sin."

"It sounds logical," Crispinus answered slowly. "But still, resurrection…"

A knock sounded on the door. Crispinus quickly made sure his uniform was neat and tidy, picked up his spear from where it leaned against the wall, and opened the door. Although the house was rented by Paul, his guards had to okay each visitor.

"Ah, Luke," said Crispinus. "Come in, and you too, Lucius – we're in the middle of a discussion you might be interested in."

Luke stood back and signalled for Lucius to enter first. Lucius, like Crispinus, wore the uniform and insignia of the Praetorian Guard, the elite unit answering directly to the emperor and responsible for guarding Caesar's prisoners.

"Is Paul still working toward his goal of converting the entire Praetorian Guard?" asked Lucius, smiling.[a]

"He may have converted you," said Crispinus, mildly, "but I'm not completely convinced yet. Resurrection still seems a bit of a stretch to me."

"Paul told me it was one of the ways God announced Jesus to be his obedient son. I like the idea: resurrection highlights Jesus' holiness and God's power."

"I suppose so, but I still need to think about it more," said Crispinus.

Luke had followed Lucius in and shut the door. "I happen to have a scroll of the Psalms with me, Crispinus. Have you ever read any of them?"

"I haven't read any, but Paul has told me about some of them, including one that gave amazing details about the death of Jesus. Phenomenal detail for something written hundreds of years before it happened. I found it very convincing. It really fits with crucifixion and the events of Jesus' death."[b]

"Agreed," said Luke. "Well, there's another Psalm which predicted that Jesus would not return to dust the way all other dead bodies do. I'll just find it for you." He laid the scroll on a table and unrolled it until he found the Psalm he was looking for. "This Psalm was written by the great King David. Near the end of it he says,

---

a   Paul obviously spoke to his guards while imprisoned in Rome and seems to have converted some of the Praetorian Guard and Caesar's household. See Philippians 1:13 and 4:22.

b   See Psalm 22

" 'For you will not abandon my soul to Sheol,
or let your holy one see corruption.
You make known to me the path of life;
in your presence there is fullness of joy;
at your right hand are pleasures forevermore.'[a]

"Do you think that could be a reference to the *resurrection* of Jesus Christ? Dead only three days, then raised to life and soon afterwards going into heaven to sit at God's right hand."

"I don't know that passage," said Lucius, delightedly. "The prophecies in your Jewish Bible are quite astonishing."

"Yet the leaders of the Jews don't believe them," objected Crispinus.

"But that didn't stop them fulfilling the prophecies of his crucifixion," said Lucius. "People don't need to believe God's prophecies to fulfil them."

"I'll have to tell my wife about that prophecy," said Crispinus. "Can I read the rest of the Psalm now?"

"Be my guest," said Luke.

Crispinus leaned his spear against the wall again and sat down, leaning over the scroll to read.

CR

After appearing before Nero, Paul was freed – he had no real charges to answer – and is believed to have travelled again, possibly to places like Spain.

After a while, he was arrested again, and this time there was no escape.

Paul is believed to have died in Rome – executed with a sword.

A courageous end to a life of tireless service to the master who would not let him go.

---

a   Psalm 16:10-11

PART TWELVE
Biographical Notes

Paul's Background

The narrative of the New Testament is dominated by two people: Jesus of Nazareth and Paul of Tarsus.

The earthly life and preaching of Jesus fills the gospels, while the faith he fathered drives the rest of the New Testament, with Paul as the main advocate for that faith.

If we imagine life as a sport, one might say that Jesus defined the playing field, described the rules, placed the goalposts and took his God-given position as referee, while Paul explained different aspects of the rules and how the teams should be organised to play together on a day-to-day basis.

Of course, Paul was not alone in this follow-up work, but his untiring – in fact almost incomprehensible – work rate as a preacher and letter writer means that almost half of the books in the New Testament bear his name as author.

So what do we know about him as a man?

His writing tells us much about his ideas and attitudes, but what do we know about his background, nationality, family, early life, education, religion and marital status?

Let's start from the very beginning, when Paul began life as "Saul", presumably named after Israel's first king. King Saul was a giant of a man, but his namesake probably wasn't since he was later known to everyone as "Paul", which means small or humble. We'll use his later name from now on.

Paul was a Jew[a] of the tribe of Benjamin[b] and circumcised on the eighth day.[c] Yet he was not born in Israel, but in Tarsus in Cilicia[d] to a father who, though a Jew, was also a Roman citizen. This gave Paul Roman citizenship[e] by inheritance[f] – an unusual situation for a Jew.

---

a   Descendant of Abraham, Hebrew, Israelite, Jew: Acts 16:20; 21:29; 22:3; Romans 3:9; 11:1, 14; Galatians 2:15; Philippians 3:5
b   Romans 11:1; Philippians 3:5
c   Philippians 3:5
d   Acts 21:39; 22:3
e   Acts 16:37; 22:25-29
f   Acts 22:28

We know nothing else about his parents, and regarding other members of his family we know only that he had a sister whose son heard of a plot to kill Paul and warned him.[g]

In one of his letters, Paul names three believers – Andronicus, Junia and Herodion – as kinsmen. Not only so, but Andronicus and Junia believed in Jesus before Paul, and were fellow prisoners as well.[h] Paul also says that the mother of another believer, Rufus, had been a mother to him as well.[i]

Young Paul was educated in Jerusalem under the tutelage of a famous Pharisee named Gamaliel,[j] a member of the Jewish Council.[k] The party of the Pharisees was the strictest of the Jewish religion,[l] but this training convinced Paul to become a Pharisee.[m]

As a very religious young man advancing quickly in Judaism, Paul genuinely tried to obey God with a clear conscience – but as part of that, he cruelly persecuted Christians[n] and was involved in the killing of Stephen.[o]

He was so fervent in his determination to exterminate Christianity that he sought to travel to Damascus and hunt for believers there. He asked for, and received, letters of authority from the High Priest and the Jewish Council to arrest and imprison any believers in Jesus that he found there.[p] However, the trip didn't turn out as expected.

Although Paul's persecution of Christians was done in honest ignorance,[q] it is obvious that by the time he met Jesus while travelling to Damascus, he was beginning to struggle. Jesus chided him with the observation that it was hard for him to kick against the goads.[r] Obviously Paul was having an internal fight against the evidence presented for Christianity and the Christians' way of life.

After meeting a living Jesus, which left him blind for three days,[s] Paul was utterly convinced about Christianity and completely reversed the direction of his life. The Paul who regained his sight and immediately began preaching about Jesus with such conviction that he "turned the world upside down"[t] was a completely different man from the Paul men had known before.

---

g   More than 40 men were involved in this conspiracy, but it failed when Paul's nephew reported it to the Roman tribune (Acts 23:12-35).
h   Romans 16:7; 11
i   Romans 16:13
j   Acts 5:34; 22:3
k   Also called the Sanhedrin
l   Acts 26:5
m   Acts 23:6; Philippians 3:5
n   Acts 8:3; Galatians 1:13-14
o   Acts 7:58; 8:1
p   Acts 9:1-2; 22:5
q   1 Timothy 1:13
r   Acts 26:14
s   Acts 9:9
t   Acts 17:6

What else do we know about Paul's background? Firstly, we know that he was a tentmaker,[a] which enabled him to support himself when necessary. Secondly, we know he had some sort of health problem that Jesus refused to cure – a problem that made his work more difficult, but helped to keep his ego under control.[b]

From that time forward, Paul led an astonishingly busy and productive life as Jesus' apostle, yet suffered many terrible things – as Jesus had warned him he would. At one stage the disciples had to lower him in a basket out of a window in the wall of Damascus to escape the governor's men,[c] while in Lystra he was stoned, dragged out of the city and left for dead.[d]

Paul was often imprisoned, suffered countless beatings and was often near death. Five times the Jews gave him "forty lashes less one"[e] and three times he was beaten with rods.[f] Shipwrecked three times,[g] he was also adrift at sea for a night and a day. On his frequent journeys he suffered cold and exposure, hunger and thirst, in danger from rivers, robbers, enemies and even his audiences as he spoke to them about Jesus.[h] He was often the target of enraged crowds who hated his message of love and forgiveness.

Paul was a God-powered dynamo who only slowed down when he was thrown in prison and forced to swap energetic preaching for energetic letter-writing.

While free to travel, he did so, walking about 7,000km and sailing about 5,000km.

His three missionary journeys over 10-12 years were followed by two years in prison,[i] a harrowing six-month journey to Rome[j] and two years under house arrest.[k] Freed after a trial before the emperor Nero, he probably undertook another preaching tour before being arrested for the last time and, as tradition suggests, executed in Rome.

As far as we know, Paul never married or had any children, and we can only imagine the family problems that might have occurred when kinsmen like Andronicus and Junia became believers while Paul was still persecuting Christians – or how others in the family may have responded to Paul's acceptance of Jesus as Messiah, which dedicated Pharisees would have seen as a betrayal.

---

a   Acts 18:3
b   See 2 Corinthians 12:7. This may have been a problem with his sight, as could be suggested by Galatians 4:13-15; 6:11.
c   2 Corinthians 11:32-33
d   Acts 14:19
e   Deuteronomy 25:3
f   One occurred in Philippi (Acts 16:22)
g   One is mentioned in Acts 27
h   Paul gives an extensive catalogue of his sufferings in 2 Corinthians 11:24-28
i   Acts 24:27
j   Acts 27:1-28:14
k   Acts 28:30-31

Paul's Biography – A Summary

Many details of Paul's background are mentioned in passing in Acts or his own letters. The following table provides a summary of that information.

Attribute	Details
Birth date	Unknown. Circumcised on the eighth day as an Israelite/Hebrew/Jew (Romans 11:1; 2 Corinthians 11:22; Galatians 2:15; Philippians 3:5).
Nationality	Dual citizenship: Israelite/Hebrew/Jewish (2 Corinthians 11:22; Galatians 2:15; Philippians 3:5) and Roman (Acts 16:37-38; 22:25-29) (both by birth).
Jewish tribe	Benjamin (Romans 11:1; Philippians 3:5).
Home town	Tarsus in Cilicia (Acts 21:39).
Education	In Jerusalem with Gamaliel (Acts 22:3).
Trade	Tentmaker (or leatherworker) (Acts 18:3).
Religious affiliation	Pharisee (Philippians 3:5).
Health	Suffered a "thorn in the flesh" that Jesus would not cure (2 Corinthians 12:7-10). Initially preached to the Galatians because of a health issue (Galatians 4:13).
Siblings	An unnamed sister is mentioned (Acts 23:16).
Other relatives	• Sister's son (Acts 23:16). • Andronicus & Junia (Romans 16:7). • Herodion (Romans 16:11). • Lucius, Jason and Sosipater (Romans 16:21).
Visions of or conversations with Jesus	• On the road to Damascus (Acts 9:3-6; 22:6-11; 26:13-18). • In the temple (Acts 22:17-21). • During first visit to Corinth (Acts 18:9). • In Jerusalem after his arrest (Acts 23:11). • Unknown time/location (2 Corinthians 12:7-10).

Paul's Letter-writing Style

We have 13 letters that announce themselves to be from Paul, enough to learn a lot about his writing style. Despite their widely differing lengths, these letters follow a consistent format.

An example – 2 Thessalonians

2 Thessalonians is among the shortest of Paul's letters but still shows his letter structure clearly. In this letter, Paul:

- Names himself as author and his co-authors. In 2 Thessalonians 1:1, these were Paul, Silvanus (Silas) and Timothy.
- Names the recipients. In 2 Thessalonians 1:1, this is the church of the Thessalonians.
- Gives a short introduction/blessing/thanksgiving. See 2 Thessalonians 1:2-12.
- Writes targeted content: praise, rejoicing, answering questions, criticising, teaching, etc. See 2 Thessalonians 2:1-3:15.
- Sends personal greetings. This is very limited in this letter. See 2 Thessalonians 3:17.
- Ends with a signature and a blessing. See 2 Thessalonians 3:16-18.

There is variation throughout his many letters, but 2 Thessalonians displays Paul's "standard" method of writing letters.

Despite the consistent format, however, each letter is carefully tailored to its audience. When directed to a congregation, his letters show Paul's awareness of the congregation's characteristics and his knowledge of individuals within the congregation. At times, they also refer to the local political and geographic situation. When directing letters to individuals, Paul's understanding of the recipient shines through.

Letters from Paul

The New Testament contains 13 letters that explicitly name Paul as their author in the text. A brief discussion of the authorship of Hebrews is provided below.

The timing of Paul's letters is not known exactly since none of them give specific dates, but the ones we have were probably written over about a 20-year period. Some of them refer to specific conditions, such as Paul being in prison, which help us to set more accurate dates.

Letters to places

Most were written to places he had visited, but some were to congregations that he may never have visited:

- Romans was probably written from Corinth during Paul's third missionary journey (for hints regarding timing and location see Acts 20:3-6; Romans 15:25-26; 16:1-2, 23; 1 Corinthians 1:14), but his first visit to Rome was as a prisoner well after writing the letter.
- Paul visited Corinth during his second and third missionary journeys and probably spent more than two years there overall. 1 Corinthians was probably prompted by news (1 Corinthians 1:11) and a letter sent from Corinth (1 Corinthians 16:17, 7:1), and it also appears that Paul had written an earlier letter (1 Corinthians 5:9). 1 Corinthians was written from Ephesus during Paul's third missionary journey (1 Corinthians 16:5-8). 2 Corinthians was written some time later from somewhere in Macedonia.
- Galatia was a Roman province, and Paul probably visited the area during his first, second and third missionary journeys. The letter to Galatians may have been written between his first and second missionary journeys or during the second.
- Paul visited Ephesus during his second and third missionary journeys and spent at least three years there overall. He wrote Ephesians from Rome during his first imprisonment there (Ephesians 3:1; 4:1; 6:20).
- Paul visited Philippi during his second and third missionary journeys, then wrote Philippians from Rome during his first imprisonment there (Philippians 1:7, 13, 14, 17).
- We do not have any record of Paul visiting Colossae, but he wrote Colossians from Rome during his first imprisonment there (Colossians 4:3, 10, 18).
- Paul visited Thessalonica during his second and third missionary journeys. 1 & 2 Thessalonians may well have been written from Corinth during his second missionary journey.

Letters to individuals

Some letters were written to individuals:

- 1 & 2 Timothy were sent to Timothy in Ephesus (1 Timothy 1:3; 2 Timothy 1:15-18; 4:19). 1 Timothy may have been written after Paul was freed from his first imprisonment in Rome, but the evidence for this is tentative and complex. 2 Timothy was probably sent in autumn from a cold cell in Rome during Paul's second imprisonment, not long before his death (2 Timothy 2:9; 4:6-8, 13, 21). Tychicus may well have carried the letter (2 Timothy 4:12).
- Titus was sent to Titus in Crete (Titus 1:5) and may have been written after Paul was freed from his first imprisonment in Rome, but the evidence for this is tentative and complex.

- Philemon, a letter sent to Philemon in Colossae during Paul's first imprisonment in Rome (Philemon 1:1, 9, 10, 13, 23) and probably sent by the hand of Onesimus, who was also carrying the letter to Colossae (Colossians 4:8-9).

Known but missing letters

In the letters of Paul that we have, he refers to other letters that we no longer have:

- A letter was written to Laodicea during Paul's first imprisonment in Rome at much the same time as the letter to Colossae (see Colossians 4:16).
- At least one other letter was also sent to Corinth as well as the two we have (1 Corinthians 5:9).

What about the letter to Hebrews?

Some people believe that Paul wrote the letter to Hebrews, and the 1611 edition of the King James Version titled it "The Epistle of Paul the Apostle to the Hebrewes" and put a note at the end that it was "Written to the Hebrewes, from Italy, by Timothie".

There are, however, a few reasons to question the claim that Paul wrote this letter.

The ones I find irresistible are:

- The author is not named anywhere in the letter. This is unique among the letters assigned by people to Paul and makes such a claim less credible.
- Paul's "standard" form of introduction is missing; in fact, there is no introduction at all. On the basis of 13 other letters which all name Paul in their introduction, this makes it unlikely that Paul was the writer.
- Paul's "standard" form of conclusion is missing.[a]
- In Hebrews 2:3,[b] the author acknowledges that neither he nor his audience had learned the gospel directly from Jesus, which is in stark contrast to Paul's claims to have received the gospel by direct revelation from Jesus Christ (see Galatians 1:11-12, 16; 2:2; 1 Corinthians 11:23; Ephesians 3:1-5).

Details of style, language and content also suggest an author other than Paul, but these arguments are too lengthy to discuss here.

---

a   While only four of Paul's letters (1 Corinthians, Colossians, 2 Thessalonians and Philemon) include the personal closing note described in 2 Thessalonians 3:17, this may have been a habit formed over time in the face of counterfeit letters being circulated in his name (see 2 Thessalonians 2:2). Nevertheless, all of Paul's letters display a similar form of conclusion, although the length and level of detail vary widely.

b   "This salvation was first announced by the Lord, was confirmed to us by those who heard Him, and was affirmed by God through signs, wonders, various miracles, and gifts of the Holy Spirit distributed according to His will." Hebrews 2:3b-4.

About the Author

Mark Morgan was born in Australia in 1963, the youngest son of Peter and Meryl Morgan. Deeply involved in religion all of his life, he has worked as a lay preacher, Sunday School teacher and missionary – trying to balance the many demands of spiritual life with those of family and paid employment.

After graduating, he worked in engineering for several years before concentrating on software development. Happily married and blessed with eight children, he has spent many years reading the Bible and learning to teach its lessons.

Writing Bible-based novels now fills much of his time.

Bible Tales Online

Other books by Mark Morgan are available from Bible Tales Online.

Terror on Every Side!
THE LIFE OF JEREMIAH

From a family of priests in the peaceful reign of good King Josiah, came a young man Jeremiah, bringing words from God to his people. It was no message for the fainthearted, either. It was a message of *Terror on Every Side!*

Vol 1 – *Early Days* **Vol 4 – *The Darkness Deepens***

Vol 2 – *As Good As It Gets* **Vol 5 – *No Remedy***

Vol 3 – *Darkness Falling* **Vol 6 – *That Broken Reed***

Available in hardcover, paperback, eBook and audiobook.

Other Bible-based novels

**Joseph,
Rachel's son**
(p'back, eBook, audiobook)

**The King's
Armour-bearer**
(h'cover, p'back, eBook)

Micro-tales

Collections of short stories about Bible characters or events, available in paperback, eBook and audiobook.

Fiction Favours the Facts
Fiction Favours the Facts – Book 2
Fiction Favours the Facts – Book 3
by Mark Morgan and others

Young Adult novels and other genres

Beyond the Western Margin
(YA adventure in p'back, eBook)

Upside Down with Paul
(h'cover, p'back, eBook)

Coming soon (God willing)

West to Moora Moora
*(sequel to **Beyond the Western Margin**)*
and ***Daniel, Man of Light***

Bible Tales Online continues to publish books.
To find the list of currently available books, visit
https://www.BibleTales.online/books

Bible
Tales

www.BibleTales.online